Praise for S

"Smart. Lonely. Rare. Weird. Otherworldly. In *Softie*, Megan Howell has done something that few can: she's made something new. This collection had me heartbroken in the best ways. *Softie* is the freak anthem I've been waiting for."

—Halle Hill, author of *Good Women: Stories*

"Megan Howell's *Softie* is a tender, sometimes absurd, incredibly impressive collection of stories about girlhood and womanhood and otherhood. What she does with these stories, with the wondrous, wandering, and whimsical women they center, is absolutely sublime."

—LaToya Watkins, author of *Holler, Child: Stories*

"The stories in *Softie* offer a bold and mesmerizing exploration of visceral grief and desire, of violence and survival, and of the body's capacity for both decay and shimmering afterglow. Expertly blending the strangeness and terror of magic with the strangeness and terror of being alive, this collection introduces Megan Howell as an unforgettable new voice."

—Danielle Evans, author of *Before You Suffocate Your Own Fool Self*

"Howell's collection...carves a needed space for female characters of color that move beyond the stereotypical white, beautiful, rich characters that dominate the subgenre."

—Kristen Gentry, author of *Mama Said: Stories*

Softie

Stories

Megan Howell

West Virginia University Press
Morgantown

Elaine Dundy, excerpt from *The Dud Avocado*. Copyright © 1958, 2007 by Elaine Dundy. Reprinted with the permission of Johnson & Alcock on behalf of The Dundy Estate, www.johnsonandalcock.co.uk.

ISBN 978-1-959000-31-0 (paperback) / 978-1-959000-32-7 (e-book)

Library of Congress Cataloging-in-Publication Data
Names: Howell, Megan, 1994–author.
Title: Softie : stories / Megan Howell.
Description: First edition. | Morgantown : West Virginia University Press, 2024.
Identifiers: LCCN 2024009297 | ISBN 9781959000310 (paperback) |
    ISBN 9781959000327 (ebook)
Subjects: LCGFT: Short stories.
Classification: LCC PS3608.O95516 S64 2024 | DDC 813/.6—dc23/eng/20240326
LC record available at https://lccn.loc.gov/2024009297

Book and cover design by Than Saffel / WVU Press
Cover image: *Untitled* by Steven J. Gelberg. http://www.stevengelberg.com/portfolio

Stories in this collection appeared in slightly different form in the following publications: "Lobes," *Minnesota Review*; "The Upstairs People," *storySouth*; "Turtle Soup," *JMWW*; "Kitty & Tabby," *Moon City Review*; "Bluebeard's First Wife," appearing as "Blue," *Nashville Review*; "Melissa, Melissa, Melissa," *Perceptions Magazine*; "Anita Garcia-Barnes," *Potomac Review*

To the girls who relate to this book.

That's the story of my life. Someone's behavior strikes me as a bit odd and the next thing I know all hell breaks loose.

—Elaine Dundy, *The Dud Avocado*

Contents

·······

Lobes

. . . .

SAM TOLD ME I was bad for his alcoholism, which had come back—that was how he phrased it over the phone. "Come back" like cancer does, because his doctors said his condition was a disease.

"But it's not your fault," he said for the millionth time. "It's just how I react to you."

"Isn't everything just a reaction?"

"What?"

I meant to say that everything in the world was technically just my senses making things up. My family, the island, every guy I'd ever slept with—none of this could really ever be proven real; it was just my brain making up sounds, sights, smells, emotions, etc., and reacting to them. The same was true for everyone else too. I'd read a philosophy listicle that talked about this theory of how perceptions differ between people. Interindividual differences. I couldn't think of the name at the time.

My eyes fixed themselves on the birthday present he'd given me last week. It was a fancy Jenga set. The blocks were tiny slabs of real marble. I thought of how much the pieces would've hurt if they'd fallen on top of me when I was small and still into playing board games with my little brother, Enzo. I'd just turned sixteen yesterday. My mom kept promising a party whose sworn luxuries grew less impressive as the days went by, the concert venue shrinking into a dinner at Rocco's for ten, five, three, two; the new iPhone devolving into money, a day trip to the beach, nothing at all. Her need for my favor was a dwindling flame that would die out when she found fault with me, then reignite once the lights got shut off or we couldn't afford heating.

"You're a really weird person," Sam said.

"Sam, I—"

The phone clicked. He'd hung up on me.

* * *

Ten minutes later, Sam called me back to ask if I was free this upcoming weekend. I was eating cereal out of the box. He didn't say that he was sorry, only that he missed me. His upbringing made him this way—clingy, unwilling to apologize. He'd told me in passing about his mom killing his dad, using the same matter-of-fact tone one might use to describe the weather. A muted shampoo commercial played on the TV, and I wondered what color his mom's hair had been. She'd probably be gray-haired now if she was still alive.

"Well?" Sam asked. "What's it gonna be?"

"Sure," I said. "Whatever."

"What's that noise?"

"I'm eating."

I heard him make that sound again, a click of the tongue followed by a grunt. He didn't think that eating was attractive. Of course, he'd never told me this outright; he wasn't cruel, only rough, an aspiring amoralist. I could just tell because he made himself easy to read whenever he got annoyed.

He talked about how much he missed me again, which led me to wonder why I'd kept the relationship going for so long when he made me feel nothing, like life could only get worse. I'd just finished my first week at a new high school. It was in Sartène. There were these two bigger girls in my grade who were telling people not to talk to me even though I'd never said a word to either of them. It had only been a few months since I'd left international boarding school, and already I felt lost. I was still getting used to speaking French all the time with people.

Sam was much older. I never romanticized the age difference because I was too busy thinking about his ears. He had detached earlobes. They were round and fat and unpierced. We'd met last year when I still worked in the back of this shoe shop that doesn't exist anymore. I was talking to the delivery lady when Sam walked in asking her for directions. I stared and stared at his ears until he asked if I had a problem, and I said, "No, I don't think so," and he said, "So what are you staring for?" Then I complimented his ears, which was enough for him to give me his number even though he'd been acting like he hated me and he was much older. He let me do what I wanted with his ears. I could bite, pull, lick, flick. In exchange, he had sex with me. I think his ears were an erogenous zone; I couldn't touch them without risking him getting aroused, not even when he was sleeping or driving, so I was always sore. He was larger than average, but I never came. Certain positions were painful to do. Marie, one of my old boarding school friends, said that men felt bigger when they knew they'd made you hurt like that. She told me this because I'd asked if my not having an orgasm meant that I might be slightly sociopathic.

Sam's earlobes were so nice. I wanted to keep them forever. They were beige and slightly fuzzed like the skin of a peach. I didn't see the problem with loving him for only a small part of himself. He was just as obsessed with my breasts. A lot of relationships like ours were only about good body parts: muscles, big dicks, large hips, pretty faces—all of it was just flesh, the same stuff ears were made of. I knew there was nothing wrong with me compared with the rest of the world even though I felt like an alien who was just visiting.

* * *

"You're always coming on to me," Sam said.

I said nothing back. His right earlobe was between my teeth. It was squishy and slightly cold, growing warmer. His breath quickened. His hands slid up my thighs. It was cool in his apartment. His warmth felt more pleasant here than it had in his car. His breath tasted strange when he spoke, which made me want to kiss him even less.

"Carla."

"Uh?"

"Nothing."

"Mhm."

We kept going until he stopped. I tried to keep going with his earlobes, but he pushed me away. He was old but strong. Or maybe I was just weak.

"I think you might be autistic," Sam said.

I shook my head, but I knew what he meant—that I was awkward, that I had a habit of talking over him or not responding at all or going on far too long about Disney trivia like the fact that the women working on *Snow White* applied real makeup to all the drawings of Snow White in order to make her lifelike. Personally, I'd never really considered myself anything even when I made myself seem like all the rich kids from my old school. I couldn't perceive myself the way I did others. When I looked in the mirror, all I saw was an avatar that sort of looked like the ones I'd customized in video games. The man I dated before Sam said I had a bland face but a good body. Like a porn star, he said. He'd graduated last year and moved to the mainland. I think he studied business at one of the grand écoles. I'd forgotten what he'd told me, and didn't check Facebook much.

"So what are you then?" Sam asked me.

"Carla."

"That's not what I mean."

"Black?"

"Never mind." He shook his head, smiling. "I feel like I know so little about you. You're just there. You never tell me anything."

"One time I saw a beaten-up lady near the playground at my old school," I said, remembering école primaire and how all my teachers disliked me for never speaking. "She didn't have on any clothes, and when I told my teacher, these people arrested her. But then it turned out that she was violated in a serious way. It was really sad. They kept her in jail for months before they let her out again, and by then the people who hurt her were already gone. I hope she's okay. She might've taken her own life."

"Jesus, that's awful."

I didn't tell him that the story was a lie. I thought that since it came from me, it was an intimate part of me, never mind that it wasn't true. When I got lonely or afraid, I liked to make up stories. Sometimes happy ones, but mostly sad, imagined articles someone might read online and shake their heads and say, "Oh, poor them" or "I hope their family sues." I used to want to be like this one girl who turned up missing because everyone seemed to care about her, even people who'd never met her before. She was pretty and had the same blonde hair as Sam minus his swarthiness. I think it turned out that she'd most likely drowned.

Sam started complaining about work again. I still wasn't sure exactly what it was that he did. Something that involved transporting goods. Tariffs, imports—that sort of thing. He didn't do any heavy lifting I don't think, though he was always heavily sunburned and had a muscular frame. His job required that he speak English, but he only talked to me in French even though I'd told him that I spoke English at the C1 level.

I listened to his story until I couldn't help but float off. I imagined him working one of the cranes at the shipping yard. It was a comforting thought: the smell of the sea, distant yells and the cry of seagulls, high stacks of multicolored shipping bins fitted into each other like Legos.

"What's your fantasy?"

Sam's voice was gravelly. Sometimes when he talked, he got so invested that spittle formed in the corner of his mouth and his throat grew hoarse.

"Your ears, I guess," I said.

"What about them do you like?"

"Well, I guess sometimes I think that I want to have them for myself. Just the lobes because they're not essential. I'd sever them. The procedure would be really simple, like piercing ears. My older sister, Camille, she's gone now, but she pierced my ears when she was still living at home. I'd felt this brief pain, then nothing. The holes closed, though. I didn't like the feel of having sharp metal inside of me."

* * *

Sam kicked me out and stopped seeing me because he found my confession about his ears bizarre.

I was bedridden with a fever when he called again. My mom was sitting at my bedside, promising me a late birthday party next month when she started a new, better job as a telephone dispatcher. The phone rang and rang, and she kept going on and on about how much better things would get, how my fever would eventually break and money would come in and Enzo would finally be able to get new glasses.

I refused to speak to her. Her hopeful act made me too angry, dialing up my body's temperature. I still hadn't forgiven her for making me drop out of the boarding school I used to go to because it got too expensive. The school would've taken care of the outstanding fees had she not yelled at one of the directors for patronizing her. I despised her for ruining my life. I despised her even worse for making me feel sorry for her, turning my anger back onto myself so that it consumed all the positive things my teachers had ever said about my upstanding moral character. That was the most unbearable part about her: I couldn't hate her, just her poverty and her resentment, which bled through her cheery veneer.

"Who keeps calling?" she asked.

I shrugged even though I knew it was Sam. All my friends texted. Aside from my mom, he was the only one who preferred talking on the phone. I'd found it jarring when Marie, my boarding school friend, called me up crying that one time to tell me that Paul broke up with her and could I please just stay on the line and listen? (I cried, too, but not because I liked Paul. He was boring. It was just that I hadn't heard her voice in so long, and even more time has passed since then.)

My mom made me pick up the phone even though I could barely speak. I tried to act like I was talking to one of my friends. He said, "I really need to see you, I miss you so much," and I said, "I'm sorry, but my mom made me drop out," and then there was a brief silence where I could only hear the sound of his TV playing in the background. My mom could tell that he was male and also very old. She made me put the phone on speaker while he went on about how much he enjoyed my body.

"Come and see me," he said.

"Okay," I said and quickly hung up.

That was the only way I could make sure he wouldn't call back right away: agreeing with him. I had to guard my face with my hands so my mom couldn't hit me there. I felt like I was going to throw up and started gagging. She told me to quit it as if I had complete control over my sickness. The last time she'd been this angry with me, I was little, maybe ten or eleven, young enough to try to run away from home. She calmed down for a while when I got older and went away for school. I thought that maybe I'd finally made myself perfect, though I also knew not to stay with her for too long in case she found a reason not to like me.

"End it," my mom said.

"End what?"

"Don't play innocent."

When she got angry at me, she acted as if everything inconvenient that I'd ever done from my fever to my birth had been an intentional plan on my part to ruin her.

"You need to end everything with him," my mom hissed. "Don't let him take you anywhere."

She made me stand outside in the rain while I waited for Sam to come pick me up. Enzo watched through the window. I saw the floral curtains flutter. Or maybe my mind was making things up. My head swam.

Sam's car pulled up. I tried to talk to him from the walkway, but he refused to roll down his window and motioned me to get into the passenger seat. He closed the door behind me, telling me I was being too slow, like a sloth. I told him everything my mom had instructed me to: that he was too old, that I was a child, that she'd make his life miserable if he ever came back. My whole body hurt so much. I started crying. Each inhale made my body ache more. I'd been coughing up phlegm for so many days and had gotten so sore that even breathing was a struggle.

Sam pulled my head into his chest, which made me feel at home in a foreign way that wasn't miserable. For the first time since coming home, my need for intimacy felt real. Before, it existed only as a memory of me kissing this one boy from my class at my farewell party. I felt pure pleasure holding Sam until I realized that I'd probably never see that boy again. It hurt so much, way worse than a billion fevers. It was just like the time I'd first gone away for school and no one would talk to me. My once pleasant memories were turning apocalyptic.

I forgot to tell Sam that my mom didn't want us going anywhere together. I thought her wish was obvious, but no. She was probably thinking it was all my fault when he drove off. But then I turned around and saw her standing by the door. She didn't go straight in to call the authorities. Instead, she went through the back gate to the small square of yard, which meant that she was going to check on her plants. When I told Sam that I was devastated that my mom hadn't gone back inside, he told me I was being strange again. I didn't know how to explain how her choice of direction meant that she'd given up on me.

We went to his place, one of the nice, new construction apartments that had a distant view of the ocean. A burst of energy went through me like it had right before my fever came. Before, when we had sex, I drifted away in my head, but now I felt trapped in my body, and could feel him fully. I felt happiness, eroticism. Regret. When he finished, he made this tiny, dying-baby-animal sound that drew attention to the wrinkles etched into his forehead, his neck, the corners of his bluish-gray eyes. It was very depressing. I had the urge to hold him close and run away. I started playing with his earlobes again.

"So soft," I said, pinching them.

"I've been thinking about your ear thing," Sam said. "I think it's the child in you."

"What d'you mean?"

"You act the same way babies act around breasts. Have you ever held a baby before? Up close like this—" he made his hands into a cradle, pressing them against the hairy plane of his chest, "Right? If they feel a breast, they just start groping. It's an innate reflex, nothing sexual at all. You're just like a child. That's what you are. You're mentally younger than you are. That school you went to coddled you too much, and now you're way softer than most Blacks."

I nodded, pretending to understand. I'd gotten to hold my niece back when she was a newborn and I was still in college. She was small, her hands even smaller. I didn't remember her trying to touch my chest. Maybe she wasn't hungry. Either that or I was too flat at the time.

"I think this was a bad idea," he said.

My body froze up. All I could do was tremble as he told me that it had been a mistake to get with me. He brought up his alcoholism again and I started crying heavy, heaving tears I hadn't experienced since early childhood. I begged to stay with him even though his words made me hate him. I hated how much power he had over me, how he could just tell me when to come and go. He said I could stay the night. I asked for more time, and he told me I needed to calm down.

Sam started drinking in front of me. I was too afraid to stop him. He pulled out a bottle from underneath the bed, being all sneaky about it, as if it hadn't been him who'd hidden it away from himself. I pretended to be asleep until he passed out beside me, at which point I decided that I couldn't stay any longer.

I was trying to find my glasses when I came across the metal scissors. They were sitting on his nightstand between the electric alarm clock and the picture of a woman who I was pretty sure was his daughter. I saw the scissors, then his ears. I reached out to touch him, poking his side once, twice, three times. He wouldn't move. I thought that maybe he'd died until I watched his chest rise and fall.

The silence of the room felt oppressive. I opened a window. The rain had cleared up, leaving behind a cool, natural odor. It was late summer. There were still vacationers everywhere, mostly old people now that all the schools had started session. I spotted a few coming out of La Sirène, two women and a man, all of them stumbling like they'd drank up the whole entire bar. In a few weeks, they'd be gone. This place was just a dream for them, somewhere to briefly escape to before returning back to real life somewhere more interesting. Nothing here felt real anymore. Each time I'd returned to my mom's for vacations, the ceilings shrunk and the walls shifted inward. I didn't grow. My mom and the house just got smaller. Nothing was real, I kept thinking. I picked up the scissors.

I didn't feel like I was in reality when I mounted Sam again. I was in my body, but the world had melted away completely, leaving just me and him, me and his ears. I started cutting without thinking. Or rather, I was thinking, just not about what I should've been, which was that it was immoral to steal a piece of someone. He screamed and tried to shake me off, but he was too inebriated to righten himself. I squeezed the finger holes as hard as I could, trying to get the blades to go down all the way. There was blood. The sight made me remember that he could feel pain even though he acted like he was pure cynicism.

I dropped the scissors and let him slap me around until he got tired. He said I was seriously messed up in the head but with more explicit language and much louder, so loud that someone—maybe the police, maybe his neighbors who'd threatened to call the police before—started banging on the door. We panicked, which temporarily brought us back together again as we decided what to do.

"The window," he said.

He led me to it and told me to climb down. It was a short fall, just two stories. I think I must've twisted my ankle when I landed. The tendons started burning.

"You're a weird bitch," Sam said. He tried to close the window, but it must've been jammed because he kept struggling with the latch.

I walked all the way home. It was a medium-length journey, but there were many hills, all of them inclines. My ankle was sprained. I didn't know because the pain didn't feel real until I tried to fall asleep.

* * *

A month later, Sam called me up again to ask to see me. I'd just finished eating pain au chocolat with my family to celebrate my birthday, which had long past. We had to eat on paper plates my mom had gotten from work because the water company had shut off the tap. Doing dishes was impossible. We took showers at her friend's place.

I'd been thinking about Sam more, mostly his ears but also the small luxuries of his apartment, the heated bathroom floors and the high-pressure showerhead. When I told him this, he said I ought to be committed. Before he could hang up on me, I told him that I'd talk to him again soon.

The
Upstairs People

....

THERE'S TWO OF THEM in the unit above Cherish's family's:
voices arguing with each other. A couple, Cherish's mom
claimed. She'd helped them carry a box of crockery up the apartment's narrow stairwell when they moved in last month. The
woman's expecting, her belly distended, her shoes orthopedic.
And the man supposedly has a condition that makes physical
exertion difficult, but from the way Cherish's mom explained it,
he just sounds lazy. Their fights are nightly, short and loud.

    Cherish is curled up on the same couch where she used to
watch cartoons. The TV's going as it always does when she's
alone, but she stopped paying attention from the moment she
turned it on. On the screen, housewives answer trivia questions for the chance to win a full kitchen makeover. She'd
given up watching kid's stuff long ago in junior high school
when this one girl, Monica Brentwood, real nasty, laughed at
her Bullwinkle impression in a mean way. Next month she'll be
thirty-two.

"Stop following me," the woman upstairs is saying. "I'm done talking to you."

"I'm not following you," the man says.

"Don't you dare raise your voice at me."

"Don't raise *your* voice at *me*."

Back and forth, on and on. The drama's repetitive, but its proximity to Cherish feels exciting: not too close to be her problem, not too distant to be just another pointless TV show—the perfect spectacle. She lights another cigarette, inhaling deeply, doing breathing exercises to cancel out the negative effects of the nicotine.

The arguing stops when Cherish has finished smoking. She hears footfalls, a slamming door, nothing. She forgets that the radiator is going until it clicks off, leaving dead air.

"I think we have our winner," the TV announcer says.

One of the upstairs people goes downstairs. Cherish's curiosity rises when she hears them walk across her landing, the sound of them growing louder. They stop outside her door.

Three knocks. Cherish rises from the couch and looks in the entryway mirror. Lucky for her, she looks presentable, her hair clean and curled, her makeup fresh. Still, panic seizes her chest.

Another knock. The woman's voice is speaking, asking if anyone's home. "Is Sandra there?" she asks.

No, Sandra isn't here. Sandra, Cherish's mom, has been out all day helping Cherish's sister, Pearla shop for the perfect prom dress, which Pearla's school says must be modest—no spaghetti straps nor strapless-ness, no decolletage, no spandex, and nothing above the knee. They probably stopped for lunch. If they haven't found anything, Pearla will have fallen back on her dieting schtick, convinced she's fat—she, Pretty Lil' Pearl, the sister with the hips and butt and flat, never-been-pregnant stomach. Then she'll cry when their mom makes her eat, then bicker, and by the time they get back, it'll be dark. The woman upstairs should just come back tomorrow.

"Hello?" the woman says.

"Hold on," Cherish says.

She re-ties the sash of her dress, strikes a pose in the mirror, and teases her hair with her fingers. For once, she's put together. This morning, she had to go back downtown to finalize the divorce. She'd set her hair the day before.

The woman upstairs is smiling when Cherish opens the door. Cherish smiles back, copying her mom's sugary voice when she asks if anything's the matter. This is the first time she's seeing her up close.

The woman's inflamed fingers fidget with the pilled fabric of her maternity dress. She has a brown pie face. Her eyes look magnified underneath her bifocals. "Sorry to bug you," she says, craning to see past Cherish.

"It's no problem," Cherish says. "Did you need anything? Something to drink?"

"I think I have the wrong apartment number. I'm looking for Sandra Foster."

"I'm Sandra's daughter."

"Oh." The woman looks surprised. "Sorry, I thought she had just the little girl." She smiles, extending her hand. She's lacquered her nails a deep shade of green. "I'm Sophia, by the way."

"Cherish."

"What?"

"That's my name."

Sophia's large, violently rouged smile feels even less genuine than Cherish's. "Such an interesting name," she says, beaming. "I've never heard it before. First time for everything, I guess. Nice to meet you."

They shake hands. Shame weighs Cherish down so heavily that she feels herself sinking all the way to hell. Her mom's trying to erase her out of shame. Such hypocrisy. It was her decision to bring Cherish into the world. Same with the wedding—she'd insisted on handling everything from the professional photographer to the handprinted invitations.

Cherish's mom's always been one to put on airs. Her life's mission: obscuring the inconvenient fact that had dominated her and her daughters' lives for a while now. The fact: the Foster women attract no-good men—didn't matter if they were Black, Spanish, or Pearla's white boyfriend who got into a fist-fight with his step-uncle. Most of Cherish's mom's friends think her husband died, when he really just jumped ship for another woman in Texarkana.

"Are you okay?" Sophia asks.

"Yes," Cherish says. "I'm sorry, what do you want again?"

"It's a bit private. Sorry."

"Okay," Cherish says, and starts closing the door.

"Wait!" Sophia says. "I don't mean to bother you. My husband has me so stressed out, and our apartment's about as big as a shoebox so there's nowhere to go. Is it okay if I come in and stay for a little bit? Not long. Just until he cools off."

"Sure," Cherish says. Her mom would get annoyed if she turned away one of her many friends. She used to always get on her for being shy toward the women at church, calling her sassy.

Cherish and Sophia drink instant coffee in the kitchen. The window captures the city's darkening skyline so perfectly that it's like looking at a picture, its crown molding and dirty scrolled corners a baroque frame in disrepair. It makes the low-rise apartment feel less cramped. One can just make out Mexico way off in the distance.

"You have such a pretty view," Sophia says.

"It is nice," Cherish says.

"The elementary school blocks most of our windows. All you can see is a big brick wall. Sometimes I can hear the little kids play, which is nice." Sophia looks down at her belly as if just remembering it. "There's something relaxing about listening to them," she adds.

Cherish looks up at the clock. It's almost six, and still nothing from Pearla or their mom. She hopes one of them remembers to bring milk on the way home. She wants to make cornbread to go with her mom's leftover casserole, maybe a hot milk cake too.

"Have you ever been across the border?" Sophia asks.

"Plenty of times," Cherish says. "My mom and me used to go there to get our teeth cleaned since a lot less local dentists in the area took Blacks, and the one we used to see near here had a kid die of sepsis in his care. I don't think he was very hygienic. I heard there was mold on the ceilings."

"How terrible." Sophia pauses to take a sip from Pearla's favorite Minnie Mouse cup. "Are you a Negro?"

"My mom," Cherish says. "My dad's from Mexico."

"What part? I have family in Juarez."

Cherish shrugs. "He died when I was really little," she hears herself lie. She purses her lips, already tired of the subject.

Sophia presses her bushy eyebrows together, pinching her face into a look of almost-sympathy. Judgment radiates from her. It's as if she's picking through the lies. Her large eyes are inquisitive, searching. They travel to the poorly plastered-over, head-sized hole in the wall that Cherish's dad had made stumbling drunk around the room. ("Get out!" Cherish's mom had yelled at him. "I ain't raising no babies with no Goddamn alcoholic." Then over the phone a few days later: "What d'you mean you're not coming back? Ramone, no, please don't do this to me.")

Sophia gets misty-eyed. "Sorry," she says, sniffling. "It's just that my husband has me so worked up. I feel like I'm gonna miscarry because of him. I'm just so tired of it all. It never ends with him."

"If you don't mind me asking, why's he so angry?" Cherish clears her throat, her shame shrinking under the woman's, her chest rising. "Maybe I could help."

Sophia throws her hands in the air. "There's way too much to explain about Ben. I'm sure you don't wanna be bothered." Then, after another sip of coffee: "It's just that he really hates my side of the family. I had him wire my sister money so she could pay off some overdue bills. It was supposed to be a loan until she got on her feet since family services won't let her see her children otherwise. She used to clean up at a cannery until it got shut down for sanitary reasons. I thought she'd find work somewhere, but then it turned out that she just upped and left with all the money. She didn't even pay her rent."

"Wow."

Sophia presses her palms against her mouth and makes a low, animal-like noise that's something between a scream and a groan. Cherish startles.

"So sorry," Sophia says. "My sneezes are all off, I know— Ben's always complaining about them. I had scarlet fever real bad as a child, so my throat's not the same as what it was."

Cherish nods and puts her hand on Sophia's. "You don't have to apologize," she says. "It must be hard. I've been having similar issues with my husband."

"Oh gosh, I feel sorry for you then."

"My husband's a psychotherapist," Cherish says, "so he has a lot of stories, and he's always on edge from the stress. I used to make him drinks in advance and put them in the freezer so that they were extra cold when he came home." A rosy feeling rises from Cherish's gut. She speaks faster: "He's such a talent, though. He used to work with shellshocked vets before he started his own practice. A lot of his patients caught on to him so well that they'd always be inviting him out for beers. Of course, he told them no for professionalism's sake."

"Does he live with you?"

Sophia's question snuffs out Cherish's rosiness, leaving her exposed again.

"No," Cherish says. "Ex-husband." The word still doesn't feel right on her tongue, its aftertaste foul and just barely familiar like rotten milk. "I'm divorced."

Sophia's mouth drops a little. "Oh, God. I can't imagine. I've heard how traumatic that can be."

Cherish makes herself laugh, but the squeaky sound that comes out of her throat doesn't sound very cheery. "I'm not sad at all," she says. "I'm happy."

"It must've been so hard for you."

"Well, it wasn't," Cherish snaps.

"Sorry."

"No need to apologize. It's completely fine—really!"

Sophia rises from her chair. She looks down at her feet. "I should probably get going," she says. "I think I might stay at my friend's place until Ben cools off."

"Hope everything works out," Cherish says.

On the way out, Sophia stops to hug Cherish. Cherish doesn't know what to do. She lets herself be embraced until she feels herself getting too emotional. She pulls back first.

* * *

A few minutes after Sophia's left, Cherish's mom comes back with Pearla. Cherish hears all of them talking in the hallway.

"That dress is gorgeous," Sophia says. "I really love the color. It's just like the ocean."

"Thank you!" Pearla squeals. She speaks over her mom, who says she can't believe the amazing deal they'd gotten—almost half-off, if you could believe it.

Pearla comes into the apartment first, dress in hand as she sings the refrain to "Isn't She Lovely." She spreads it out on the kitchen table, the light of the overhead lamp turning the rhinestones into starlike twinkles of light.

"Well?" Pearla says. "What d'you think? It's perfect, right? The fabric's taffeta. Don't touch, though. I can't have wrinkles."

Cherish offers generic compliments even though she finds the blue and white pattern a bit tacky. "How wonderful," she hears herself saying. "So nice. What a pretty color." She's not thinking. She can't. Her divorce clouds her thoughts like a thick smog. She can't stop remembering those words that had taken shape in her head after the first miscarriage: *broken woman.*

"That's exactly what Sophia said," Pearla says, "but I feel like the outer layer's darker than aquamarine. The lady at the store said the color's called 'Promise.'"

Their mom goes into the kitchen to start dinner. The clanging of pots and pans annoys Cherish on an irrational level. She just wants her old place back, not this one with its ancient furniture but the other one with Darryl.

When Cherish doesn't respond right away, Pearla waves a hand in her face. "Are you still alive?" she asks.

"I don't know," Cherish mumbles.

"What's wrong?"

"You know. The usual."

Pearla rubs Cherish's back. She's getting sad for Cherish, which makes Cherish feel even sadder because today's supposed to be Pearla's day—they've been saying so for weeks, Pearla slowly collecting her savings for the outfit of her dreams. Cherish can't risk having her misery infect Pearla too. Peppy Pearla with her sparkly dress, rainbow-painted fingernails, and purple-rimmed glasses; her automatic, high-fidelity record player and comedy records; her youth and blemishless face. Her boyfriend's supposed to be taking her to the dance, but she hasn't said anything to their mom yet—only Cherish—and when she does, there'll be an argument for sure, because this boy's been to reform school while the farthest Pearla's ever been from home was Bible camp in Galveston one summer.

"Lemme hem that for you," Cherish says. She doesn't wait. She gets out the sewing kit from the wardrobe.

Pearla whines as she puts on the dress, saying that she's starving and also that she can't ever have carbs. She mounts the old baby stool she used to climb to reach the bathroom sink when she was little. She probably doesn't remember him, but their dad built it.

Cherish wears a pin cushion like a bracelet. She thinks of her childhood, motherhood. She's the mother of two miscarriages and, before that when she was really little, a plastic baby doll that her mom has pictures of Cherish trying to nurse.

"You always wanted to be a momma," her mom used to say, which wasn't a lie. One time, when Cherish was pushing baby Pearla through Kroger in her stroller, this lady, white, stopped her and said that she had the most darling little daughter, and Cherish didn't correct her.

Cherish's hands work on the dress as her mind hurdles back to her old life with her ex, their old apartment in the nicer part of the city, and the horse ranch he promised that he'd buy one day for her and all the children she was supposed to give him. She wonders if things would've worked out different had she met her ex in high school instead of in her thirties at the Garden Inn's taproom. Would he have loved her more deeply then? Maybe. If only he'd grown up here with her instead of in

Chicago. Maybe then their bond would've been harder for him to break. She'd pretended not to be jealous when he told her in passing about girls he'd fallen for as a kid in Bronzeville: pretty girls from school, his mom's friend, a bank teller, a play-cousin who turned out gay, a nun, Jayne Mansfield.

Fat tears roll down Cherish's cheeks. Her mom comes up behind her, whispering, "Baby, let's not do this right now," and Cherish nods, wiping away snot with her free hand while Pearla pretends not to see. Pearla redresses in her overalls. Then she and Cherish set the table while their mom deshells shrimp.

Their mom spots the two mugs in the sink. As she washes them, she asks Cherish if Sophia was doing better or if that man of hers was still giving her a hard time.

"The second," Cherish says, her eyes going toward the window again. She peers down and sees what has to be Sophia, wearing the same creamsicle-colored maternity dress from earlier. There she goes, Cherish thinks. An orange blip, that's what she is.

A taxi pulls up and Sophia gets inside, looking over her shoulder before she closes the door.

"Poor lady," Cherish mumbles. She looks up. "Hey, Ma," she says, "I think Sophia might be leaving her husband. She's getting into a taxi now."

"Her money situation is a nightmare from what she told me," Cherish's mom says. "Five hundred dollars—that's how much her cousin stole. Can you believe it?"

"I think it was the sister."

"Was it now? I can't remember. The woman's a real talker."

"At least I stuck it out with Darryl. I didn't run away. Didn't work out all the same, but still. I tried."

Cherish's mom clears her throat. She doesn't say anything. The silence speaks for her, telling Cherish to be quiet, to mind her business and help her in the kitchen with the black beans she's draining. Still, Cherish goes on, talking about all the future she has now that the divorce papers are signed. Seeing the taxi pull away makes her feel optimistic but in a sad way, like a lone survivor escaping a housefire. A few months stuck at her mom's is barely any time at all compared to the decades she still has to live.

"It's not too late for me," Cherish says. "There have to be millions of women in the world who have it way worse, and I'm nowhere near being them. Marielle from work says we might be getting a raise just like the rest of the accounting department, so there's hope in a way."

"Mhm," her mom says.

"I don't have to have kids to be happy. Maybe I could go into teaching. Or babysit on the side. It'd be like being a part-time mother."

"There's no such thing as a part-time mother. A caretaker, sure."

"I just want to be happy."

Cherish regrets saying these words as soon as she hears them. She waits for her mom to tear her down, to tell her for the umpteenth time that she should've done this, that, and the third if she'd really been serious about Darryl. After the first loss, her mom had been supportive in her usual overly instructive manner, giving Cherish big jars of vitamins and recipes for soups that were supposed to improve circulation. "Don't change the litter box," she'd warn at the end of every call. "Have Darryl do it." She'd read somewhere that cat feces cause birth defects. She liked Cherish's husband, but not his pet tabbies, which she said looked dirty, more like alley cats than the cute purebred ones with the smushed-in faces.

"It'll work out," her mom says now.

Cherish nods, smiles, her eyes still red. "Thanks."

She looks out the window again. All that's left is a long strip of mostly empty road save for the two clunkers parked on the opposite side. Also, the horizon. The sunset has painted the sky pinkish orange.

Thank God Cherish isn't Sophia. Cherish has money. Options. Though the old apartment's gone, the divorce settlement is enough to get her out of her mom's. All she needs to do is figure out where to go, what to do.

Cherish should feel lucky. Her breakup hadn't been violent. Darryl was gentlemanly, the well-bred child of two teachers with six very doting daughters. There was never any hitting or screaming with him, no police visits, zero arrests. Cordial, the lawyers called the divorce. One of them had a client who'd tried to poison her husband with the little packets of silica gel that keep new shoes fresh. What a nightmare. Darryl was never like that at all. It was his disappointment that hurt Cherish. He'd given her so many clues after the second miscarriage. He never wanted to be the one to end anything, not even when the relationship was new and strong, always waiting for her to hang up first on those long, pining calls. He just wanted to move on, he said now. He was tired.

All Cherish could give him was death, and though he never said so outright, she knew him well enough to feel his emotions swelling up inside of herself, his disappointment and hidden disgust becoming hers forever.

* * *

The next day, they're at it again: screaming, crying, and carrying on. Sophia's returned and Ben is beside himself.

"You were out fucking Ronny again, weren't you?" Ben says. "It was him. I know it was him. Don't lie to me."

"Give me back my shoes," Sophia says.

"Say one more word and I'll go find the bastard myself."

"You'd better not. I'm warning you, Ben. Ben? Ben! I'll leave barefoot if I have to."

Cherish drinks wine and shakes her head. "How terrible," she keeps saying as she massages Pearla's scalp, "so terrible."

"I wish they'd shut up already," Pearla says.

Pearla starts coughing again, squinting as she tries to watch *Little House on the Prairie* without her glasses. She's curled up in a tight, catlike ball, her head on Cherish's lap, her forehead balancing a frozen water bottle.

Pearla's dance is tomorrow, but their mom says she can't go because her fever won't break. She must've picked something up at one of the dress shops. Her skin is hot to the touch. Their mom should be coming back soon with more Tylenol.

Cherish wants to take this private moment to tell her sister so much, mostly warnings, but can't figure out how to without sounding like their mom. Don't stay with people who break your heart, she thinks, imagining the words traveling down her fingers and directly into Pearla's brain like electricity.

"D'you think we should call the police?" Pearla asks. "That guy sounds insane."

Cherish puts a finger up to her lips. The upstairs is silent now. Then there's a loud crash.

Quickly, Cherish gets up, moving Perla's head, her heart beating fast. She's pretty sure Sophia's okay, there's no screams of pain. She almost sits back down when she hears Ben say, "Look, I'm sorry," and then Sophia's light footfalls echo through the stairwell. Cherish feels like she's about to choke on her heart.

Clop, clop, clop. Sophia must be wearing heels this time.

"I'm leaving you!" Sophia yells at the top of her lungs.

"Fine," Ben says, yelling down at her.

"Will you two shut up already!" yells a third voice, that of the elderly Black woman who lives across from Cherish's family. She slams her door as the fight rages on in the stairwell.

"Come on," Pearla whispers to Cherish, her hoarse voice almost gone, "let's just call the police. Please."

"Okay," Cherish says.

She walks up to the phone only to pass it for the door. When she goes out into the corridor, Pearla rushes behind her.

"What're you doing?" Pearla whispers. Cherish ignores her.

Sophia's still in the stairwell. Cherish rushes toward her, her stomach a turgid water balloon of excitement and dread. Then she looks up and sees him hovering one flight above them: Ben, his face swarthy, his hair mussed.

"If you gotta leave," he says, "then you better take your stuff with you. All of it."

He disappears back into the apartment, and for a moment, there's peace. Then he comes back out again and starts throwing things over the railing. First small things: candles, books, newspapers, a tied-up stack of *Reader's Digest* issues. Gradually, his rage increases, and with it the objects' sizes: shoes, a lazy Susan, a drawer full of panties and bras, kitchen bowls, pots and pans, a birdcage with a parakeet squawking inside. He keeps coming back out, surprising Sophia over and over as she rushes to pick up the broken pieces of her life with him.

The whole time, Cherish and Pearla take cover and scramble like they're at war. Pearla helps Sophia retrieve her things. Cherish tries to pull her back, but Pearla keeps pushing her away. Pearla's bigger. Stronger. Though the mean girls at her school sometimes make her cry, she can punch a hulk-sized dent into metal, having demonstrated so on the souped-up truck of a boy who wouldn't stop following her.

There's a loud crash. A mini fridge, its door swung open, beers everywhere, some of them leaking brownish-blond foam. Cherish goes for Pearla one final time but slips on a puddle. She falls on her side so hard she feels her soul rattling around her bird-boned body.

All Cherish can see is the ceiling, the dim, exposed lightbulb and the water stain that's kinda shaped like Florida or maybe Italy. She doesn't see the exercise weights when they first land. She just hears more screaming. The silence that comes after is what alerts her.

"Oh my God," Sophia is saying, "No, no, no, no."

Over by the fridge that looks like a bomb went off inside of it: a new puddle, deep red and growing. Cherish sees Pearla on the floor and closes her eyes, shaking her head. Panic takes hold of her. Her mouth tastes like it's full of pennies.

* * *

On the drive home from the hospital, Cherish stops at the gas station near the local pool. She's craving the fifty-cent tamales Pearla's obsessed with. She's not hungry. She just misses the rough feel of the corn husks and the way her sister used to lick them clean.

"We're all out, ma'am," says the overly freckled white girl working the register. "We've got other stuff, though. Check the freezer section."

Cherish thanks her. She thinks of buying more smokes but stops herself, remembering what her mom had read about nicotine and fetuses, as if the information matters anymore.

Not knowing what else to do, she walks through the aisles, studying the bright packaging of pork rinds, Circus Peanuts, potato chips, Moon Pies, beef jerky, popcorn, licorice, Twinkies—on and on, endless rows of junk food. People pass by her without looking. Nothing, she keeps thinking. There's nothing in the world left for her.

As she's about to leave, she comes across that boy Pearla's dating. She's seen him a few times before, mostly at Pearla's volleyball games. She creeps closer. Yep, she thinks. That's definitely him: same dirty blond hair, same lanky frame. She thinks of telling him what happened but can't find her voice. Tonight's the dance.

The boy's talking to the cashier. She gives him a skeptical look, swishing her lips as if he's a flavor of soda she can't decide if she wants or not.

"I can give you my number if you don't wanna gimme yours," he says.

"You must think I have 'stupid' written across my face," she says. "No way. I've heard the rumors. You're trouble."

"Aww, come on, girl, don't go listening to those people. They don't know what they're talking about." He leans into the counter, resting his hands against its surface. "I'm a real good person when I try to be."

The cashier crosses her arms. A moment passes where they just look at each other.

"Naw," she says. "Like I said: you're trouble."

Cherish rushes outside. She thinks she's going to throw up and doubles over by some shrubs. Nothing comes out of her. She gasps for air.

It's late. The sky is dark with no stars. This morning, Cherish overheard one of the nurses calling Pearla's case hopeless, and though she knows the woman was probably right, she can't help but hate her. So much hate. She's bursting with it, its sources too heavy to sift through. There's that nurse but so many others; even people Cherish hasn't thought of in years are starting to grate at her. She tries not to think about them as she drives home, blasting the radio, but then a reporter comes on and starts talking about Pearla's accident without giving her name and she almost has a head-on collision with a station wagon.

She should go home. But she can't. The apartment is too empty. Ben's in jail. Pearla's on life support and their mom's been by her side since the tragedy.

Then there's the issue with the stairwell. The mess is gone but not cleaned. Everything still smells like beer. The linoleum is sticky. The gas station was a spotless oasis by comparison.

But Cherish goes home because there's nowhere else to go. She makes it all the way to the unit's door and freezes when she hears a noise from upstairs.

Clop, clop, clop. Cherish's heart's about to explode.

"Sandra?" Sophia says.

"It's Cherish," Cherish says.

Sophia hugs her belly as she comes around the corner. She's trembling. This is the first time she's shown herself since the accident. Her hair's matted. She's in a threadbare housecoat and a slip, no bra. When she gets closer, Cherish can see the dark half-moons underneath her eyes. "I'm so sorry," she says. "You have no idea. I've been praying!"

"You need to calm down," Cherish hears herself say, her voice cool and even. "The baby—remember?"

"I just don't know what to say," Sophia says. "This is all my fault."

Cherish shakes her head, but Sophia keeps going.

"How bad off is Pearla? Is she gonna make it? I've been up all night thinking about her. Do you need money? I can give it to you. I want to help."

"She's fine," Cherish whispers.

"But the blood."

"I said she'll be fine."

"I'm sorry, I can't imagine the pain you must be feeling."

"No," Cherish whispers.

"What?"

Right as Sophia's about to speak again, Cherish slaps her across the face. Sophia whimpers, but she doesn't seem stunned. She just nurses her face. It's not the first time she's been hit. Blood trickles out from her nose.

Cherish offers her a silk handkerchief from Brooks Brothers. For the first time since the accident, she lets herself smile. It's a close-lipped smile. Nothing can get past it.

"You must be so desperate right now," Cherish says. "Can't imagine what it's like having a husband in jail."

Vacuum Cleaner

·······

CHEYENNE IS WALKING to her second job when she sees the protest going on outside the abortion clinic again. Cluttering the entrance is a religious group hoisting blown-up pictures of pulpy fetuses into the air. They're taking up the whole sidewalk. A construction crew ripped up the other side. Though it's a sunny Saturday afternoon, the workers are all gone. The steamroller they left behind blocks off Indian Head Ave. so that Cheyenne has no choice but to walk through the throng of people yelling Bible verses in her direction.

An old man, white, pulls her aside. His hands are soft and slippery like oil-tanned leather.

"Don't go in there, miss," he says.

"I'm not," she says.

Cheyenne doesn't mean to imply that she agrees with him. She's pro-choice, a progressive. She was treasurer of the feminist coalition at her school, a selective women's college in Maine. Her people are all no-nonsense types from Brooklyn. Both her mom and her oldest half sister Leticia would've popped him in the jaw if they were her.

"Do you know what they do to babies in there?" he asks, still holding onto Cheyenne's arm. He draws her in closer. His breath smells like tooth decay.

Cheyenne tries to pull back, but he won't let her go. She's afraid she might break him if she pushes too hard. She's never been the fighting type. In her family, which is her mom and three older sisters, she's the brainy one and sometimes the smart-alecky one, but never the one to assert herself physically.

A yellow-jacketed volunteer from the clinic yells at the old man, shooing him away with an umbrella that knocks Cheyenne's bifocals off her face. Cheyenne doesn't see the volunteer in his entirety, only catches blurry snatches of the umbrella and his outstretched hand. As she stumbles away, she hears the crunching sound of her Birkenstocks crushing the three-hundred-dollar antiglare lenses. She wants to stop and pick up the pieces, but the noise around her is overwhelming.

The old man, reduced to an abstract whir, struggles against the volunteer's hulking frame. "They kill them! They use a vacuum and suck them up like they're just dirt!"

"I said stand back!" the volunteer says.

"Like dirt!"

"*Stand back*, sir. Don't make me say it again."

Cheyenne pushes through the rest of the protestors and breaks into a sprint. By the time she gets to the end of the block, she's already out of breath. She regrets all the nights in college she spent chain smoking behind the library with her old roommate Sarah Tso. Her lungs are burning like she's trying to breathe underwater. The southwestern sun beams down on her like a huge spotlight. Sweat streams down from her temples.

Without her glasses, she feels more naked than on the hot nights she has to sleep in just underwear.

Yesterday, Cheyenne had answered a Craigslist ad that was looking for a part-time caretaker. Over the phone, the woman who'd posted it, a widow, asked Cheyenne if she had experience with eldercare (yes, if grandparents counted) and children (yes). She gave her the job after just three minutes of talking mostly about her late husband dying in a car wreck. All Cheyenne has to do is watch over the woman's ailing child, Daniel, on Saturdays for sixty bucks an hour. Ms. Halladay—that was the woman's name—said he was a handful, but Cheyenne doesn't mind. In the five months of Cheyenne adventuring out to the desert on her own to teach high school math, she's administered Narcan to a tweaked-out boy on Homecoming night and broken up a fistfight. When she caught two white boys greeting each other with "my nigga," she made them read Peggy Mcintosh during detention.

Still, even as she thought of her triumphs, she couldn't help but feel sorry for Ms. Halladay as well as all the burnt-out teachers at the school—"veteran" teachers, the news calls them—who've been working for decades. Ms. Halladay's voice sounded desperate and sad and old, which reminded Cheyenne of her own mother. Cheyenne asked her for Daniel's age twice, but each time Ms. Halladay acted weird, sighing and saying that Cheyenne would have to come and see for herself. She assumed the woman must be the overprotective mother of a special needs kid. When she hung up, she texted her mother's cellphone, reminding her to take her hypertension pills before her shift at the insurance call center.

At twenty-three, she knows that people never cease being their parents' children even after they're grown. That's why Sarah and her are always saying they want to be rich, hot, childless aunties whom all their nieces look up to. That way they don't have to risk the pain that comes with pulling smaller, more vulnerable people from their insides and into a dying planet. Cheyenne still hasn't completely forgiven her mom for refusing to apologize after killing Barker, their poodle. She'd accidentally given Barker a fatal dose of sedative so that she could clip his nails without him fighting her. The cake she baked for everyone the following day only exacerbated the push and pull of Cheyenne's love for her, torturing Cheyenne. Everyone could hear her sniffles up until she turned on the blender. Unlike her older sisters, strangers in their late thirties and forties raised by a foreign, crueler version of their mom, Cheyenne can't make herself hate her mom completely.

It takes Cheyenne an additional ten minutes to make it to Ms. Halladay's front door. She's already sweat-drenched and tired. She feels like she'll slip out of her clothes if she moves too fast. She rings the bell and waits.

Ms. Halladay's house is a whitewashed Mission Revival with a small succulent garden and two cars in the driveway, a sports car and a VW bug painted like a ladybug. Standing on the grand veranda makes Cheyenne feel poor and miserable even though she'd grown up in a world of relative privilege compared to the other kids in her neighborhood. She remembers how, when she came home from her gifted and talented program as a girl, she used to go through the Long and Foster catalogues that appeared in her mom's mailbox. The houses they advertised were just like this one, grand and old and still way beyond her price range. To think that she used to believe that she'd be living in a place like this by now. She'll have to empty out her savings account to pay for a new pair of glasses. She wishes Ms. Halladay would hurry up and answer the door already.

This crummy job is just her side gig, Cheyenne reminds herself. She's not someone's help. She's an educated Black woman, a college grad who finished a math–education double major with a 3.98 GPA unweighted. She teaches calculus to bright, low-income kids who are always coming into her class bleary eyed but also desperate for an escape. It doesn't pay well, but she gets to live out her virtues. She could be like her overzealous friends from her college's poli-sci and econ departments, most of whom are working for the corporations they used to criticize in academic papers with titles like "The Perils of Privatization: How the World Bank and the IMF Destroyed Africa." Though she knows she's doing what's right, she can't help but feel a pang of sadness whenever she goes online and sees that Sarah Tso, a financial analyst in Manhattan, has posted even more photos of her and her new boyfriend, Li Jing, "#adulting" together at fancy restaurants.

A teenager opens the door. He's wearing a quilted bathrobe and fuzzy brown slippers.

"Is this the Halladay residence?" she asks.

"Yeah."

She can't see the contents of his face clearly without her glasses. He talks, but her astigmatism makes it look like he has no mouth, only a vague line.

"Oh. You must be Daniel. Your mother—"

"You can come in, you know. My mom'll get angry if she sees me letting out the AC."

"Great! So excited to be working with you."

He grunts.

Lining the foyer's buttercream-colored walls are framed photographs of men and boys who must be family, maybe Daniel's siblings. There's a polaroid of a little boy in overalls, a smaller picture of a man in a cap and gown, and a circular one of a middle-aged man standing in front of the Eiffel Tower with a curly-haired woman. Cheyenne has to squint to make out all the details. Her head starts to hurt.

"Are they your brothers?" Cheyenne asks.

"No. They're me."

He doesn't even look up to see which pictures she's referring to. There's no difference between him and her students. All kids his age have been like this until they open up to her: solipsistic, indifferent. Cheyenne wants to think that Daniel doesn't look all that sick—that he isn't bedridden or a wheelchair user—but stops herself. She knows from college sensitivity workshops that illness can oftentimes be invisible. Ms. Halladay hadn't specified why Daniel needed a caretaker, and Cheyenne didn't press her, not wanting to force a widow to relay her personal trauma.

Ms. Halladay's sitting in the living room. *Fixer Upper* plays on a giant flat screen, which makes Cheyenne think of home—not her current efficiency apartment that's across the street from the clinic or the old terrace apartment near Kennebunkport, but her mom's rent-controlled apartment in Dumbo. Her mom's obsessed with makeover shows and home decorating shows—really anything that involves well-deserving housewives crying tears of joy over refurbished kitchens, blonde highlights, Spanx, etc.

"Howdy!" Ms. Halladay says, unironically.

She's wearing a tunic with yoga pants and cowboy boots. She sounded white over the phone but possesses the same even terracotta skin as Daniel, only darker. Cheyenne assumes that her late husband, or whoever Daniel's father was, must have been white. Halladay sounds vaguely Dutch, maybe English—more lily-white than whatever this woman is. And she's so old, more so than the parents at school or even Cheyenne's mom. If she and her husband had gotten married at Cheyenne's age, would they have had to go to another state because of the antimiscegenation laws that used to exist? Cheyenne wonders why Ms. Halladay waited so long to have children. Maybe she was hoping for the world to get less racist. Cheyenne sometimes feels like she has to do the same, saving up for a future that might never come. She counted five houses with Trump yard signs on Ms. Halladay's street.

They shake hands. Ms. Halladay's gray hair is cut into a stylish bob that sways with the languid way she moves her body. Daniel's gone off into the kitchen. He yells out about there not being any Fig Newtons left in the pantry. They ignore him.

"I'm so glad you came on time," the woman says. "The last person we had was always running late. And then she just stopped showing up altogether. She said Daniel's affliction was scary."

"Sorry to hear." Cheyenne pinches her face up in exaggerated concern. All she wants to do is lie down, watch TV, and eat the big bag of pita chips that's sitting unopened on the coffee table.

"The worst part is that I can't really blame her. Daniel's such a hard case." Ms. Halladay sighs. "On my worst days, he honestly makes me wanna side with all the people who left him. I'm just so desperate for just the tiniest break."

"I'm sorry."

Ms. Halladay makes a swatting gesture with her hand as if to say the past's not important. "But if you need anything, you have my cell number. I'm only going to be gone for an hour, just to test things out. I might stop for coffee at the Riviera Club. Did you want anything from there? Their beignets are to die for."

"Thank you," Cheyenne whispers.

"I saw the résumé you sent. I'm sure you don't want to teach forever. Have you looked into aeronautics? My husband did it all his life. It's still a really good field to go into, especially if you work for the air force. You can raise a whole family without worrying about the future."

Cheyenne says she'll think about it, but the truth is she doesn't want to work for the military just to raise a child. She's read about the military industrial complex and seen pictures of deformed Agent Orange babies. The mere idea of doing what her mom and Ms. Halladay's late husband have, giving their kids the world while also making it worse, pains her.

Daniel calls out for his mom again, this time louder. "You're not listening," he says.

"Teenagers," Cheyenne says, trying to find some semblance of solidarity with the gray-haired woman standing in front of her. She's doing that thing her mom did with the other moms on their block when Cheyenne was Daniel's age, bonding by complaining about stubborn children who never listen.

"Oh? Daniel." Ms. Halladay starts laughing. "He's not a teenager, Cheyenne. He's forty-two. Here, I'm never good at explaining these things aloud."

She reaches into her purse, the same leather clutch all the rich girls from college used to carry, and hands Cheyenne what looks like a business card. Cheyenne has to squint to read the card three times, and even then she's still confused.

Whenever Daniel gets uncomfortable, his condition flares up. It developed after an attempted suicide following a very unfair divorce (if you read this, Traci, you're going to hell for stealing my grandkids). His memory isn't as good as it used to be, please be patient. I'm the only one taking care of him because his ex-wife refuses to help out as usual (you are a LEECH, Trashy Traci), and all the doctors just want to study him like an animal.

Ms. Halladay won't look at Cheyenne. Her eyes are staring at the TV's glowing screen. Cheyenne can tell she's trying to be flippant when really she just looks scared. She recognizes the familiar sadness clouding Ms. Halladay's eyes.

"I don't understand," Cheyenne starts, stuffing the card into her pants pocket. "What—"

Daniel tromps back into the living room, an empty box in his hand.

"Daniel!" the woman snaps, which makes Cheyenne jump back. "Why can't you just calm down for once!"

"But you said you went to the store!"

"Well, I guess I forgot. You know, this universe doesn't exactly revolve around you. Hard to believe it, I know."

Daniel lets himself collapse onto the couch. He gives her the middle finger. The woman shakes her head and leaves, slamming the screen door on her way out.

Cheyenne is unmoving, still standing in the same spot where Ms. Halladay has left her. She hears one of Ms. Halladay's cars pulling out of the driveway and onto the main road. The sound of the engine grows distant until there's nothing left in the air but a sudden, deafening silence. She thinks Daniel might cry like the kids who sometimes come to her office hours when they've failed an exam. Instead, he turns the channel to a baseball game.

"Can you move?" he says. "You're blocking my view."

* * *

It doesn't take Cheyenne long to realize what Daniel is. When she goes to use the bathroom, passing by him real close so she can get a better look, he looks just like a teenager. He keeps feeling the cystic acne on his cheeks with his hands, the fingernails of which are grubby and dark. He has a baby face that clashes with his broad football-player shoulders.

She times herself so that she can maximize the length of her solitude without having Daniel think she's taking a shit. She sits on the toilet lid and reads through the texts she got this morning. There's one from Sarah Tso, who says she saw their old RA on the PATH train into the city this morning. Apparently, their RA is now pregnant even though she's only twenty-five, just a few years older than both of them, a distance that used to feel vast when they were freshmen and she a junior. If it had been anyone else, Cheyenne would freak out. But she's fine because the RA came from a small religious commune where women are expected to do that—grow up, find a man, get pregnant, create an army-sized family that can protest abortion clinics. It's different for women like Cheyenne. It's 2016, the era of third-wave feminism. This isn't *The Group*, after all. Still, she feels like time is running out, like the futures she used to have to choose from are tumbling away like fallen fruit from a tree or the eggs in her uterus.

Cheyenne is in the process of composing a response, a jokey question inquiring who among all the hardcore partiers from their floor freshman year would make the worst mom, when she hears what sounds like a baby crying. The cries are coming from the living room. Cheyenne sighs and puts her phone back in her back pocket. Ms. Halladay never said she had to take care of a baby too.

"Fuck this shit," she says to her reflection.

When Cheyenne steps back into the living room, Daniel's not on the couch anymore. In his place is a wailing, naked toddler. It's crying so hard that its face is all red like the inside of its gaping, gummy mouth. She looks down and sees its thumb-sized dick. She doesn't like looking after kids below high school age. She's told her mom that little kids can't be taught, only taken care of. They lack subjectivity, babies especially.

She thinks of calling for Daniel, but decides against it. He'd be no help. She turns off the TV right as a commercial for weight loss smoothies begins playing. She picks up the toddler and sees that he's been lying on top of Daniel's bathrobe. She nearly trips over Daniel's slippers, which he's left carelessly on the floor.

That's when it happens. The toddler's rolls of fat begin rippling like small waves. She can hear his bones cracking and groaning as they change form, distending the flesh. She screams, but doesn't think of dropping him until he's no longer a toddler anymore but a little boy that's also totally stark naked.

He shoves her away and goes behind the couch, laughing. He looks like he could be eight or nine, though she's always been bad at discerning the ages of little kids.

Cheyenne runs back into the bathroom and splashes water on her face until he comes in, his reflection filling up one of the bottom corners of the mirror. She squints and sees that he's dressed in Daniel's bathrobe, which trails behind him like a French king's cape. He's just standing in the doorway, staring at her with a moony expression. She latches both hands onto the porcelain basin, suppressing the urge to scream. Slowly, she turns to him.

"Are you my babysitter?" he asks.

"I-I have to go now," Cheyenne says. "Your mom should be back soon. I'm sorry. I don't feel too good."

"You can't go!" he says. He stamps his small foot.

She tries stepping around him, but he grabs onto her leg.

Cheyenne screams.

"What are you?" she asks.

"I'm Daniel!"

Cheyenne remembers the card. It crinkles in her back pocket as she backs out into the hallway. She feels like she did that one time she came across a legless amputee on 131st Street. The beggar had grabbed ahold of her pants leg and told her how he wanted to suck her tits raw. He burst out into a high-pitched laugh that stung her ears like bits of shrapnel, driving her into a hipster-y coffee shop. She waited over an hour for him to go, watching him until he scooted down the road on a skateboard. She felt herself growing smaller with him as he disappeared into the giant swarms of people.

She can't just leave Daniel alone. But she also doesn't want to stay.

"How about I take you to you mom. I can drive you. I saw you had a second car. If you know where the keys—"

"No, no, no. She's mean. She locks me in the closet."

"I'm so sorry."

"I wanna play Stormtroopers. Play Stormtroopers with me."

"I don't think that's a good idea." She tries to use a polite, high-pitched voice. It comes out all squeaky. "Maybe next time, alright?"

"No!"

"Watch your tone, please."

"Fuck you. Dad says I can do whatever I want."

"Please. Be kind."

The kid lets go of her and dashes into the kitchen. She runs behind him. He's so fast it looks like he's everywhere at once, a lagging blur that can't keep up with his fury. He's screaming and jumping and pushing all the wrought-iron barstools onto the floor. Cheyenne opens her mouth. She thinks she's telling him to stop, but she can't hear her own voice over the sound of him self-destructing right in front of her.

He's gotten into the cabinets now. He knocks over the millennial-pink canisters, the sea-glass bottles and mason jars. A bag of flour explodes, filling the whole kitchen with a thick plume that rains onto the floor and countertops. He smashes a spice rack and a lazy Susan. The whole room suddenly smells like turmeric and cloves and garlic and chili powder all at once. He stops yelling, focusing all his energy on chucking canned goods against the wall. One of them breaks open and sprays Cheyenne with a briny liquid. She tries tackling him, but keeps tripping. He's strong for a little kid. He throws a cast iron pan like a javelin.

Daniel only stops once she starts screaming, beating him at his own game. She's not saying anything. She's only making noise just like him. By now, the kitchen is destroyed. She looks at the oven and sees that he's shattered its window. Cheyenne grows quiet. She's not paying attention to him anymore. She's thinking about the kitchen and how Ms. Halladay will fire her when Daniel inevitably pins the blame on her somehow. Cheyenne would offer to fix it, but doesn't have the money. She can barely cover rent with the paltry checks she receives from the educational NGO that assigned her to the town.

"Are you angry at me?" he asks.

She gives him the silent treatment.

"Ms. Babysitter? Are you angry?"

Silence.

"I hate this. I wish I'd never been born. This isn't my fault. If you'd just—"

Cheyenne plugs in the Dyson vacuum that's propped up against the kitchen table. She takes out one of the nozzles and starts cleaning the hard-to-reach places, working her way to the center of the floor where the real mess is waiting.

When she looks up at him again, he's a man, maybe in his forties judging by the gray streaks in his hair. He's still sniffling, still naked. He looks confused. Cheyenne pretends not to notice him. Her eyes dart back on the floor, desperate to avoid his sad eyes and sadder flaccid penis. She hears him rushing to put the bathrobe back on.

"I'm sorry," he says. He follows her around as she vacuums up the spilled spices, tracking flour across the hardwood. He talks extra loud over the mechanical sucking noise. "I don't know who did this, but if I did, I'm sorry. I swear I'll clean it up. I have a temper, but I'm working on it—I'm going to therapy now. I must've blacked out. I was bleeding out in the tub and I saw a light and now I'm here. Are you one of the maids my mother hired?"

Cheyenne just shakes her head. She wants him to go away without telling him. But he keeps talking.

"*¿No sabes ingles?*"

She shakes her head again, which makes him break out into giant, choking sobs.

When she looks up again, his body is melting. He's still crying as he shrinks into nothing. His skin tightens around him, making him smaller and smaller and smaller until he's just a pulsating, quarter sized blob of pinkish flesh on the floor.

She drops the nozzle and steps backward, knocking her back against the butcher's table. In kindergarten, her class watched baby swallows hatch one by one in an incubator. She imagines their skin now, featherless and gooey like the yolks they emerged from.

The nozzle jumps around on the floor. Then it sucks him up. She can hear him coming unraveled as he travels upward through the nozzle. The force is ripping him to pieces. The vacuum slurps and sputters.

Her hands are shaking so badly that she misses the switch the first two tries. When she finally turns the machine off, she pries open the plastic reservoir and sifts through the layers of filth until she finds him at the bottom. He's a formless nothing. She picks up the pulsating blob, cradling it in her hand as she watches the time on the microwave's clock. Two minutes go by. She's waiting for him to change, to transform before her eyes once more. She pokes it, curiosity overtaking her horror.

Her pocket vibrates. She takes her phone out with her free hand and taps the screen. Her fingers tremble as she undoes the lock and sees that it's not Ms. Halladay but only Sarah Tsao wanting to know if they can FaceTime later tonight. She puts the phone back away so she can cradle Daniel with two hands.

Her heart is beating so fast that it feels like it's all the way in her mouth, choking her. She spots a stainless-steel grilling skewer on the center island. She's not trying to hurt him when she presses its sharpened tip against him, only change him, remembering the card, but then blood comes out. Though she's speechless, her mind is yelling, telling her this is all her fault, that she's destined to suffer for what's out of her control—for Daniel, but also her broken glasses, ailing bank account, and Ms. Halladay's destroyed kitchen—because she's powerless and thus always at fault. Cheyenne hears Ms. Halladay's car pulling up into the driveway. She looks up at the microwave again and realizes that it's already time for her to come back.

The sound of the engine swells. She bolts out the front door, still holding onto what's left of Daniel. As she runs with no clear direction in mind, she envisions a pair of giant hands ripping the world into shreds of flesh. She picks up speed, trampling a flowerbed and narrowly missing a work truck.

Cherry Banana

·······

HENRY WAS ALWAYS talking about checking out of the Regent, though by now his room had developed the cluttered, lived-in feel of a home. His messes were too intimate for a hotel: grease stains on the wall, mud all over the little shoe rack he'd brought from his place. There were dishes and a hot plate and pulp magazines with pretty blondes on the covers.

He'd also brought his kid's baby blanket, though he admitted that she'd been too old for that sort of thing when she eloped with that no-good boy of hers. But as soon as his kid came back, he told Cherry for the millionth time, he'd pack up everything and leave this place forever.

"But what if she doesn't?" Cherry asked.

"She will," Henry said. "She checked into this room with that loser, and she's gonna check back out again with me. He didn't even pay the bill. The cheat."

"But you said she went away on her own. She wasn't kidnapped."

"She'll realize her mistake. The private investigator I hired deals with these sorts of things all the time, and he said not to worry."

All Cherry could do was nod. She was one of the Regent's receptionists, the light-skinned one from down south. Freckles, red hair—real cute. She often spent the night with Henry, just the two of them in this tiny room where his daughter had reunited with her fling. She lay in Henry's arms with pouting lips, the uncommitted type of pretty girl who wanted everyone to look at her and no one at all. They used the fold-out couch, not the bed—that was off-limits.

Cherry had gotten her job around the same time that Henry had checked in, and she'd started sleeping with him a little bit after. That had all been close to a year ago. Summer had cooled into autumn, which froze into the harshest winter she'd ever felt through the thin fabric of her peacoat. This morning, she'd heard from Pamela downstairs that there was going to be a snowstorm sometime tonight. It was late now. Outside Henry's window, a black sky hovered above the lit-up city. No snow yet, but maybe later.

"Can't wait to be out of this dump," Henry said.

"I'll miss you," Cherry said.

He smiled. He didn't say he'd miss her too. Instead, he kissed her on the cheek like she was a child. Cherry felt a sting in her chest. She didn't like his messes and despised his stubbornness, but she'd come to like him. He was different, but also familiar. His family was Algerian, which he said the French looked down on. He had money from his accounting job and his father's wealth. Being with him was like rereading one of her favorite Westerns because she got to be close to someone who felt too interesting to be real. She'd just left South Texas for Chicago, her need for something new fighting homesickness and winning just barely.

Cherry buried her head in his side. The couch's metal frame groaned under their weight. She wondered if it would ever give.

The hotel was a place of ill repute. There were women who wore fishnets and strong perfume, mostly Black but some white. They left wet condoms on the floor that Cherry had to pick up by hand before she vacuumed (management made her clean in addition to her desk duties; they refused to hire enough people). She wasn't one of them. She wasn't with Henry for money because he hadn't given her any. And obviously, they weren't married. She didn't know what she was after with him, figured she just liked the feeling of him. His minty cologne made her brain tingle—it was just that good; she'd lap it all up if she could, and sometimes, when she was drunk enough, she tried.

Henry cleared his throat. "Deena"—his daughter, the one who ran away with a boy—"still has her key to this room. She didn't return it, and I don't think anyone changed the locks. She forgot her hat. It's her favorite. She'll come back for that before she tries going home. Her and her mother can't stand each other."

"What if she doesn't like it that much?" Cherry asked.

"She does. You just don't know."

But I do, Cherry thought. She knew what runaway girls were like. He of all people should know that about her by now.

A part of her wanted to push Henry a little. Not to the point of making him angry but just enough to try and

understand him better. He and Deena fascinated her, Deena
especially. What she knew was that Deena was sixteen, rebellious and dangerously in love with the older boy she'd eloped
with.

"I wish I had your life," Henry said.

"You wouldn't like it," Cherry said. "I already told you
about my ma going crazy. She chased me around with a hot
iron when I told her to go to hell. Imagine all of that happening
to you in a little room with a bunch of screaming babies inside."

"I'd take all the poverty and everything else if it meant erasing all this pain. You just don't get it. You've never had a child."

"But I do get it." She had more to say, but her voice was
in knots. She was thinking about the hot iron again, how her
mom was always threatening to burn her with it before beating
her instead. Her head started paining her again.

Her mom liked to say she was a seamstress, and though she
could sew—taught Cherry everything she knew—she made
most of her living washing clothes. Every day, she'd dragged in
big, fat bags of rich white people's day clothes, eveningwear,
night clothes. The apartment always reeked of lye even with
all the windows open. Once Cherry asked about who her real
daddy was, asking if it was really the redheaded white man who
ran the post office, and her mom shoved a huge chunk of laundry soap into her mouth for repeating gossip. "It's none of your
Goddamn business!" her mom screamed.

"You've got a kid?" Henry asked Cherry. He grabbed her
shoulder when she turned away, making her look at him. "How
old did you say you were, again?"

"*Had*," Cherry corrected him. "I had a son. And I'm almost twenty-one."

"How old is he?"

Cherry struggled to swallow. "Five," she heard herself say.

Henry nodded. "I was young when I had Deena." He laughed, then sighed. "My parents threw me out, so my girlfriend and I moved in with her family. I don't know what I'd do without them. They were so kind. Very progressive. They could've just sent her away and told me to beat it. Her dad said I had to stay with her if I wanted his support, which I was more than willing to do, of course, because I loved her and she loved me back."

"Are you still in love?"

Henry paused. Cherry thought that maybe he didn't hear her, but then he told her not to worry: he and his wife were separated except at dinner parties where they pretended to still be intact. He dragged her closer to him. His warmth made her sleepy.

"I'm guessing your son's a ward of the state," he said.

"I don't feel much like talking," Cherry mumbled.

"What was the reason for you losing custody?"

Cherry shrugged. She had half a mind to smother him with a pillow. She had to wake up early for work tomorrow, and also find a way to avoid the nosy cleaning woman whom she suspected had caught wind of the affair. A dead taste filled her mouth.

The wind was so strong it made the window rattle like the porthole of a ship in crisis. They weren't that far up, only two stories—the building itself was small—but Cherry still had nightmares of the Indigo collapsing, killing everybody inside and leaving her trapped alone in the rubble. She'd read an article in a magazine about that happening to a baby boy during the Second World War. Somewhere in Europe—she'd forgotten where. He survived; his mother and older brother perished.

"You don't have to talk if you don't want to," Henry said. "Just know that your son's still around. You can still see him. You just have to be patient. One day, when you least expect it, he'll phone you. You have to be ready."

"That's silly talk," Cherry said. "He's probably buried somewhere I'll never know."

"Did you see him die?"

"No. I just know. I can feel it."

"So you don't know, then."

Cherry closed her eyes, thinking, her memories of the past so deeply felt that they were an emotion of their own. When she opened them, she felt tears dribbling down her face. He'd unearthed something in her. It was too big to put back. She was bawling. She'd never felt so sad and yet so relieved since the day she crossed the border into Oklahoma.

Henry stroked her hair, running his fingers over the part of her neck where the freckled skin met the red, woolen curls that men loved so much. He squeezed her hair tight like a sponge and watched it expand back again.

"Is Cherry your real name?" he asked. "Or a nickname?"

"Neither," Cherry said, sniffling. "I made it up when I came here. People used to call me Banana when I was little because someone said I was all splotchy and sweet like one."

He started kissing her. She giggled until she thought she might throw up. "Banana," he kept saying in a funny voice. The name still stung a little, but his hands felt good underneath her chemise. "Cherry Banana."

* * *

Cherry hadn't known what to do with her pregnancy. She was so young. Her stomach wouldn't stop growing no matter how hard she willed it to flatten. It made her ill. Her breasts ached. She started wearing her sister Monica's old clothes, which were baggy even with her pregnancy, Monica being six-foot-something and buxom like most of the other women in their family.

Cherry's mom didn't say anything in the beginning, so no one else in the house did either, though her dad grumbled more about all the mouths he had to feed. When Cherry had to drop out of school—there was no pregnancy school where she was from—and almost confessed, she told her mom that she preferred doing real work. She convinced herself that her mom didn't notice any change in her. Her mom wordlessly handed her the washboard. They cleaned clothes together in silence for what felt like forever, the hours stretching into weeks that pained Cherry's back. Her mom took breaks. Cherry did more work: the cooking, the cleaning. She had seven siblings who still lived at home, all of them young and loud and very needy. Monica, the second oldest, had run away the previous summer.

So when her mom finally did say something, Cherry's surprise was genuine. Cherry was complaining about her feet being swollen when her mom snapped and called her a lazy whore. She knocked a brush out of Cherry's hand.

Her mom's accusations came out of nowhere. They'd been cleaning, her mom playing the radio for company, Cherry hoping that she'd have a boy who could save her somehow— and then her mom started carrying on again.

"People keep talking," her mom said. "D'you know what this is gonna do? All the shame and staring, and all because you wanted to open your legs."

Cherry shrugged. "People talk."

"*People talk.*" Her mom snorted. "You've got some nerve."

Cherry smiled, though she didn't want to. It was just something she did when she got yelled at. When her mom came at her with the iron, Cherry started laughing so hard that she could barely run. So strange, she thought the whole time. Nothing about her body made sense.

Her mouth felt dead like it had when her mom had made her ingest soap over the postal worker. He probably was her real father, too, even her dad—her mom's husband—had said so while playing cards with a friend, oblivious to Cherry, who'd been lingering just out of view. He'd taken a long sip of beer, slammed the bottle too hard on the packing-crate-*cum*-table, and proclaimed that his crazy Jenni might've killed that po ol' girl had she been left alone with her. It took a moment for Cherry to realize that she was the po ol' girl. Jenni was her mom.

"Who was it?" her mom asked. She was holding the iron in front of her like a loaded gun. "Tell me right now. Who'd you let do this to you?"

Cherry tried to escape. She ran outside onto the wooden landing, slamming the door behind her when her mom smacked it wide open.

"You tell me or else," her mom said.

"That's none of your Goddamn business," Cherry yelled at the top of her lungs. She kept dodging her mom's blows as she was coming toward her, hopping left and right and backward like a boxer.

Cherry's mom slapped her hard and fast across the face. Cherry fell backward, the floorboards disappearing from under her feet. She became breathless.

Her mom was big, much larger than Cherry. Up close, she was pretty, her lips bee-stung, her eyes large and expressive and honey-colored. But from a distance, as Cherry went flying down the perron staircase that connected their apartment to the unit below, her mom was a giantess poised to devour her. Cherry felt her head knock against something sharp. Then she was out.

The miscarriage wasn't painful. Not at first. The blood pooling in Cherry's underwear was warm like bathwater as she faded in and out. Time sloshed around in her head, leaking out onto the pavement.

Cherry thought of the crazy woman who used to live below them, the one her mom had driven away all those years ago. She'd barely been walking age, but she remembered the floral pattern of the crazy woman's couch and the headache she'd gotten crying for her mother. The woman wanted a child because the state had taken all of hers.

"So she tries taking one of my own," her mom explained to Cherry once she was old enough. "Crazy-ass bitch. I knocked down her door and beat her so bad she had no choice but to not come back. I told her if I ever saw her sorry face again, I'd kill her."

The story was the closest thing Cherry had to a mother's affection. She liked to hear her mom tell it over and over. That was the only time she savored her mom's violence, which felt too nuanced for anger alone to drive it, its meanings so varied it could be a language of its own.

Her mom might not like her very much, but she'd kill for her, and that felt like enough for a while. Cherry found pleasure in the idea of other people going mad for her. The woman downstairs had watched her play dolls with other girls from the apartment, older, impressive girls with nymphlike figures and playground wits that felt wise—but it had been Cherry who was chosen. If only she hadn't been insane, maybe Cherry might've stayed. Cherry could've hidden under that couch until her mom left. Maybe then she would've been able to keep her baby.

Her baby. Cherry knew he was gone from the moment she woke up in her mom's bed. Was there a body? As she pulled the quilt off of her, a searing pain jutted up from her armpit to her back. She cried out as one of the little ones in the house rushed to put a hot water bottle on her stomach. She kept shaking. A life had passed through her like a terrible disease.

Cherry couldn't decide if her mom had meant to burden her with this much pain. No matter what the answer might've been, she knew that staying with her wasn't an option. But she couldn't run away right now—not when she was still so weak. She was helpless. She never did get to go back to school. And the pastor's son who'd gotten her in trouble moved away. He'd never know he was a father, much less a bereaved one. What luck.

When Cherry looked back on her pain much later, she couldn't help but think of the hotel. In her dreams, amalgamations of the past and present, Henry was right there next to her in the bed. He told her there was someone out there who loved her. It wasn't her mom. Nor was it the pastor's boy because he'd only been fooling around with her out of boredom. And friends from school didn't count because they had all been casual. It had to be her own son who loved her because he was gone. That had been the only thing that ever gave her warmth: nothing, no one.

Cherry bore the emptiness. There was so much room for hope. Her son could be anywhere, be anything. All she had to do was close her eyes and there he was.

* * *

The following week, Cherry got a new, better job cleaning up at a furrier's place in Edison Park. She meant to tell Henry, but work got in the way until the fantasy of seeing him devolved into an obligation that she neglected like a dreaded appointment. But his words stuck: there was still hope. On the bus one morning, she decided that her son's name was Matthew. That was the hospital where he should've been born: Matthew Earlham Memorial. She was pretty sure it got shut down over a mold infestation. Her mind got sidetracked. She wondered if Henry had forgotten about her.

Cherry's period didn't come. The rest of her life went on anyways, changing its shape into something more promising, less predictable. A month passed. The furrier's assistant quit. The furrier asked Cherry if she could sew. Cherry said yes and the furrier gave her a white smock to wear.

A familiar sickness took hold of Cherry's stomach. It wouldn't let go. She kept having to go to the bathroom. The trips became more frequent as the furrier's busy season picked up. Cherry cut and sewed pelts, feeling their softness, measuring their sprawl, and taking frequent breaks to throw up in the toilet. It was just like when she was sixteen, lots of work and discomfort, no one she could talk to about it, only now she was completely alone. The furrier's cold indifference had replaced Cherry's mom's rages.

"You're pregnant," the furrier said. "Aren't you?"

"Yes," Cherry said. She put a hand on her still-flat stomach. "And I'm keeping him."

The furrier clucked her tongue. She was an old white woman who was icy all over: cool disposition, piercing blue eyes, skin as colorless as blank paper only more ravaged. Though she didn't seem to give much thought to Cherry, her passive contempt was obvious.

"Well, you know, I don't normally deal with single mothers," the furrier said.

"I'm not single," Cherry shot back.

What she really wanted to do was scream. She closed her eyes and felt herself falling from a great distance as her feet stayed planted on the floor. That day she lost Matthew, when she was recovering, she wondered if her mom had been trying to save her or kill her. Her mom seesawed between one of the two possibilities, back and forth—she loved Cherry, she loved her not. Cherry had made herself stiff each time her mom helped her get dressed, ignoring intense pain as she raised her arms. Later, when people in town asked where she'd been as if they hadn't already heard, she said she'd had the flu. She was lying for her mom's benefit, which was also her own. Sometimes she added that she almost hadn't made it.

"I didn't realize you were married," the furrier said. She gestured to the other employees, two mousy white girls busily, nervously, trimming the guard hairs of a leopard throw. "My female assistants wear their rings to work."

"I'm getting married soon," Cherry said.

She didn't know where the lie had come from, but it sounded convincing. "Next month," she added. "To my fiancé. He's an accountant. He's living out of a hotel until we can find a place that's decent."

"How wonderful," the furrier said. Her face was blank.

"Very," Cherry agreed.

"You're cutting too much."

"What?" Cherry put down the scissors. "Oh."

She'd meant to let out the skin of a pelt but had made one of the strips too small. She'd come so close to ruining everything.

"Oh God," the furrier said.

She grabbed the strip from Cherry, studied the tiny flaws and threw everything in the overflowing bin of scraps. The place was in desperate need of a new cleaner. The furrier ran her business out of her apartment, her work spilling out from the "factory" (read: living room) to the kitchen with its sink full of dirty dishes.

"I have to leave early," Cherry said. "My husband. It's an emergency."

"I thought he was your fiancé," the furrier said.

"Yes. That's what I meant."

Again, the furrier clucked her tongue. "Well, just know I'm a pragmatic Christian. I'm not charitable to sinful types, and I certainly don't employ them."

"My fiancé's waiting."

"Whatever you say."

The furrier lived far from the Regent. On the long bus ride, Cherry thought about Matthew and reincarnation, a funny idea she'd heard from a friend of a friend who'd become Buddhist. She wondered if the eggs inside of her shared the same soul. But what about siblings? Weren't they separate entities? No, no, no, Cherry told herself. She shouldn't be thinking about the spiritual like this. Matthew was still out there. Alive. Or maybe he was more than alive, a persistent force flickering inside of her like a kind of hope.

By the time Cherry made it to the hotel's side door, it was already late. One of the cleaning women came out, a new girl from the looks of it. Cherry pushed past her, and the girl just let her through. She bolted out into the sitting area and up the stairs before anything could stop her.

Henry was in. He looked surprised to see her. At first, she couldn't make herself speak. All her mind could do was chastise her for coming this far when she should've just gone home. She braced herself for his rejection of her.

"I thought you'd quit," he said. "What happened?"

"I'm pregnant," Cherry said.

The confession didn't seem to affect Henry. He just nodded and let her in. They sat next to each other on the end of the bed, eyes facing the wall. They were so close. Cherry could feel his breath.

"I'm running low on money right now," he explained. "My wife. She wants a divorce. I told her how bad it would look, especially after what happened with Deena. And of course, the details of our marriage weren't the best, but I thought we'd made up for it. But then Deena."

"You're waiting for your wife too," Cherry asked. "Aren't you? You love her."

"Yeah."

"That's what I thought." Cherry was about to get up to leave when Henry grabbed her hands.

"Please," he said. "I can still love you, I swear. Just don't go."

"I don't know," Cherry said.

"Don't get rid of the kid, okay? Not now. I'm not in a position to choose right now."

"I'd never dream of doing that, Henry."

Henry reeled her into a tight hug. She kissed him. He made her promise that she'd never leave again like that. She apologized. She hadn't realized that he cared about her so deeply.

"They pass through me like water in my hands," he said.

"Who?" Cherry asked.

"Everyone." He looked her in the eye, his face getting hard. "I didn't expect to, but when you stopped showing up, I thought of giving up. I wanted to go home and pretend none of this ever happened. I thought I could forget Deena."

"Henry," Cherry said. She couldn't think of anything better to say. She felt like she'd been miscast in a romance movie about some other girl named Cherry.

"Of course, I didn't leave," he said. His grip grew tighter still. "I thought: No, I just need to stay here and wait. She'll come back. They'll all come back. And then you did."

Though part of her recoiled, Cherry made herself smile. He seemed more desperate than she remembered. His skin was sweaty to the touch.

Everything around her felt grimier and ill-lit. His room hadn't been vacuumed. There were bits of hair embedded in the carpet. Crumbs everywhere. Most likely, the cleaning women had all grown tired of picking his junk off the floor.

Cherry wondered if management would ever throw Henry out. People here normally got the boot when they stopped paying their bills. But Henry was rich, or at least he was compared to most of the building. She'd never been to his real home, but from what he'd told me, it had four bedrooms, three levels, and a sunroom where his ruddy, Scandinavian-American wife painted landscapes all day. Their backyard was big enough for their children (three plus Deena) to go egg hunting each Easter. Cherry imagined all their kids having fun together in church clothes, the girls in crinoline-stuffed dresses, the boys in suits and new leather shoes still stiff from lack of use.

"I have a name for my child," Cherry said. "Matthew. I'm hoping for a boy so I can call him that."

"And if it's a girl?"

"Who said there can't be a girl named Matthew?"

"Matthewla, perhaps."

Cherry made a face. "Maybe something else."

Henry laughed at that. The sound was strained but genuine. "Matthew," he said, nodding. "How very biblical of you. How'd you come up with it?"

"It was my other son's name," Cherry said. "The one I told you about."

Silence. A moment passed where all she could hear was breathing, the hum of the radiator and a man hollering for someone named Jeanetta down the hall. Henry laughed again, this time meaner.

"I'm sorry," Henry said. "It's just so ridiculous: replacing one kid with another like they're parts to a machine." He shook his head. "Unbelievable."

"I'm not replacing anybody," Cherry said.

"Then what are you doing?"

Cherry tried to organize her thoughts, but they wouldn't come out right. They all sounded ignorant once she heard them out loud. She talked about God and eggs and the friend of a friend who became Buddhist.

"Hold on just a minute," Henry said, his voice getting louder. "Don't act all flustered just because I caught you red-handed. I bet you thought you could replace my kid, too, while you were at it. How many Matthews have you had?" He wouldn't let her speak. "See? That's the problem with people like you: you don't value human life."

"What's gotten into you?" Cherry asked.

"You know what, just get out. I don't care what you do with your baby. I want no part of your deception."

His face was too much to take in. His eyes were hard. The lines across his face and around his mouth got deeper. Cherry looked down at her feet.

"I'm not going," Cherry whispered.

"Fine."

Henry started dragging her out of the room, yanking her bad arm so hard that she yelled out. The pain was unbelievable. She couldn't fight back anymore. All she could do was scream.

"You must've lost your damn mind," Cherry yelled.

Henry pushed her against the hallway wall. Bits of her hair caught onto one of the sconces. It yanked on her scalp as she slid to the floor. His hands were now balled-up fists.

"Keep it up," she warned, "and I swear I'll do something." She paused, thinking, mostly trying to catch her breath. "I'll kill you."

The hallway was quiet. Empty. Cherry braced herself for a fight. She got back up, legs wobbly. For a long moment that refused to end, she waited for him to strike.

"You're touched," Henry said finally.

He went back to his room, closing the door but not slamming it. Everything got quiet. The lonely buzzing of the wall sconces gutted Cherry. She was on her own again.

* * *

At first, the Regent had been the private residence of a fruit heiress. When she died, it became a finishing school, then an art gallery, a nursing home, a reform school, and all the while, its structural parts were rotting from increased neglect. The scrolled cornices became worm-eaten, the white-painted siding weather-beaten and grimy. The hotel was the building's last, worst incarnation.

A cracked foundation was what led to the condemning of the Regent. By then, Cherry hadn't worked there in two, almost three decades. She had her own business dealing and revitalizing fur, a house in the suburbs, and her daughter, Matilda, who was grown. No husband, though; she'd grown tired of searching long ago. She was older. The furrier who'd fired her was certainly dead by now.

From what Cherry had read in the papers, the Regent had been scheduled for demolition for a while. The problem was the squatter. He was disheveled, unwieldy. Allegedly, he pulled a knife on a construction worker. One of the hotel's new owners had tried to have him killed—"*Removed*," he insisted to the press—so now the hotel was of national interest. There was a criminal suit and a civil one, protests and counterprotests. The mafia was involved. A courtroom brawl left a bailiff with a broken nose.

Cherry listened to the latest updates on the radio. She was sitting in her Corvette at O'Hare, waiting for traffic to move. In front of her, a family, Black, took their time disembarking from a cab. The littlest boy struggled to pull out a suitcase from the trunk. The teenage one took over with ease, and the younger one protested, stamping his feet. They started walking to the gate, the kids trailing their parents like a gaggle of ducklings, the youngest still pouting.

For a moment, Cherry's vision dissolved around the family. She didn't see who was coming toward her until she heard a knock. Her body jolted to life. She became aware of herself. It was a terrible feeling sometimes. She switched off the radio and opened the passenger door.

For the millionth time, she went through her mental check-list: get Deena, reunite her with her dad, go home. Anything to get Henry to leave the Regent. She was tired of journalists ringing her up. How the hell had they even found her? She still couldn't believe Henry was the squatter. The humiliation. Matilda hadn't forgiven her for saying that her dad had died in Vietnam.

Cherry rolled down the window. "Hey," Cherry said. "How was the trip?"

"Long," Deena said as she fiddled with her seatbelt. She didn't have any luggage with her, just a patent leather purse. She was bigger than what Cherry had imagined. Older too. The light wrinkles on her forehead made Cherry aware of her own.

Cherry laughed, her mood getting heavier, darker. "It's about to get longer."

They didn't talk about much in the car beyond the nice weather. By the time they made it to the old hotel, the camera crews and rubberneckers were already taking up the entire entrance. She had to park three blocks away. They walked as calmly as they could. No matter how much the guards beat back the crowd, it kept lurching for the two, yelling, reaching and begging for interviews.

Henry frowned when Cherry came into his room again. There were two police officers with her this time. And also Deena. When Deena appeared, his frown deepened. She pursed her overly rouged lips, her eyes darting around the dirty room.

The air smelled sulfurous. Darkness shrouded the filth. The city had cut off the Regent's electricity, but Henry still refused to budge. Somehow, he'd shaved, and yet he still looked feral. His hair was wild, the well-pomaded curls now a matted, almost clothlike material. Once muscular and taught, his body now reminded Cherry of that of a shipwrecked man left to languish on a desert island: thin and wan, matchstick appendages and a small potbelly. He sat on the edge of the bed with his hands on his lap as if he'd been expecting them all this time.

"Deena's here," Cherry said. "You can leave now."

"You think there's a solution to everything," Henry said. "Just replace everyone with someone new—isn't that right, Cherry?" He spat out her name like it was a curse. His memory was sharp. Clearly, she had hurt him badly. Or rather, his memory of her had. He shook when he breathed.

Cherry rolled her eyes. She hadn't gone by that name in years. It was so silly sounding, something a kid would invent. But it still felt like hers, more so than her real name or the new one she'd since come up with.

"Well?" Cherry said.

She turned to Deena. Deena was no help. She just fiddled with her tennis bracelet. Carefully, she raised a hand and waved.

Deena was too old for this type of weak behavior. It made Cherry despise her as much as she felt connected to her. They were close to the same age; back in their youths, a few years difference would have been an insurmountable chasm, but now they were nothing. Both had children who were older than they were when they'd run away. Matilda was a senior at

UIUC. From what Cherry had heard from the investigators, Deena's eldest, a boy, played baseball for the minor leagues.

"Daddy, please come out," Deena said in a pipsqueak voice. "Please? I'm sorry."

Henry sized Deena up. She was chubbier than she had been in those snapshots of her on her high school softball team. But her face was still the same, sweet with high cheekbones and a widow's peak that bisected part of her forehead.

"I have nothing to say to any of you," he said.

"I divorced my husband," she offered. "You were right. He was bad. Very mean too. I'm married to someone much nicer now. His name is—"

"I don't care," Henry said. "Go away. You're just an imposter now."

"So you'll leave?" Cherry asked.

"No," Henry said.

Deena cried into her palms. She rushed out of the room, her wails turning into coughs as she struggled to keep up with her upset. Poor girl, Cherry thought. That's really all Deena seemed to be: her father's daughter—a child. People like Henry could seamlessly belittle those who stayed too close to them.

"What do you want, Henry?" Cherry asked.

"Don't think I've forgotten what you did," Henry said. "I bet you tried replacing our kid, too, just like you tried with Matthew and Deena. That's what people like you live for, right? Always throwing people away and looking for the next best thing. You don't know what commitment is."

"You've never even met our daughter. And my other child's been dead and gone for years. I'll never know where he is. My mother died before I could even ask her what she did with him. Now can you please just leave already? You're humiliating everyone."

"I'm staying here until all the lost children are found. All of them." He stood up and shuddered as if something inside of him was hurting. "You've replaced everyone." He pointed at the empty hallway. "That's not my daughter. That's someone else. You can't trick me."

Cherry backed away. She should've left with Deena. Her being here was a mistake, and it was her fault. When the hotel's owner phoned her, she hadn't known there was already a plan for her. She didn't know where Deena was or if Henry was alive. Unwittingly, she'd joined a team of investigators, lawyers, PR specialists, etc. who all worked for the same property developer, and they were all much more knowledgeable than her and yet so unaware. They told her everything: his history of drinking, the allegations of domestic abuse. She felt sorry for him when she learned that his wife had passed away last year.

"I have to go," Cherry whispered to Henry. "Good-bye, Henry."

When she turned away, Henry lost it. "Evil!" he shouted.

Cherry heard his rushed footsteps and started running. She stopped by the door when she heard him fall, her heart banging against her chest as she searched the room for a danger that had already fizzled out. The two cops had Henry pinned down. He bawled like a hurt baby as they cuffed him. They dragged him out into the hall and down the stairs. She heard his yells long after he'd left her sight. The hotel had become echoey.

A bright yellow splotch shone in the dark room. Deena's baby blanket. Henry had left it draped over the bed's headboard. Carefully, Cherry picked it up. She petted it as if it was a living creature. Time had worn down the synthetic fibers. The color was faded. Sunlight made it look more vibrant than it was.

Something glass shattered. She looked around the room. Nothing seemed out of place, but there was danger—she swore she could sense it lingering in the room.

Cherry dropped the blanket, childlike fear filling her chest. She thought she heard her mom's voice calling out to her, and though she knew the sound was just the wind beating harder against the windows, her body tensed up anyway.

Right before she'd left home, her mom had warned her about there being monsters in the world. Better watch out, she said. If Cherry had the guts, she would've told her mom to go look in the mirror if she wanted to know what monsters were all about. Instead, she left silently, out the door and into the world.

Turtle Soup

....

MY BRAIN ATE up the rest of me so that I was just my thoughts. I couldn't feel the scabs on my arm that I'd been picking bloody. The whole world became Emma—prickly—and all because she wouldn't stop telling other kids lies about me no matter how many times I asked her to please stop it, it wasn't funny anymore.

When I got dressed in my uniform, I was thinking about Emma pointing out how weird my scars looked. And when I went down the stairs for breakfast, I was thinking of Emma telling me I walked like I weighed eighty tons even though I knew I didn't, that she was just being mean to see how deep she could cut because that was what she did when she got bored—cut, cut, cut, and if not me then other girls online. She said, "One day, Tard, you're gonna be fat like your mom and you'll have to waddle like you have a big sausage between your thighs." She swore she could tell just by looking at me because she knew me best. She was my best friend. She was the second-meanest person I knew, except she'd never been to jail.

Mom was drinking 7Up because she couldn't tolerate coffee anymore. There was food on the table, fish, but I wasn't hungry and even if I was, I didn't like fish. Mom's face was puffed up and raw and really hard to look at.

"I don't wanna be here anymore," I said. I didn't know where the words came from. I hadn't thought them up before they tumbled out of my mouth.

"Sweetie, what's wrong?" Mom asked like she wasn't all bruised up.

First, random words had come out of me. Now: nothing. My throat was hurting me. I thought maybe David had given me strep. We'd kissed at recess because Emma dared us to—we didn't like David because he smelled like a dirty house and wore cheap sneakers—and told everyone I was obsessed with him even though I wasn't.

Mom's face got tighter, which meant she was thinking of Emma. Or my dad blowing up at her last night, but she didn't like it when I talked about him—that was gossip, she said. She didn't like Emma either. She thought her family was trash, especially Emma's mom after what happened between her and this other kid's mom who was best friends with mine.

"It's that girl again," she said, "isn't it?"

"She has her moods," I said.

"You shouldn't be hanging around her. Hey, whatever happened to that girl down the street you used to play with? The one with the pink cowboy boots?"

"Martha's boring, Mom. And she's a third-grader. I'm *twelve*. She still plays with dolls."

"I don't get you anymore. Hanging out with that friend of yours." She took a long sip from her cup. "You know it was her mother that got into a shouting match with Ms. Brinson over a parking space." (I did know; she'd told me a million times, and this one was the one million-and-first.) "A parking space. You would've thought she'd witnessed a murder by the way she was screaming and carrying on." She shook her head. "It's a shame your school accepts people like that. They give out scholarships to the anyone, I swear."

"Emma's not on scholarship," I whispered.

"The school's probably getting money from the government to take in certain kids."

"They don't."

"Such a shame," Mom said, looking past me. "I didn't send you there to be with trash."

"Emma's parents are rich."

Mom clicked her tongue. "Having money doesn't make you classy. Just look at that redhaired girl from that movie you like." Another sip. Her bruisy eyes looked down at the Barbie placemat. "Whatever you do, don't go chasing after people just because they have money. That girl's no good. I can tell. I know things. If you need anything, ask me. Not her."

I nodded even though I already didn't care if Emma was rich or poor. I was friends with her because she listened to me. She used what I told her against me, but she still listened, and I kept telling her things, hoping she'd become the type of best friend that came on the Disney Channel. For example, Emma knew that I like-liked Martha's older brother, which was why she'd told everyone. *Tard loves Arthur, Tard loves Arthur, Tard wants to suck off Arthur!*

"She only hangs out with you 'cos of Arthur!" Emma had yelled at Martha. We were riding bikes and passed by Martha playing Barbies with this other little girl on her front lawn while her brother, Arthur, watched from the porch swing. I told everyone I didn't want to play with Martha anymore—playing was for babies—but she'd been the one to end things first. She made fart noises when I passed her and her baby-friends at school. It took me a minute to realize that the falling feeling in my stomach was me missing how we used to play Fashion Models with her mom's old clothes. So unfair: the people who hated me most were always the ones who were hard to hate back.

"How would you feel about moving?" Mom asked, which meant that we were moving because she never let me have a say about anything.

"I wanna be with Emma," I said.

"We can stay with Grandma. You'll love Connecticut"— that was where my dad's mom lived; she'd just finished renovating her new place, and prided herself on knowing how to fix impossible things like wiring issues—"and all the space she has. She lives next to an animal sanctuary. There's a petting zoo where you can go to see llamas."

"S'not the same."

One last sip. Mom had finished her drink. She played with the cup, running her fingers over the half-heart-shaped handle. "I wish you'd forget that girl, already," she said. "I heard the way she spoke to her father when she came over. It's atrocious. Don't invite her to my house anymore."

"You say that every day," I said.

"Well, I'm saying it again."

"It's not even your house. It's Dad's."

Mom leaned back in her chair. She folded her arms. Her face was too messed up for her to raise an eyebrow, but I still knew I'd said something dangerous. The fear had already started burbling in my stomach before I'd finished speaking, when it was too late to take everything back.

"I'm gonna remember that one, girl," she said. "I'm not trying to raise any Emmas. I'll wring your neck before I do that."

"I know Dad's a bad person," I whispered. My throat hurt so bad I thought for a second it might close off completely and kill me. "I'm sorry," I said quickly.

Wrong answer. Mom whistled like I was Emma's mom acting out. She felt like a huge, super difficult test that I hadn't studied for. I made myself a plate, taking a baby-bit of the fish and dropping the flecks on the clean saucer she'd put out. Her eyes narrowed, squeezing my middle with just their spite. My throat started hurting worse.

"You know that's your father you're talking about," Mom said.

"And Emma's my friend," I shot back. "My *best* friend."

Mom wasn't in her yelling mood, so she laughed instead. Last night, she'd spent all her anger talking to one of my grown sisters on the phone, arguing, begging. My mom'd been the one to call the cops on my dad last night, and now she was trying to get the money to get him out of jail. Made no sense.

"In a few years," Mom said, "you won't even remember that girl."

I stood up and left. I got it in my head that I was running away even though I knew I was too chickenshit for that. School was the only place I knew. The mall was too far.

"Don't you dare slam that door," Mom said.

I slammed the door. When I thought I heard her coming for me, I ran. She might actually kill me if she knew I'd told Emma all her secrets. The fear made me faster. I almost tripped.

Though I wanted to hate my mom, I hoped that she was right about forgetting because being with Emma hurt too much. She was a lot like Emma in that way. I dreamed of getting back at her while hanging on to every word she said, burying the meanest ones deep inside of me so they'd erupt much later.

* * *

Emma was starting to feel like one of the townspeople in this video game I liked. The game was called *Queen Quest*, and the point was to collect a bunch of gemstones to give to this queen who was secretly evil and also the final boss.

The townspeople were super dumb. They walked into walls while saying things like, "I heard there are mermaids on Emerald Beach" or "Did you want to buy some turtle soup, lad?" But what made them really dumb was that they never remembered anything. You could hit them a million times, and they wouldn't flinch. They'd say, "Hey!" or "Watch out!" or "You lookin' for a fight?" and go right back to saying boring things like, "Are you sure you don't want turtle soup?" like you hadn't been trying to kill them.

But Emma was just like them minus the part about the walls. Every day, a new start. If she'd made me cry the day before, she'd say she didn't remember, and if I'd yelled at her for making me cry, she'd say she didn't remember that either. "Better to forgive," Mom said. Not about Emma—God, no— but people in general, which included Emma.

When Emma called me Tard again, it felt more like a real insult than a fake one. We were out on the blacktop during lunch. It was me, her, and these older girls. Emma and me were sixth graders. Lower-school babies. These girls were thirteen and fourteen. One of them had done nasty things with this boy Emma liked but I thought was gross. The boy wound up telling his friend, and that friend told Emma's cousin, who told Emma, who told me and that girl. (Emma, while talking online to the girl, pretended to be this other, older girl from California whose pictures she'd stolen: "ur pussy must smell like beef juice lol.")

Such a nice day. Springtime. Sunbeams, lawnmowers, blood-fattened mosquitos—blue-skied weather that made birds sing and older boys take off their shirts on the soccer field. Since morning assembly, I'd been thinking about telling Emma that I never wanted to speak to her again, and also that my dad was in trouble with the law again and I didn't know what to do. My problem was that I was as dumb as the townspeople too. I never really spoke, and when I did it was always pointless stuff that sounded fake. Like, "Hahaha, that was funny, Emma." I'd waited too long to speak up, and now we weren't alone anymore.

These girls we were with liked Emma. I think they liked her because she was a lot like them: older-seeming, her boobs bigger than theirs on account of the women in her family being beyond DD. That and also because of the chain of liquor stores her parents ran. They were supposed to be crummy-looking places, but they must've earned them a fortune because they had no problems paying for her tuition or her horse or its board. She stole stuff for kids she liked. Once she brought me a pack of sour-flavored bubble gum.

My stomach started hurting, growling. I was hungry, but I didn't feel much like eating. Emma asked me if I had to take a shit. Everybody laughed but me.

"What's wrong with you today?" Emma asked. "You barely speak."

"I don't know," I said.

"Why're you acting so weird?"

"I don't know."

"Jesus, can you say anything else?"

I said nothing back, so she started talking about my worst memory ever like I wasn't there.

"Did you hear about it?" Emma asked the girls. "It's insane. Tard thinks so too. Right, Tard?"

I shrugged.

"Jesus, I hate you sometimes."

More laughter from the girls. This time it sounded more like a "Jeez, this is awkward" laugh than a genuine "hahaha" one. These girls were different from the ones we were usually with, so they didn't know anything about me. I couldn't tell if they were laughing at me or Emma. Maybe it was both.

It always hurt hearing Emma bring up the same old story about me. It was true, but it sounded like a bunch of lies coming from her mouth. The way she told it made me sound like more of a baby than even Martha. The worst part was that she was super good at telling stories. She could make the most boring-sounding sci-fi books she read into stories that made me cry and laugh and panic about nuclear winter. Then I'd try reading them and get bored after the first chapter.

My story went more like this: Mom crying, then perfect quiet and the scratchy feel of my quilt, then boom—everybody screams. I'd called the police that time, but I don't remember. Sometimes, when I got really upset at Mom or Emma, I got the feeling of that memory minus the memory, which was all smeary. It clouded my vision like smog.

I think I was seven at the time. Mom said younger. But I knew this all happened before I'd met Emma, who seemed almost sad that she hadn't been around then. Mom decided that she couldn't take living with Dad anymore and she tried to take me to her mom's house, but Dad stopped us. That night, she wound up sleeping in the spare bedroom because she couldn't stand him and said so about a million times. She took pills she shouldn't have with beer her addictionologist said to keep out of the house. If she'd remembered to lock her door before collapsing, she might've died. Sometimes I think what happened was worse.

"There was vomit everywhere!" Emma said. Her eyes got wider, sparkling. "Tard found her passed out. Her dad wouldn't let them go to the hospital. It's a miracle her mom didn't die. She should've, if you ask me. Bad parenting all around."

Normally when she got to this part, I acted grateful like she was my interpreter. One time, when Emma told the story to one of the aftercare workers, the one I had a crush on, he pulled me aside and said that I shouldn't be friends with her. "You're being bullied," he said, and I shook my head because back then I still liked Emma and didn't like the idea of being easily hurt.

I always defended Emma. Always, always, always. Like when we were in the fifth grade and Emma jumped into this giant mud puddle at the school harvest festival, and I jumped in, too, so she'd look less ridiculous standing there all dirty. But I didn't feel like jumping in mud puddles for her anymore. I just stared and stared at everything but her: my penny loafers, a smashed-up grape and the ants encircling it.

"Fuck," one of the older girls said. "That's horrible."

"Her dad still lives with them too," Emma said.

"Really?"

The girl turned to me. My face felt like a big sunburn. I started crying. My nose ran so much that I could taste the snot above my lip. One of the other older girls, the one with the butterfly clips in her hair, kept asking if I was okay, if I needed water or was having a medical thing.

"She's fine," Emma said. "I know her."

When I looked up again, I looked at Emma real hard. She'd never called me her best friend. She just knew me. One time I'd asked her, "Emma, we're like BFFs, right?" and she said, "No, Stacia is." (Stacia was a girl she'd met at her horse stable. Emma told me she'd kissed her and also this boy, but pretended she hadn't when I asked her about them the next day.)

They came down hard and fast: one strike, two, three. They hurt so bad that I saw white light.

Emma liked to play-fight when she felt like it, when she hated me but didn't want to seem bothered by me either. Her punches still hurt, it wasn't like in the movies where Tom Cruise only pretended to hit the evil henchmen. The only difference between her and someone like my dad was that she laughed when she punched, and I laughed, too, but not this time. My dad, he was the type that stayed straight-faced and closed-fisted.

When Emma hit me again, I fell down screaming. Other kids were looking at us. No one said anything. The boys playing four square stopped, the fat one hugging the ball tight in his arms. They just looked, no one really saw me, just the drama. One of the teachers yelled, "No roughhousing," and that was it—everyone went back to four square and hopscotch and MASH and rumor-spreading by the broken water fountains. Emma and the older girls started talking about this show I'd never seen about a teenage werewolf who falls in love.

I thought about home, about Mom's TV and the one in the sunroom. Mom played movies about sad ladies while she folded laundry in her bedroom. I always watched cartoons after school. Sometimes the TV sounds came together so that it felt like Mom's sad ladies were talking to SpongeBob or Timmy Turner. One of them would cry, "I'd do anything to love again!" and Squidward would say, "Wake me up when I care." Our house was small. You could hear everything.

I was like the sad ladies. Emma was the cartoons. She heard bouncy-ball-hitting-pavement sounds each time she hit me. I just hurt.

When I walked home from school—the walk was super lonely because Emma lived in the opposite direction of me, and even if she didn't, her parents drove her everywhere—but when I was walking home alone, I pretended there was depressing violin music playing. I remembered Emma saying that David kinda looked like a blobfish and how I'd laugh even though she was mean. The good parts about her soured in my head. I hoped someone called her ugly. She had really big ears for a girl who'd supposedly been elected Most Beautiful at her sleepaway camp.

"Tell me why you're friends with her," the aftercare worker had said. He wouldn't let me play with the other kids, with Emma, until I explained myself.

"Because she's nice," I said.

"What does that mean?"

"She lets me tell her things."

He frowned. "But what does that mean?"

"She understands what I say. Even when I don't."

He shook his head. For the whole year he worked there, he kept me and Emma separate. We ate at different tables, went to the blacktop at different times, me with kids our own age and Emma with the really, really little kids who still wore regular clothes instead of uniforms.

* * *

My dad's shoes were at the front door. Mom was airing them out on the porch so that I almost tripped over them coming up the stairs.

I went back down the stairs and kept going, thinking. When I walked in on my mom that one time, in the story that was also my real life, I thought she'd die and that I'd be alone. She didn't die. I almost wished she had when she forgave my dad, but I didn't want to be like him.

My neighborhood felt sadder. There was Martha's house, the group home, the park, and the artsy house that was painted black and white to look like cowhide. When I got to Main Street, I sat on one of the benches. The wood was wet, but I didn't care.

"Promise me you won't tell anyone," I'd whispered. Those were the first words I remembered saying to Emma.

We didn't have to tell each other our names because our fourth-grade class was small, thirty-five in total. We hadn't been friends until then, just classmates who sort of knew each other and sometimes got put together for group projects.

"Just tell the freakin' story already," Emma'd said.

So I told her everything. The sounds. My mom passed out on the carpet, heaving. Dad yanking the phone from my hand and smashing it against a wall. Don't you dare, he kept telling me because he wanted her dead. Was that murder? I asked Emma. Was I normal? Of course, Emma said. She had plans of emancipating herself like her sister at sixteen and moving to her place. Her own mom had mental breaks. She'd threatened Emma with a knife one time, but Emma didn't care because she was going to be famous one day, and if not famous then a secretary who married rich.

Talking to Emma was like talking to a ghost. It was really late. Dark. This all happened on the overnight Civil War trip to Manassas. Emma and me and the rest of the class were all sprawled out across a church basement that smelled like dirty dog. Emma said she couldn't sleep. That morning, one of her older brothers had dared her to drink a Four Loko for twenty bucks and she'd drained the entire can. On her wrists, new bracelets—ten dollars from the giftshop at Bull Run that sold mostly random junk. I could hear the fake pearls clatter against her wrists.

I couldn't sleep because of nightmares about my dad killing Mom. It was worse than the old, boring ones where aliens tried to cut my head off. I got put into foster care and taken in by violent Bible freaks and perverts—the kind of people abused kids on *Oprah* brought up when they talked about getting locked in closets with nothing to eat. I couldn't understand how my dad could be so violent. He was always mean, physical, but the choking and everything else was new to me.

"My mom didn't want to press charges or anything," I'd said. "She said she wants him to stay and keep his job and everything. I don't get why she just can't get a job. Or why not divorce him and get money that way? It's like she actually likes him. I thought maybe she was just acting, but I don't think so anymore."

"She's probably just lonely," Emma said.

"There's a million people in the world she could go after. My dad's awful. This one time, I was playing with my dollhouse, and he randomly came into my room, yelling at me for having too many lights on. I told my mom, and she just said I was being rude for bringing it up."

"What'd he say to you when your mom almost died?" I could feel Emma move closer, feel the bitter moistness of her breath and smell the sweetness of sweat mixed with fabric softener and Hidden Fantasy eau de parfum.

The memories came, tumbling out of my mouth before it could remember what Mom had said about shutting it. "Just crazy stuff," I said, "like, 'I'm not paying for you anymore when you're eighteen.'" He said that my mom used me to trap him because she's too lazy to work on her own, which I guess is true, but he's really frightening when he's mad like that. He could say that the sky's blue and it'd be insulting."

"Does he beat you?" Emma pointed at the scars on my arm. I didn't know how she could make them out. Her memory was good. She picked up on things. People like her were good at that sort of thing: scrounging for weakness, searching for an opening to crawl inside.

"I pick my skin. It's a bad habit."

"Because your dad beats your mom?"

"Right."

"You know what your mom's problem is?" Emma didn't wait for a response. "She relies on other people too much for everything. People who're like that are super annoying."

"I guess," I said.

"No, really."

The thought of my dad exhausted me. For a long time, Emma and me said nothing. I waited to talk until I thought she was sleeping, remembering an article I'd read about people listening to Spanish radio in their sleep to help them learn the language subconsciously. I wanted to be a good dream to her, nothing but pleasantness. I wanted to tell her everything and nothing about me; to hide her words in my pocket and sneak away before she could notice anything off about my personality, looks, tastes.

"Emma?" I whispered.

No response. Somewhere off in the darkness: snoring.

I felt attached to her in a way I hadn't with anyone else. Even when I was with other girls, I was alone, me with my problems and them with their imperfectly perfect sitcom parents whose worst crime was getting them the wrong American Girl doll for Christmas.

"Are we friends?" I asked. My voice was so small that it was mostly air.

"Go to sleep," Emma said. Then, when I thought I'd cry, she said, "You're really interesting, you know, with your crazy family and everything," and my heart started yo-yoing between hurt and hope, up until now.

The walking signal clicked on. A lady pushed a stroller across the intersection. I thought about running away again. I knew that if, when, my dad started hitting me, too, it'd never stop because that was how cruelty worked—like clockwork.

I remembered Connecticut and got excited. I'd never been, didn't really like petting zoos—the concept felt cruel to me, all those animals locked up in pens for nothing—but the idea of leaving didn't seem that bad. Dad would never agree to the move. The financial place where he worked only had offices here and in really big cities like New York, London, and Tokyo.

Connecticut. The idea felt empty to me like a room with nothing inside, mostly because I knew we'd never be going. It was the type of lonely nothing that was hidden so deep inside of me that no one could hear it until I opened my mouth when I wasn't supposed to.

Kitty & Tabby

....

HER FULL NAME might've been Catherine, but she went by Kitty when we were still failing out of Saint V's together. Sometimes our geometry teacher, Mr. Bell, called her Cate, and she wouldn't bother correcting him because she hardly came to class anyways. That was the main difference between us: she was the type of slacker who skipped. I endured each test, failing miserably, never scoring anything higher than 55 percent in any of my classes. Not that the distinction mattered. Somehow, a fifty was just as bad as a zero, an F. The logic of the world evaded me.

She befriended me around April, I think. I was walking home, taking a long, winding route for the exercise. It was cool out, but not frigid. When I took off my coat, I shivered, and when I put it back on, I felt suffocated. I undid the buttons and let the air circulate between me and the heavy quilted fabric, hoping that the warmth and cold would cancel so that I'd feel nothing again.

Kitty came outside of the bungalow on Grant Street, the one with the purple shutters. I'd seen her hanging out in the yard during the warmer months, so I guessed she lived there. There was a guy who stayed with her, an older goateed man whose face I couldn't remember. She was new to the area; she'd moved in less than a year ago when she first transferred in the middle of the spring semester. Kids gossiped about her and the guy making out at the mall together.

Sweat shellacked Kitty's skin in a glamorous way that made her look as though she were made of fine glass. She was taking out the garbage. A putrid smell kept me from going any closer. I watched as she hoisted the trash bag into the trash bin. The whole time, I avoided looking at her eyes. She was more popular than me. Consequentially, everything she did felt more important than my existence as Carissa Constantine's ugly cousin.

"You're Tabitha, right?" she asked, turning to me. She dusted her hands on the jean jacket she had on and came closer. "Carissa's cousin?"

I flinched. She was pretty and aloof like Carissa. She captured the attention of boys I used to fantasize about. I say "used to" because one of them, Uriel, my best friend in the whole world, a lifelong crush, ended my dreams when he said he could never love me—not because of my gender but my looks, which he said he found repulsive.

I stuffed my hands into my pockets. I'd started biting my nails down to the quick again, piercing through the flesh until I tasted blood. I had no dreams or desires, only a vague urge to destroy myself. I wanted to bash my face against a steel door so that my mother would have no choice but to pay to fix the hump on my nose; hack the fat from my legs like meat off a rotating spit; jump off of City Hall, the tallest building in our town, and be reincarnated as either a girl who was Victoria's-Secret-angel pretty or nothing at all.

"You should go by Tabby," Kitty said.

"No one ever calls me that."

"We could be Tabby and Kitty together."

"Sounds like the name of a cheesy sitcom."

"What's our theme song going to be?"

I laughed. When she didn't say anything, I finally realized she was being serious. "Something by Beyoncé?" I said.

"What's that one song? You have to know it. It goes: *Da-dun, da-dun, da-dun dun dun dun dun.*" She started doing an awkward dance. "It's about friendship or something."

"I don't know."

Silence passed between us. I wanted to leave but felt like the conversation was still going. Kitty furrowed her brows like she was thinking of something serious to say.

"You know," she started, "I can't stand Carissa. She's not even that attractive, if you ask me. But your other friend. Uriel. Wow. If I didn't already have a guy to take care of, I'd definitely want him for sure."

"I have piano practice." The lie felt strange on my mouth as I turned to leave. "I need to go soon. My teacher, she's testing me on the scales or whatever."

Kitty called after me, her voice loud enough for people indoors to hear. "You should be careful walking home. There's bad people." She paused. "You don't want to get hurt again."

Again. I started fast-walking. The word echoed in my mind: *again, again, again.* My heart felt like it was going to burst. What did she know? Had she talked to Uriel? Carissa? The principal's daughter who'd hated my existence since the second grade? Had the Discord server of Saint V's students come back together to share more awkward candid shots they took of me in PE?

My thighs chafed. My chest swelled. Eventually, I struggled walking and breathing at the same time. I stopped at an intersection and watched my mom's pet peacock, Percival, strut past me. He'd strayed too far again; my mom's house was almost a mile away. His sprawling train was folded in on itself like a closed fan. I petted his crown and he followed me all the way to the front porch where my mom had laid out his dinner, candied yams in an old casserole dish.

Kitty was just playing mind tricks, I thought as I watched Percival eat. She might know embarrassing things about me, but that didn't mean she knew me. My mind contradicted me, bringing up the look of knowing that had illuminated Kitty's eyes. I'd blocked it out when I first saw it, but my subconscious preserved the memory anyway. She'd been toying with me, treating me like some little kid who said funny nonsense that adults find amusing. Her eyes, an unnatural shade of green, were the only ugly thing about her. They were so scary. Their depth resisted definitions.

* * *

I spent the weekend crying and, when I couldn't make myself feel anymore, rewatching a cooking show Uriel and me both liked. The feelings I still had for him softened the melodramatic music score, giving each episode a false sentimentality I hadn't felt since we saw *The Notebook* with Carissa. I cried as a group of chefs struggled to keep a tiered cake from collapsing, thinking: How could he be so cruel? He'd been sleeping with my cousin Carissa for over a year, back when he still said he was gay and not bi.

My dad came home late in the evening from wherever he went now that he was jobless and without purpose. He threw his steel-toed boots onto the ground and chastised me for not greeting him like I used to. My eyes didn't break from the TV. He was pointless to engage with, always punching walls when someone didn't say the right thing to him, so I didn't say anything at all. Dealing with his sour moods was like trying to fight a petulant toddler piloting the mech from that anime Uriel was obsessed with. He couldn't understand the fact that the degradation of our relationship had been a gradual progression that started years ago, before the hooker, when he cheated with an old neighbor, and, before that, his coworker's wife.

I despised him not just because his transgressions made the abuse I faced at school worse but because I couldn't blame the bullying on him. My looks were what ultimately attracted people's derision—hardly anyone here cared about morality for real. Why else would Nancy Tadwater still be beloved by practically the whole school after leaking her best friend's nudes?

"When's your mom coming home?" my dad demanded.

"Don't know."

"Yes, you do, bitch. Now, where is she?"

"A friend's house. They're playing cards together."

"So you were just lying about not knowing, then."

"You didn't ask me where she was. You asked when, and I said I didn't know."

"Lying bitch."

"Okay."

He went upstairs. My attention bounced from him to the TV commercial for vitamin-enhanced dog food to my phone. My phone's cracked screen kept lighting up with angry texts. Carissa was trying to guilt me over giving Uriel and her the silent treatment.

I realized that I'd never liked her. The two things we shared in common, Uriel and a vague commitment to family, had finally, mercifully broken. I deleted her messages as they came in, imagining that my phone was my memory and that I was slowly wiping all trace of her. *I didn't want to tell you because of Uriel.* Delete. *Ur seriously being so selfish.* Delete. *Uriel said he wasn't trying to hurt ur feelings. U literally were the one who kept pushing for details. U just can't accept hearing no.* Delete. *I'm done playing nice with people like u. Ur a narcissist. Hope u flunk out of school and go to prison already that's what my mom thinks about*—delete, delete, delete.

Another message, this one from a number with a foreign area code: *It's Kitty! Look outside ur window* ☺. Carissa, I thought, my body growing hot with anger. I guessed that she'd heard about me talking to Kitty somehow and wanted to taunt me for something else that was out of my control. I imagined one of her friends joining in on the fight just to make it more exciting for them.

I opened the blinds and studied the backyard. The grass was still overgrown and interlaced with weeds; the old playhouse basked in the sun, which had turned the hot-pink roof salamander over the years; empty beer bottles from Mom's birthday party collected rainwater on the deck. The striped umbrella leaned up against the fence, its wooden base snapped in two. Carissa was playing mind games. I thought about blocking her.

Another message: *The front yard, dummie lol.*

I ran to the front door and looked through the peephole. Kitty was waving, smiling. In her small hands was a blue package. I wondered if Carissa had sent her. A pretty-girl alliance had formed between them—I was convinced. I imagined that the bond was so powerful it transcended race.

"Open up!" she said.

My mind went numb with panic. While my mom hadn't banned visitors, she had an acute dislike of Kitty's type, wild girls like the university students who lived two doors down from us and had parties practically every day it seemed. Kitty was also Black. Though my mom never spoke of race, her silence toward my older sister, Melina, and her Somalian husband screamed out. When she and my dad were still close, they used to threaten to drive me to the Black part of town when I was being bad, making up impossible stories about superhuman dope fiends who lived in the dumpsters there. My dad would slow down the car when we passed through, even when I was saying nothing, pumping the brakes and putting the car in park like the dumbest character in a zombie film. "Uh oh, folks," he'd yell over my screams, my mom's laughter, and my sister's silence. "Looks like we're all out of gas."

I let Kitty in. She wore a floral dress that was too small on her, especially around the chest. Though she was tiny, she had mammoth boobs. She said her back was hurting, then walked into the living room and plopped down miserably on my mom's recliner. I asked if she wanted anything to drink. She reached behind her back, digging into her dress to unclasp her bra's hooks.

"We have Diet Coke," I said because she was cool and I suddenly wanted her to be my friend. I prayed that she'd say no. We didn't have any Cokes. We could barely afford to keep the house, let alone waste money on soft drinks.

"Do you have any beer?"

"No."

She peeled off her flats and sighed. Her expression stayed blank. She picked up the remote and turned the channel to the local news. The anchors were talking about a sanitation worker who'd found half-eaten scraps of human remains at a landfill. She started channel surfing, whistling a tune that sounded made up.

"Oh my gosh, I almost forgot!" Kitty offered me the colorful package. "I got you a present. It's nothing extravagant. Just sweets."

"Wasn't Easter last week?"

"Yeah. That's why I got the stuff. It was on sale at Walgreens."

"But why?"

"Um, because I'm broke. I had to get rid of the guy I was dating. He was unhinged. Said I needed either an exorcism or a bullet to the head."

"You should call the police on him. People like that only get worse if you leave them be."

"Nah."

"Oh." I looked down at my feet, trying to feel at ease while my heart cried out with anxiety. I was so lonely. Being around people only added to the pain, making me worry that I was always on the brink of losing a friend.

"But why did you buy me a gift?" I asked. My throat got tight like it always did when people talked around me.

"I heard what happened with Uriel and was like, wow, that sucks. He's so hot too. I'd be pissed." She plopped her feet onto the coffee table, knocking over the small village of Precious Moments figurines. "I hate this body. It's been such a pain, but it's not just that either. I'm done with being a girl. It's too much stress."

"Me too. I mean, like, I hate myself too."

"I have a bunch of medical conditions because of this guy I was with before my new boyfriend. He didn't tell me how messed up he was before we got together."

"Did he have STDs?"

"No. Fibromyalgia. I thought it was an old people's disease, but apparently not."

I nodded, assuming that whatever she was talking about was sexually transmitted. I lived in a small conservative town, very red, very religious. Carissa had informed me last week that it was possible to get pregnant while swimming in a pool with a chronic masturbator because of how strong their sperm was, which was why she said she couldn't go to Davis Cottingham's pool party. Not because he'd spread a rumor about me being a pedophile for liking a freshman—no, she just didn't want to risk getting impregnated by super sperm. The worst part was that I believed her.

"I hate being pregnant."

Kitty delivered the words flatly as if she'd just said she hated waiting in line or going to the dentist. She didn't look pregnant. Her stomach was flat. I started blinking hard.

"What're you gonna do next?" I asked.

She sighed and asked if I had anything that could treat pain. I brought her a bottle of aspirin and a cup of water from the tap. She took three times the recommended dosage of pills. All I could do was watch. She was strange in a way that made people want to get closer to her, which was how she'd made the Most Fuckable Girls list at school. She probably knew that this strangeness would eventually make her a target, which was why she kept her distance from most people. She and Saint V's were still in their honeymoon phase. The whisperings about her past—riveting tales of world travel, orphandom, and a vague tragedy that couldn't be named—hadn't had the chance to sour.

The way she shifted in her chair, wincing as she popped her spine, reminded me of my mom, who was complain-y and pretty and big-boobed like her. My mom did calisthenics to ease the pressure of what she coyly referred to as her "womanly afflictions." I was flat by comparison, not that I minded. My dysmorphia concentrated around my face and weight. I didn't envy Tamara Russo or Emma Rosa, womanly looking girls from school whom people called slutty even though they were some of the more devout kids in the class.

I trained my eyes on the TV screen. A commercial for weight loss supplements was playing. A fat cartoon woman unzipped her skin, revealing a thinner, bustier body underneath.

"If only people could actually do that," I said.

"Do what?"

"Just jump out of their own skin, you know? Like, it would be awesome if I could just pull all this pig fat off my arm and just be done with it."

Kitty shrugged. "You could always have children. Live through them."

"That's a bad idea. For me, at least. Besides, even if my kids were way better than me, they'd just leave me eventually. And then my body would be in a million times worse shape than before, so I'd have nothing."

"Oh"—she popped her palm against her forehead—"I completely forgot. Sorry."

"What do you mean?"

"I'm not like most women. I can change. I forget sometimes. Part of me wants to think there's other me's in the world, but then I have to tell myself: *no, fool, it's just you*. I guess you just reminded me of myself. You look like someone who gets sick of being stuck in the same ol' skin every day. Not Carissa, though. Boy, will she be in for a shock when she turns thirty. Milky skin spoils. I learned that the hard way a while ago."

"How can you change yourself?" I asked.

"For you? You can get a name change, surgery. You can move. Or kill yourself. You have a ton of options."

I rolled my eyes. "How would *you* change yourself? You're not that different from anyone else."

"I can change form," she said as if the answer were obvious. "I've lived through all the women I'm descended from. My spirit can't rest until I give birth to a boy. Then his daughter can replace me."

I'd read somewhere that pregnancy hormones could drive women crazy even after their babies were born. Sometimes even the thought of being with child was enough to addle the mind if the fantasy was strong enough. Or maybe, I thought, Kitty was just in some niche religion I didn't know about. I'd once known a girl who was a Wiccan.

Kitty reminded me of a made-for-TV movie I'd watched with Uriel and Carissa. It was based on a true story, but the poor writing made all the true parts feel more funny than real. The main characters, a group of high school girls, make a pact with each other to get pregnant. Carissa had purposefully chosen the movie to cheer me up, which it did because I wasn't a teen mom. I temporarily forgot about all the rumors about me secretly getting facial masculinization surgery. We laughed at the stupid girls who'd willingly made themselves so vulnerable. How could they believe that having babies would make their boyfriends stay?

"Don't you care what people think?" I asked. "I mean, whatever the reason, the whole school's gonna think less of you when your stomach gets big."

"Why would I?"

"Like, you don't want to be, like, a racial stereotype or whatever. Then people'll think of you in only one way."

Kitty snorted, making a theatrical display out of trying not to laugh. She thrust back her head, clasping both of her hands over her pursed mouth. Even as she got up and left, she laughed. She clutched her stomach as though the baby were already threatening to shoot out of her.

"What's wrong?" I asked.

"I'm not Black," she said.

"Yes, you are."

"No, I'm not."

"Then what are you, then?"

"I'm no one," she said and slammed the screen door so hard it bounced back open.

I watched her flounce down the flagstone path my dad had installed the summer before his arrest. Desperately, I wanted to be her minus her strangeness. What I'm trying to say is that I wished I could feel free like her, even though she obviously wasn't.

* * *

Carissa spread a rumor about me having limerence, a condition that I had to Google after a random kid messaged me saying that I needed psychiatric help. According to the internet, it was "the state of being infatuated or obsessed with another person, typically experienced involuntarily and characterized by a strong desire for reciprocation of one's feelings but not primarily for a sexual relationship." According to everyone else, it meant that I, Tabitha Drinkwater, had stooped as low as unrequited love or possibly even the lower, isolated hell of sexual predation where my father languished. I could normally alchemize other people's cruel words into flippant jokes I'd learned from fat male comedians. Now, there were too many new rumors to process. They kept evolving before I could pin them down. They loved to see me in pain, "they" as in my schoolmates whom I repelled so hard they all morphed into a single, contemptuous unit that was against me.

I tried begging Carissa and Uriel for help. I cried at our lunch table. I sat with them even though I still hated Carissa for starting the rumor. There was no other choice; I had nowhere else to sit that was familiar. The abuse of strangers was scarier than Carissa's hate, its depths unknown.

Uriel hugged me, which only made me cry even harder. I viewed kindness as unstable energy that could collapse into hostility at any moment. I wanted to pull away, but the familiar scent of the lavender fabric softener his mom used made me feel nostalgic for a romance that had only existed inside my head. I told him that I was sorry, that I was happy for him because I loved him, I wanted him to be happy and for everyone in the cafeteria to stop staring at me as if I were some wounded, dangerous creature on display.

Other rumors about me, which had existed since middle school when my body first turned ugly, grew exponentially in size, threatening to break me down like a pair of giant breasts. According to the hivemind of my classmates, I was a predator who looked at other girls in the locker room, a maniac who wanted to kill Carissa so I could have Uriel for myself, a victim of incest, a product of incest, a slut, a prude, a homophobe. Someone, probably Carissa, had told everyone about my mom being my dad's former foster kid (a true fact, for once), and now the world couldn't decide if I was pathetic or a monster or both.

I could hear the voices carry over from a nearby table. A group of lower classman girls talked at full volume, staring right at me, the short brunette scrunching her nose like I was a bad smell.

"Look, she's doing it again."

"She's so creepy."

"Did you hear about her dad?"

"Yeah, he got arrested because the prostitute-lady was, like, sixteen."

"I heard twelve."

"I thought she was fourteen."

I lied to Carissa and said it wasn't her fault that people hated me a million times more than she must. She gave a cautious smile. I went on, telling her it was natural that she'd confide in her friends from the soccer team about Uriel and us. Never mind that the same group of girls used to dare each other to poke me with the sharpened tips of their pencils, trying to get me to "pop." I wanted to hurt her and love Uriel, an action that was impossible because they were now an official item. He'd bought her a silvery locket that shone brightly against her freckled décolletage.

For the first time since wetting my pants in elementary school, I decided to skip school and watch TV at home.

* * *

Carissa called me that night to say it was safe to come back to school, that I was no longer the target of everyone's ire because Kitty was pregnant and might be dropping out.

"It's so crazy," Carissa said. "One day she looks completely normal, and then the next day it's like she's about to pop. She came into Geography twenty minutes late, and Mr. P had to send her out of the room again when he saw her stomach. Oh, and she claimed she was hundreds of years old. I swear, she's just like that girl who wears a fake tail everywhere but worse."

She didn't say that she was sorry for what she'd done to me. I pretended to be oblivious, acting surprised at the news of Kitty's downfall. Kitty's visit had been over a week ago now. It felt significant to me, though I was sure she was too preoccupied to ever think of me again.

"Sounds like a lot of BS," I told Carissa. "People love spreading pregnancy rumors. They've done it to me too."

"Someone asked her point blank to her face, and she didn't deny anything," Carissa said. "I was there."

"So?" A part of me snapped. I couldn't help it, laughing. "And that's supposed to make your story more believable?"

"Oh my God, Tabitha, don't be like that. Do you have any idea what I'm going through right now?"

Carissa shifted the subject to herself again. I listened as she told me about how she and Uriel were fighting. Apparently, Uriel thought she was controlling and manipulative.

I wanted to care about them both, but my mind brought up the memory of him calling me repulsive and I shut down. He'd told me after school, after confessing his bisexuality, which Carissa had slowly awakened. Something about her doe eyes and long, luminous curls turned his appreciation of her features into a full-on make-out session in his Jetta. I joked about us having a threesome. He laughed and called me repulsive in a light tone that weighed down on me still. I made myself smile.

"Isn't that crazy?" Carissa said. "He's so abusive. I can't take it."

"It's super"—I stifled a yawn—"crazy."

"You were right about him. He's so fuckin' hurtful."

"Totally."

"I know, right?"

This went on for a while. When I hung up, all the light had disappeared from my window. I tried to look into the backyard again but could see nothing but blackness.

* * *

I went to bed early and woke up energized but still sad. I prepared an extravagant breakfast. I cut melon while bacon cooked in the microwave under a sheath of dampened paper towel. I came into math class fifteen minutes early and stayed after the bell rang, staring at a midterm whose questions felt like an alien language. Kitty wasn't there—gone with no excuse as usual, maybe forever this time. A boy occupied her old seat near the helm of the class, the least popular one where the late kids had to go. We were the last to leave. The teacher yelled at us for taking extra time we weren't entitled to.

At lunch, Uriel and Carissa talked to me while ignoring each other. The attention felt flattering, then quickly turned into an exhausting task that dragged. I gave up on trying to make myself eat the cafeteria food. The creamed corn had soaked the undercooked chicken.

When the subject of Kitty came up, the invisible, sound-proof partition separating them disappeared. Uriel repeated what Carissa had already told me, only with new bits of information. He said that she'd thrown up by the soccer field, leaving a mealy lump of regurgitated food that someone posted a picture of online as a joke; that some thought she'd been wearing extreme shapewear all these months, which was why no one had noticed her baby bump until it broke through all constraints. Carissa took pride in Kitty's defeat. Though she didn't believe in God like her parents—didn't think a benevolent, omnipotent deity would've let them lose their old house to the bank—she still clung to all the puritanical aspects of her religious upbringing. She didn't think Kitty deserved to go to hell, but rather the earthly equivalents: poverty, prison, early death.

I had the urge to kill my cousin. I winced and smiled, thinking: I should've drowned you in your kiddie pool while I was still young enough to get away with murder. I didn't just want to kill her. I wanted to erase her from existence so that she'd never been born. The energy behind my hostility grew too large to contain, pouring over into my interest in Kitty. Guilt quickly followed. It was the worst type, the one that made me feel guilty for having sex with Uriel in my dreams.

"Where is she?" Carissa asked. "Kitty, I mean." She turned to Uriel, who knew everything that went on at the school.

"I feel bad for her," he said. "It sucks to be in her spot."

"But why isn't she at school?" Carissa said. "Is she at the hospital?"

"I get what you mean, Urie," I said. I smiled at Uriel, savoring the beauty of being able to ignore Carissa completely.

He broke down. "I'm sorry," he told me, his voice shaky. "I didn't mean to hurt you."

"I'm sorry too."

"I'm sorrier."

Carissa rolled her eyes and tried to change the subject to a concert she and Uriel had apparently gone to last summer.

Uriel ignored her, revisiting the subject of Kitty with a more sympathetic tone. He said he hated how the administration had given her the boot, then made us both promise not to tell. He had a family friend who worked in the school's business office and didn't want her to get into trouble even though the news would probably leak anyway.

"It's all so hypocritical," he said, squishing mashed potatoes with a spork. "It's always the worst people here who pretend to be compassionate, but they're lying."

"Definitely," I said.

"We should create a petition for her."

"Totally!"

"I'm sure we could find a bunch of people who'd sign it if we can get just get it off the ground."

"Yes," I said, clapping, feeling my heart grow lighter with each suggestion.

Uriel asked Carissa if he could borrow a sheet of notebook paper to start the petition. She swatted him away, giving him a pouty look.

He put down his pen, pulling her into a hug like they hadn't ever despised each other. They were fickle. Or maybe their relationship was just that strong: they couldn't stay angry at each other for long. My throat got tight as I realized that I didn't know what true love was.

"Carissa," he said. "What's wrong?"

Her voice wavered, cracked. She broke down in tears. "You never pay attention," she said.

"That's not true and you know it."

"You're always leading me on like this. Why'd you bother sitting next to me if all you do is pretend I'm not here?"

She cried into his chest. He cradled her head, burrowing his face into her hair, which had come undone from the loose French braid she'd been wearing all morning. I waited for him to bring up the petition again. The bell rang.

* * *

Another Saturday. The same message, but from a different number with a foreign area code. *It's Kitty! Look outside ur window* ☺.

Kitty looked pale. Her glassy glow had become a curtain of sweat that dribbled down her face. Her stomach bulged through the cotton fabric of her oversized shirtdress, which only made her look more inflated. She announced that she was anemic and let herself inside. This time, she opted to lie down on the couch. Both of her legs were wrapped in gauze and bandages. She said she was taking morphine that her boyfriend, a medic, had given her.

I didn't mind the intrusion. I welcomed it. My mom was visiting a family friend and wouldn't be back until early tomorrow. My dad was staying at his mom's because the rest of his side of the family found him too shameful to keep. I'd thought my mind would mimic the calm of the empty house. Instead, it raced, filling with memories I hadn't had the time or concentration to think of for months, maybe years. At least people at school had finally stopped harassing me.

"How's your back?" I asked.

"Awful. The pain's spread to my whole body now. I just want it to be over soon. I've been eating nothing but meat to make the pregnancy go faster. It puts my body in so much pain. Oh, Tabby, I'm just a mess."

She pulled off a large bandage from her arm. Underneath was a really deep, bleeding gash. She stuffed it with Kleenex. The sight made me gag and gasp at the same time. I choked on my spit.

"Don't be so loud," she hissed.

"You should get medical treatment," I said. "Maybe a surgeon."

"You sound like my boyfriend. He didn't take me seriously either. Hardly anyone does."

She put the bandage back on, slapping it down to her skin, trying and failing to get the weak adhesive to stick.

"Just go to your boyfriend or whatever."

"I already told you: he's gone. He was fickle." Kitty let out an animal-like groan. "Can you please just help me? I can't go to the hospital. I don't trust doctors."

"What do you want me to do?"

She rolled her eyes. "Help me give birth."

"You're not in labor."

"Look. I just need you to make sure the thing doesn't choke on the umbilical cord. I don't want to go through this alone again."

Again. I said nothing. My hands felt clammy.

"If I wasn't so light-headed," she said, "I'd just rip your face off."

"I think you should go."

She stood still, staring at the fleur-de-lis-patterned wall-
paper. She started biting her nails, chewing on them like I did.
She swallowed, and I felt my stomach go sour. She did this for
what felt like forever, prying off each well-manicured nail with
her teeth and devouring them. Blood dripped down her fin-
gertips. She kept going, finishing off all ten fingernails so that
there was nothing left but their bloody beds.

Then she ate her hands. I started to scream. There was
so much blood, a cascade of it. Pools of red formed on the
carpet. Her face looked pained. Devoted. She fainted, collapsing to the ground in a bloodied heap. Her head knocked
up against the coffee table. A moment passed. She didn't get
up. I looked into her face. Her eyes were open but vacant.

"Kitty?"

My voice sounded small like it was coming from all the way
upstairs. I couldn't make myself check her pulse, but I knew she
was dead. My body started trembling. Though I couldn't move,
the world around me surged forward. The phone rang. My
next-door neighbor turned on his lawnmower. The leak in the
kitchen ceiling was growing. The staccato rhythm of water hitting the pail grew faster. Children squealed at the park across
the street. "Ready or not," one of them cried, "here I come!"

Red bloomed from between Kitty's legs, puddling onto
the carpet. I heard the baby before I saw it. It crawled out on
its own, its body wrapped in slimy tubes that looked too large
and important for any of them to be umbilical cords. I made
myself pick it up. I tried cradling it. It suckled my finger, then
bit down hard on the meat of my hand, drawing blood. The
baby had teeth. The pain felt like electrified needles.

I dropped her—it was a girl; there was no penis—and nursed the wound she'd left on my palm. My mind swam from pain but also fear of death. I remembered how, a few years ago, during his rebellious atheist-slash-wannabe-palmist phase, Uriel had told me my fortune. The memory exploded in my vision: "Yep," said his voice. "There's something big waiting for you in your future." I asked him jokingly if I was going to marry Jake Gyllenhaal, and we both laughed.

The baby didn't cry. Instead, she crawled up to her mother's breast, biting through the cotton fibers of the dress and into the skin. She suckled, then ate, devouring the flesh with her incisors. I watched her swell in size as she continued to eat Kitty. Her development happened all at once. There were no bright puffs of smoke, no explosions, or awkward, liminal phases that temporarily left her with limbs of differing sizes. She was a baby, and then she wasn't.

"What are you?"

The words felt like sandpaper against my throat. I was trembling so violently that I heard my bracelets clacking against each other.

"It's still me, Tabby. Obviously."

As she talked, I saw the semblance between the corpse and the new woman who stood in front of me. They had the same snub nose and big, anime-like eyes. Only, the new Kitty was tan instead of brown. She was taller and thinner. Her chest wasn't as big.

I watched as the woman undressed the corpse of Kitty. Sweat drenched my shirt.

"Can I get some help over here?" she said.

I opened my mouth. No words. Only a cold, familiar silence. I watched as she put on the corpse's ruined dress even with the hole over the breast. She smoothed down her hair, smearing the dark curls with more blood. The sunlight filtering through the blinds grew stronger. It hit what was left of the corpse, dissolving it into a bubbly red liquid that evaporated into nothing.

"Are you coming to school tomorrow?" I blurted out.

It was supposed to be a test. I wanted to know if she was really Kitty or some imposter. I thought of that one cliché I'd seen all the time on TV growing up: two copies of the same person, one a doppelgänger and the other the original. The latter's friend, armed, has to shoot the former to save them all. The friend asks the two a question that only the original would know the answer to. The copy falters.

Kitty laughed. "No way am I staying in this place, Tabby. I only came here to get a break from city living. I think I might go to Paris. Or maybe London."

"Who are you?"

"I already told you: I'm no one."

"Are you still Kitty?"

She shook her head. "Even when you get it, you're still just as ignorant."

* * *

The days surrounding Carissa's miscarriage were a blur. They followed Kitty's disappearance, a collection of random events that added up to nothing: Carissa crying at school but refusing to say why; me going to the grocery store, buying root beer, exchanging pleasantries with the checker; an unopened can of Pabst growing warm in my hands that night I hung out with Carissa and Uriel on the latter's deck; my dad coming back, leaving, coming back again, getting kicked out.

I became especially numb to the changing seasons and silly school events. My dreams where Kitty devoured me felt more real than anything that happened when I woke up. The wound she'd given me hadn't healed right. There were two bloodless punctures left in my palm.

"Oh my God, *you* got a present?"

Carissa came into my room without knocking, her face still pallid and pinched from her hospitalization that she insisted had been for mono. My mom must've let her in before leaving for her Saturday shift. Or maybe it was a Sunday.

In Carissa's hand was Kitty's gift. It'd been so long. I'd forgotten about the package until now. For months it had been nothing to me, but I still wanted to yell at Carissa when she started opening it without asking. I thought of the snottiest way that I could bring up her miscarriage, which I'd only heard about through rumors.

I forced myself out of bed and watched my cousin devour the sour candies Kitty had brought. She threw the royal blue wrapping paper into the trash bin, then collapsed into the bean-bag chair I'd stabbed with a pen upon realizing for the millionth time that Uriel didn't love me, that no one loved me romantically and never would. A steady stream of plastic beads leaked onto the carpet. I thought about blood again.

"Your mom said it'd been sitting on the coffee table for-ever," Carissa said. "She was about to throw it out and gave it to me instead. Do you have a secret boyfriend or something?"

"No," I said.

"An online friend?"

"No."

She started giggling. "Kitty?"

"Yeah," I whispered.

I already told you, I'm no one. What are you then? No one.

I wanted so badly to be Kitty. I wanted to be no one—not a nobody that everyone saw and ridiculed, but a shapeshifter who could grow around the expectations of others who pinned me down. For the first time since discovering Carissa's rela-tionship with Uriel, I let myself remember that time in middle school when I'd let Uriel kiss me. He'd called me beautiful then and, though I knew this wasn't true, I'd felt the bones in my face reconfigure themselves into something beautiful. I let his tongue part my lips and infect me completely with his attrac-tion. I didn't care that we were just supposed to be testing what it must feel like to be loved.

My eyes got irritated. I felt tears coming down my cheeks, wetting a dry, angry patch of stress acne.

"Are you really crying?" Carissa asked. "Come on. I'm sorry. I can buy you more, I swear."

"It's fine," I said. "I don't care anymore. She's gone anyways."

"She left a note. *To: Tabby.* Jesus, that's an awful nickname. Oh my God, she's legit insane. Like, serious serial killer energy. She didn't write her name or anything."

I jumped up, my heart racing. "What does it say?"

"To a wonderful friend. I wish you could be like me too."

I went to read it for myself, ripping the card out of Carissa's hand, feeling the bones in my face move again. The transformation felt more intense. Painful. I looked in the mirror and imagined my face hatching like an egg. Gradually, a new life emerging.

Bluebeard's First Wife

. . . .

I WAS SIXTEEN and scavenging my best friend, Lachlan Lovely's, house for the Kool-Aid packets he and his older brother used to dye hemp necklaces with. Lachlan had told me to look on his desk in the bedroom they used to share, but I'd found nothing there, so now I was absent-mindedly going through the clothes Merle—that was the brother's name—hadn't taken out of his dresser when he'd last packed for college. You could tell their mom did all the laundry by the department-store-quality folds of her asshole son's T-shirts. There were sachets of lavender in every drawer. Eyeleted ribbon kept them cinched closed. Both brothers were spoiled—Lachlan hadn't felt like helping me search—but I couldn't say I wasn't, too, when my own mom had let me paint my bedroom black.

I'd been to their house a billion times before. I thought I already knew for sure what their whole family was like deep down, so I wasn't being intrusive examining the logos of dress

shirts out of boredom. Lachlan and me went to the same
school where Merle had graduated. According to the alum
magazine, they're both pharmaceutical reps now, but in high
school Lachlan was the closest thing I'd ever had to a real boyfriend. He was a boy that happened to be my friend. Merle was
the opposite: shy in a cruel and calculating way, which was why
he made these weird, pursed-lipped expressions whenever we
locked eyes. I still hadn't forgotten how, last summer, while I
was waiting in the self-checkout line at Safeway, I'd witnessed
him glare daggers at the Black cashier over the five-cent-per-
plastic-bag charge she insisted that he pay.

I thought I was avoiding trouble by skipping over the
underwear drawer, but then I came across a weathered copy of
The Bell Curve in the one where Merle kept all his ties. One of
my sisters was studying sociology at the local university, so I
knew it was a book that racists liked. The area we lived in, an
overwhelmingly white township in Northern California that
had previously been known only for grapes and hippies, was
going through a hate crime problem that attracted the ire of all
the progressive newspapers. I kept thinking of it as safe anyway
because a lot of my friends at the time were white and none
had never called me the n-word. I didn't even really consider
Merle all that bad, trying to convince myself he was just anti-
social since we barely ever talked, him being one year ahead of
me and all.

My heart started racing. I remembered the fairytale "Barbe
bleue" and how the titular blue-bearded man forbids his young
bride from entering a secret room in his castle. She goes inside
anyways and sees the corpses of the wives who'd come before

her, all of whom disobeyed him like she had. What could've been inside that secret place before the corpses?

I flipped to a random page and read the first sentence over and over again until it ceased to make any sense, dissolving into random words and those words a string of letters, shapes. I hadn't yet pinned clinical terms like *race-based trauma* to my emotions, which swirled together in my mind like unnamed colors. What I remembered from the book was this: endless jargon, Black people being lesser, their kids and those kids' kids even more inferior.

There was a tangent against affirmative action penciled into the crammed margins. I could tell it was Merle's handwriting. I'd seen the notes he'd left to his mother on the fridge from when he still lived at home—*please get more bread love you I'll be back at four.* I put the book on Lachlan's bed with the spine splayed out to the page that'd haunted me even before I'd read it. I wanted him to see. I didn't know I'd wind up being more afraid of him than anyone else in town, fleeing from him forever the moment he let go of me.

I tried to convince myself that Merle couldn't be like the real hateful types who'd staged a riot in Sacramento, but couldn't. I'd always sensed that there was something wrong thickening and spoiling in the air around him. I'd felt this force even in his absence, mostly at school whenever one of the meaner senior girls bumped into me on the way to Assembly. She'd hung out with Merle.

When I went out into the hallway, I thought about going back and putting the book in its proper place. I stood there unmoving for what felt like forever.

I heard his mom coughing in the master bedroom. The soft glow of a television lit up the crack underneath her closed door. The local news was on. I heard the anchorwoman's voice talking about the Black boy from the public high school who'd been killed. Just last week, his purpling, bloated body had been discovered in an irrigation canal near Paradise Shopping Center, a fact that had made my mom tear up when she'd finished reading aloud the *Times* article about his murder to my dad. There were a lot of cases like that happening, lots of dead Black boys popping up throughout the country, only this time, according to the anchorwoman, he was gay too. A panel of experts wouldn't stop mentioning how he'd used Grindr despite being under eighteen, yelling over each other. They didn't mention the murder suspect, a man who'd worn a Celtic cross necklace to his desk job at a company that sold inground swimming pools.

The channel clicked. The Empire Today jingle piped up and, as if a curse had been lifted from me, I could walk again. I left the book on the bed.

In the kitchen, Lachlan was still playing that anime puzzle game on his phone like when I'd first gone upstairs. I tried cheering him on, giving him unsolicited instructions like I did whenever we played *Ocarina of Time* on his dad's vintage Nintendo. It took him ten minutes to complete the level he was on. He let me play. I lost pretty quickly. The big-boobed schoolgirl I was supposed to control tumbled off a cliff.

"Did you find the stuff?" he asked.

"No. They weren't where you said, but that's fine."

We'd wanted to make Hawaiian Punch shots from this recipe we'd found online. We started preparing overflowing mugs of strawberry milk instead when Lachlan came up with the idea of going to a roadhouse for dinner. We made a competition out of seeing whose drink could turn colors the fastest, stirring the Nestle powder into light pink whorls that marbleized the white of the milk.

"Whoever loses has to pay for the food."

I forgot who said this, me or him. We shared almost everything together—same words, same tastes. He flashed a perfect smile. I smiled right back, showing off the glow-in-the-dark bands my orthodontist Dr. Wen had put on my braces. It was impossible to tell who won, so we called it a draw.

The happiness we both felt was so obvious and cliché to me. I'd trained myself to become so aware of these moments of pleasure I couldn't fully enjoy them, my gratefulness for their presence morphing into dread of their ephemerality. The memory of Merle's drawer dangled over me like an anvil, but somehow, I kept smiling.

His mom, a rheumatic homemaker who was always asleep when not busying herself with simple household tasks, kept earthenware crockery from Williams Sonoma in their pantry. The mugs bore a hefty weight that made everything taste luxurious to me, even the overly sweet milk. Lachlan and me took a few sips and tossed our half-full cups into the sink. Neither of us liked the chalky aftertaste, which Lachlan said reminded him of the bubble-gum-flavored amoxicillin that was supposed to cure strep throat.

I went to go put on my sweaters, which I'd left puddled on the living room floor. It was winter break and Lachlan's dad had just left his family for the third time. A greater absence than usual permeated their split-level. The artificial Christmas tree stood half-finished in the spot where his dad's stereo system used to be.

The house was small and you could hear everything. Lachlan jogged upstairs to his bedroom, opened his door, paused, shifted things around, paused again, and came back downstairs. The whole time, guilt washed over me. I tried to think of something to say as we laced up our boots by the door.

"It's supposed to snow tonight," I said. "Three feet."

He cleared his throat but said nothing.

"Is something the matter?"

"What? No. Just trying to undo this knot."

We talked about school as we walked along Main Street. There was a rumor floating around that the religious girl who'd dropped out of the grade below ours was enrolled in a special program for teen moms because she was pregnant. I felt like I understood her. I told him that people just liked to talk, especially when they had an excuse to make their nastiness seem pure. Lachlan's face got all serious. He breathed in and said, "I get what you're saying." It was a sudden change from his usual sticks-and-stones philosophy, which had always secretly repelled me the same way Merle's bitterness had drawn me in.

* * *

The roadhouse was crowded. Everyone was talking at once; their conversations morphed into a singular droning noise that was hard to speak over. I could just barely hear "Jingle Bell Rock" playing on the crackly speakers. The floors smelled like Fabuloso. I breathed in the scent, comforted by its sterility and the familiar way the sticky residue clung to the bottoms of our boots like flypaper.

We were able to get a booth seat. Our waitress was an older woman who said we looked adorable together. I watched Lachlan shift in his seat. He was too polite to reject her compliment.

"We're just friends, ma'am," I said.

"Aww. Don't be like that, sweetie. You might break his heart."

Lachlan and I ordered burgers. I watched the waitress disappear behind the kitchen door. Her winged hair was teased into a messy ponytail. She reminded me of a mother from an old-school family show, one of those perfectly imperfect TV white women whose worst crimes never went beyond burning food in the oven.

"I have something to tell you," he said.

I froze. My mind became blank save for two memories: Merle, the contents of his drawer. All the childhood nightmares I'd had of Barbe bleue and his bludgeoned wives flooded my mind.

Lachlan told me he had dreams of having sex with attractive men. He never used the word *gay*. *Lesbian, gay, queer, sex, feminism*—these words felt off-limits to us at the time, too adult, too intellectual.

"That's awesome," I said. "Please just be safe."

"How does it make you feel?"

"Happy? I mean, you don't have to pretend to yourself anymore."

"Is that a good thing?"

I shrugged.

So many people at school were convinced we were a couple because our friendship had become more consistent than most high school romances. Their conviction had only grown stronger after he broke up with his ex, a mousy girl who went by a boy's name because her real one took too long to say. I suddenly thought of how, on the last day of midterms, a few days before the breakup, she'd widened her eyes like a spooked deer when a senior girl hurled a chunk of ice at my face by the bus stop. My breathing got fast remembering the stinging feel of the cut that'd formed, which hadn't hurt half as much as Lachlan later telling me it had all been an accident even though he hadn't been there to see. I didn't know what to make of his ex. She was Chicana, light-skinned with an aquiline nose and sin-black hair that ran down the length of her back.

"Is that why you broke up with your ex?" I asked him. "Because of what you realized about yourself?"

"Hmm." He mimed stroking an invisible beard, which made me laugh. "That was so long ago."

"It was November, Lachlan. One month—not a year. And you still haven't told me the reason."

"Okay, okay. Yes and no. Yes, we broke up because I never really felt anything with her. And no because I would've still stayed friends with her if she hadn't acted all weird the last time

Merle was home. She started this political thing that totally set him off."

"She's pretty meek. Sometimes I forget she even goes to the school." I touched the faint scar on my cheek. It didn't sting anymore but I flinched anyway, expecting to feel something. "Pretty sure most people do."

"Yeah, I guess. But I have to support Merle. We've been through so much together, you know. More than you can imagine."

I wanted to ask him about the political thing, but the memory of her terrified expression and the terrible secrets they no doubt bore silenced me. My mom had taught me to never get involved with other people's relationships, which was why I'd always tried my best to avoid looking Lachlan's parents in the eye.

The waitress came back with our waters. I tried to take a sip. It was a struggle to swallow. The environmentally friendly paper straw went pulpy in my mouth. I wondered if Lachlan had seen the book at all. I kept searching for the answer in his face until I remembered that Merle was coming home next week. Lachlan had told me, but I'd forgotten up until now. All at once, the smell of cooking burgers, burning flesh, made me ill.

* * *

In a way, the kids from school were right: Lachlan and me fit the definition of a couple, but that still didn't mean we were one. We'd been having secret sleepovers at his house since middle school when we first met, slowly falling asleep in the spare bedroom as we talked about what the world might be like in a thousand years. He believed there'd be a cure for cancer and teleportation machines, and I believed that World War III would end humanity in fifty years.

A few weeks before I'd made the mistake of opening Merle's secret drawer, Lachlan and I made out at Winter Formal. We'd just come from pregaming with all his teammates from swim team in the captain's backyard. Top 40 music blared in the gymnasium. His lips tasted like orange peels, probably the orange-flavored Chapstick I'd given him. I felt the same awkward, mushy feeling I'd had with my first kiss, a dreadlocked boy from the Novato Horeb Haitian Company whose grandparents were being deported. He told me that he'd always been curious about how I looked without any clothes on.

In that moment at the formal, I only noticed his ex sitting alone on the bleachers with her cocktail dress hiked up awkwardly around her knees. But on the taxi ride to his parents' place, as the tipsy haze of cheap beer lifted from my eyes like a veil, I remembered all the other faces that had stared blankly from the semidarkness. Some of them had been older: blandly dressed chaperones. I tried to pick out their faces individually, but they were all just a whir that swam beneath Lachlan's ex.

The intimacy I shared with Lachlan was a one-time thing, an experiment. Just once, as a test, we tried having sex in his bedroom that night. His mother was too deep in an Ambien-induced slumber to care. He tasted like citrus not just on his lips but all over, like a clean floor. He seemed like two separate entities. Staring into his eyes, all I could see was the sexless image of Lachlan, a boy from school who eagerly dedicated all of his free time to the Seventh-day Adventist Church and Pokémon. And hidden in the darkness of his grandmother's handmade quilt was the rest of his body, an incubus that made me come so violently I lost myself, forgetting that Lachlan was even in the room at all. The incubus jabbed his fingers inside of me and I realized I could alchemize the pain of their presence into pleasure simply by letting go. He kept going soft in my hands and mouth, and after a while I gave up and let him touch me without reciprocating. I was new to sex, greedy to be felt as much as possible without having to do any work.

"How did it go for you?" he said when he stopped.

"To be honest, more sensuous than sensual."

"There's a difference?"

"Yeah. Sensual is more romantic. Sensuous just means you felt something good, but not romantic-good."

"Oh."

"Weren't you in Ms. Nowak's class last year? That was all she talked about in my section when we were going over *Bovary*."

"That class was the bane of my existence. She only gave As to people she agreed with."

"How was it, by the way? Just now, I mean. Not school."

He made a vague motion with his hands.

I spent the night at his place without thinking anything of what we'd done. We slept until noon and made blueberry pancakes for brunch. Merle was home for the weekend to see off their dad before he moved out. Cardboard boxes waited idly in seemingly every room of the house. He walked into the kitchen and started talking to Lachlan about video games as if I wasn't even there. Lachlan didn't seem to notice. I stared at the floor and listened to them laugh at an inside joke Merle told about a comic book I'd never heard of.

After an hour or so, I went home without a good enough lie to explain away my absence. My parents smelled all of my sins on my breath, discerning not just the alcohol but also Lachlan, a boy whom they'd always been suspicious of. For the umpteenth time, Dad told me the cautionary tale of his aunt who'd thrown her life away, children and all, for a man who'd only wanted to use her body for sex. Mom made me clean our already spotless kitchen as a character-building exercise, too progressive to out-right admit to punishing me. I still associate the egg-plant color of the Fabuloso bottle with a longing type of sadness unique to my childhood. Its nostalgia feels as bittersweet as the fairytales, TV shows, and toy commercials from my youth, all of which provided fantasies so realistic that some part of me eventually became convinced I'd experienced them firsthand.

I came to believe the things people thought about me and Lachlan. In my mind, being punished for a deed made that deed automatically true. We had to be lovers because of our races. He was a white boy going out of his way to choose me, a fact he often complained his friends from the swim team wouldn't let him forget whenever he was about to eat something around the same color as my skin but usually much darker—chocolate, coffee, all consumable things that never lasted long.

* * *

"Should I tell my parents?" he said. "Merle thinks I should. Parents first and then everyone else."

We'd left the restaurant after splitting the bill. We walked aimlessly through the township with no destination in mind, too reluctant to part just yet. We chose where to go based upon which intersections gave us a walking signal first. It was starting to get dark. The sun lowered itself over the horizon, turning the whole sky pink. We passed by Paradise Shopping Center. Of all the stores, the 24/7 laundromat was the only one still open.

"You already told Merle?" I asked.

"Of course. He's my rock. I told him after Formal."

"Oh."

Last year, Merle had graduated from school a year early because he was a genius of sorts. A parenting magazine had profiled him when he first got accepted into that selective engineering college in SoCal. According to a different magazine, the school had only nine Black students in its freshman class and the security guards there kept pictures of them to better know who among the campus's predominately Black neighborhood belonged. I'd convinced myself that Merle wasn't that bad based on the things Lachlan told me about him: He was a meteorology major who believed in global warming. He had a half-Japanese, half-Jewish girlfriend named Earth and a Woodstock poster that he kept in his dorm room. He had Lachlan.

"I think you should tell them," I said. "Your parents, I mean. But only if you want to. I want to say I know them well enough to say, but I'm just not sure anymore."

"It's not that I think they'll kick me out, though."

"Then what is it?"

"I just don't want their perception of me to change. I don't want to be 'the gay son.'"

"I'm sorry."

Lachlan grabbed my hand and for a moment, I forgot myself.

He led us to a small park he told me he used to go to back when his parents' marriage had first started to crack. It was almost empty; all of the children had gone home. He led us underneath a poplar tree. We had a habit of doing this: standing around waiting for the other to leave first so that we didn't have to, extending our time together for as long as possible.

Sitting on one of the benches was a girl around our age and an older man with flowy Jesus hair. She had on hoop earrings and a bubblecoat that swallowed up what I assumed was the clothed part of her otherwise bare legs. She kept pumping her legs as if she expected the bench to take flight like one of the swings. Both were laughing. I wondered if the girl was secretly thinking the same thing as me: that her mom was going to give her hell when she inevitably came home late. They were white, but so were most of the people I'd grown up around. All my life, I'd only noticed people like me, all of whom stuck out even though I pretended we didn't.

When she saw me, she stopped to wince her nose. She pointed at us. A Doberman was lounging at her feet. Its eyes lit up when it saw us, its slobbery mouth wide and welcoming.

"Aww, look at the dog," Lachlan said. "He's smiling."

"Yeah. Cute."

I didn't trust the way the man kept smirking at us. I felt something in the air choking me. I had to let go of Lachlan. I took off one of my layers so I could breathe right. The couple with the dog started whispering to each other as I tied my favorite chenille sweater around my waist. I felt a sudden guilt assuming they were together. Still, the fear bubbling up inside of me refused to go away.

"What's on your mind?" Lachlan asked.

I was thinking about Merle and the drawer but also Formal, Lachlan's ex's stares, the strawberry milk. The couple wouldn't stop looking at us; even when I turned away, I could feel their eyes trained on me. I tried to open my mouth to talk but started crying instead.

Lachlan hugged me. I tried to pull away, but then he buried my face in his chest.

"Why are you upset?" he asked. "Come on, you're scaring me."

"I can't be friends with you anymore," I said. My voice was all muffled.

He stopped breathing for a second. I could hear his heart beating through the layers of clothes he had on. He pulled away.

"Merle," I said. "Merle's a racist. I saw. In his room. He had this book and I put it on your bed because I wanted you to see."

"Is that why you're upset?"

I nodded my head.

"Merle reads everything. It doesn't mean he believes what it says." He laughed. "Everything's going to be fine."

He stepped back to put his hands on my face. They felt like ice. I was barely listening to him. "Everything's going to be fine," he kept saying. "Listen. Look at me. Everything's . . ."

From above Lachlan's shoulders, I could see the man walking over to us. He was still smiling. My whole body focused on his. Time slowed. I tried to pull away from them both, but then Lachlan reeled me into another stubborn bear hug.

"Going. . . ."

The man held an Evian bottle of something yellowish in his hand. He'd probably found it in the trash. I saw him thrust back his hand dramatically and for a second, I thought that maybe he was only going to pretend-throw it at us. The bottle gleamed underneath the tepid glow of the streetlights. Its cap was gone.

"To be . . ."

Time surged forward. A sticky liquid splashed us, releasing a scent that reeked of wet pennies and human stink. When Lachlan finally let go of me, the man was already half-way down the street. I turned toward the bench, but the girl and her dog were already gone.

Devil's Juice

. . . .

FINN WAS WAITING outside Starbucks when the big dog came flying after the smaller one. It had humanlike muscles and a giant bobblehead that outsized its legs, which were scrawny but also agile, very fast. Its jaws latched into the small dog's side, killing it, throwing around mottled fur and flesh and spastic limbs. Finn hugged onto his guitar case as if the bass inside were a living thing in danger.

His old classmate Anne Favreau appeared, pale and awkward. He'd begun to suspect she'd canceled their hookup, but there she was now, trembling, crying. Telegraph Avenue came back to him all at once. Bikes, cars, the faint odor of coffee beans and trash. Blood. The ADT security ad on the side of the bus shelter asked him in bold lettering if he knew where his children were (he had none, so nowhere).

The little dog was dead, but the big one wouldn't let go, just kept swinging the carcass around with its mouth. The vape shop guy tried choking it with his hands, but this lady in raspberry soft shorts came running up behind them screaming. She started beating him with her purse, saying something like, "Don't hurt him!" or "Don't hurt me!" or maybe both. She didn't understand what was happening. Or maybe she did. There was blood everywhere, all over her shorts. How could she not know? The little St. Mary's girl looked lost standing there in her uniform. Long braids curtained her face, lots of beads and barrettes, the plastic clattered when she started running.

The big dog shot across the street, narrowly avoiding a Horizon milk truck that laid on its horn. Everyone waited for the police, Anne and Finn and the whole crowd of people who'd gathered around the little dog's body. The soft shorts lady owned the big dog. She didn't go after it. Instead, she yelled at this other lady who Finn was pretty sure was—had been—the small dog's owner. The big dog came back on its own, stopping again at the little dog's corpse. A cop car pulled up. More onlookers came, more shouting.

Finn had to drag Anne away. She couldn't talk. She kept shaking her head as he tried to find the hotel. He asked for a name, but all she could do was move her head around. The address came to him after they'd started off in the wrong direction. It was only a block away from the carnage, which turned into four because of the convoluted path they took. There was a line for the elevator. He took the stairs. She followed.

"Ten," Anne said.

"What?" Finn said.

"Tenth floor."

He'd taken his time getting ready for the Waldorf's show tonight—he was just a musician, he hadn't wanted to do the engineering program that his mom wanted—but now sweat was bleeding through his new shirt. The fabric grew heavy. The idea of sex with Anne became unbearable. He preferred the stairs over her. There was only one bed in their room, a queen. They sat on the end. She said she didn't want either of them taking off their clothes tonight. But also, she still wanted sex, just not right now.

"Give me a moment," she kept saying.

Thirty minutes went by. They did nothing, said nothing. How many moments made up an eternity? Finn plucked pills of fabric off his angora sweater. Outside, the steady rush of traffic, birdsong, children's laughter. There was a playground across the street. It belonged to St. Mary's, their old K–12 school. All the students there wore uniforms, girls tartan jumpers or skirts, boys dress shirts with khakis. His mother used to teach English at the upper school for the tuition discount, but retired as soon as he graduated to avoid the new, worse director. Sometimes, when Finn needed money, the admin let him work in the front office mailing donation slips. He was so desperate for money, his mom's help and cramped apartment were all he had. The band's travel expenses had gotten costlier, and though indie magazines liked their style, none of them were widely read enough to make any real difference. Finn could always go back to Holland, but that would require being completely optionless. He'd rather suffer here than with his dad and new girlfriend who his mom said was around Finn's age.

Anne's eyes were still glazed. Her mind was far away from here, with the dead dog probably. She'd been a big animal lover at St. Mary's. Her folders always had pictures of horses on the front from the first grade all the way up until their last class of senior year.

Anne reached into her satchel and pulled out one of the old folders, one with a sparkly unicorn on the front. "Geometry," read the label. Inside was the check, which had a faded picture of puppies in the background. They wore matching red bows, all of them squishing together in a giant wicker basket. Finn crushed the check into the part of his wallet where all the old receipts and parking stubs were. He looked around. Now his leg was jangling too. Fear was like an infectious disease. He couldn't stop thinking about the little dog.

What he was doing with Anne was prostitution, which meant having sex for money. It didn't matter that Anne was only paying him for a baby rather than the feel of him. She'd suggested the idea as a joke at St. Mary's five-year reunion, and they laughed until they both got serious.

Finn started laughing again now when she gave him the paperwork she'd been talking about over the phone. Without hesitation, he signed over his paternity rights (could he do that without a lawyer?), daydreaming about the slides at St. Mary's until he remembered the dogs and grew sick.

The violence of the day made him feel less secure in the world. Detached. He didn't know why, only that the little dog's death had affected him in such a way that he couldn't stop himself from grinning. There was nothing happy about the situation. He felt like he was being used. Anne's continued infatuation with him felt predatory and pathetic. She used to go to all of the band's concerts when it was still called One Time. Now it was Devil's Juice. She told him softly that she was sorry she hadn't been to the recent performances, but that the new house had taken up all her time. Her parents helped her get this newly renovated American Foursquare. She showed him pictures of it on her phone. The house had scalloped wainscoting, pressed tin ceilings, and an old well that the HOA required she keep boarded up for safety reasons. Her life was a pleasant blur. He couldn't relate, much less care.

Anne went to lie down on the bed, strawberry-blonde hair fanned out on the pillow. He touched her thigh, pressing her nylon tights against her flesh. She didn't pull back. She didn't react at all.

"Let's just get it over with," she said.

"I don't really feel anything," Finn said.

"It doesn't matter. Doesn't have to be enjoyable."

Finn laughed until he realized that she was being serious. "I mean," he started. "It's kinda necessary. Otherwise, I can't, you know."

Anne said nothing. The AC clicked on. Dust fluttered toward the ceiling, trickling down like snow. He imagined himself talking about this moment with his bandmates. He was close to them all like a family. Everyone had gone to St. Mary's save for Joe, who'd gone to public school. The alums all remembered her because of how pitiful she'd made herself. She used to talk to herself in class, mumbling as she drew odd shapes on her arms that people said were satanic.

And then she asked me if I'd have her baby, Finn was telling the band in his head. *She was all up on me and everything, and I'm just like, "You really need some help."*

The others laughed until one of them asked if he went through with it, at which point the fantasy fizzled out. Finn's memories were the only place where he still had power over

Anne. Her wealth trumped the popularity he used to enjoy. All he had left was music and his friends.

"What are you thinking about?" Anne asked.

"Nothing," Finn said. Then: "Why do you still like me?"

She shrugged. "I like your face. And your hair. Really your whole body. I want my child to have your features. They'd look just as good on a son as a daughter."

"Why not just marry someone?"

"I don't want to share." Anne sidled up next to him. The feel of her wasn't intimate. She radiated fatigue. "The idea of someone taking my kids away from me—I'd scream if it ever happened. Your parents are divorced. I'm sure you know what I mean. Did your mom get sad when you had to go back to the Netherlands in the summer?"

"I don't wanna talk about that right now."

Anne yawned. "I think I also just prefer to be superficial when it comes to choosing my child's future dad. I don't want to have to sift through guys who won't hurt me because then I might not be left with anyone, or at least not anyone attractive."

"That's a glum view of things."

"I have a right to be. All the St. Mary's girls used to be so awful to me. Some of the boys were complicit too. It's really weird how those memories have stuck. Like, I can't even think about the TV shows that were popular then. Jesus, everyone was so obsessed with TV. When I see those shows, all I can think about is how awful people can be."

Finn rolled his eyes. She saw, though he didn't mean her to. He was only thinking how petty it was to care about the past when she had everything she needed right now: a house, no money problems, bright thoughts of gurgling babies on her mind. She'd gotten plastic surgery to fix her face, and now she looked normal, pretty almost. Her parents' fortune would last her for all of her life the same way Finn's mom's poverty might last him for the rest of his. His dad refused to send them any more money now that Finn was grown. His mom had been putting off paying a bunch of old debt, and now a collections agency had started ringing up the apartment all day, torturing them both but Finn more since he slept in the living room where the landline was.

"I know my problems are boring," Anne said, reading his mind, or rather his face. "But you feel everything more when you're growing up. It's the most vulnerable time. I was so small. A girl shoved me against a concrete wall in the fifth grade. I didn't even know who she was at the time. She was some random new kid who wanted to fit in." She took a long, pained breath. "Humans are no different from animals."

"That's not true."

"You're right. Humans are worse."

"What about the vape shop guy?"

"Who?"

"Never mind."

Anne was more introspective than Finn had thought, which made her more exploitative. He was convinced that she sensed his money issues and took pleasure in paying him to debase himself like this. She knew that their school viewed her as repellant. She was using her ugliness against him. Finn had cried to himself in the bathroom that one time in middle school when someone spread a rumor about him being in love with her.

"I've always wanted to possess beauty," Anne said dreamily. "I used to have dolls, then crushes. Then men. A lot of them don't even care if you're pretty or not. But it doesn't matter. Everything goes away eventually. I was talking to my doula, and she said that people continue living through their children even after they die. I don't want mine to be pathetic like I was. I want a new life. New body."

Finn wanted to leave so bad. But the idea of going back outside felt suddenly impossible, like stepping out into space without a spacesuit. His head might explode if he had to see all that blood again. And the people. Why hadn't they done anything? Most of them had just stared like him and Anne. He'd become so weak. But he also couldn't risk having a dog bite off his hands, his real livelihood. He looked at Anne until he couldn't. Something about her had changed, it wasn't just the surgery. He wanted to remove it from her. She looked too pleased with herself. Her practiced misanthropy had come too late; most in their grade had outgrown it. Only a stunted person thought they could achieve moral purity by cutting themselves off from humanity.

Anne tried to make herself out to be like the protagonist of a sappy romance, mewling as she touched him. He buried his head into her body so that he didn't have to look at her face. He acted violent, letting his anger blend together with the eroticism of Anne's small frame, entering her as hard as he could, first his fingers, then fist, his manhood last. The feeling of her was liberating, like being in a relationship with his ex, Charlotte, minus the obligations or care. He grabbed the back of Anne's neck, imagining that she didn't like what he was

doing and that he'd ruined her. She cried out. He was pretty
sure Charlotte had been the one who'd pushed Anne against
a wall.

Shame, so heavy and unwieldy. It enveloped him like a
haze. He knew it would go away eventually. He went to the
bathroom and pissed. When he came back out again, he got
so overwhelmed he had to lie down on the bed. His mind kept
playing the image of the small dog dying over and over.

Anne wiped his face with a washcloth, whispering to him.
"It's fine. You'll be fine. We'll be fine."

"I don't want to bring kids into this world."

She hugged him. "It's not your kid," she said.

* * *

When Anne had first decided that Finn Loevinsohn was the
closest she'd ever gotten to really loving someone, she was sitting in her sister Shandra's old room. Right at this moment,
her high school graduation was gearing up on St. Mary's front
lawn. She'd opted not to go last minute, complaining of a stress
headache.

Before, she would've probably said that she loved her little
nephew best. He'd reached out for Anne's breast when he was
a baby, recognizing her womanliness and humanity back when
Anne first started suspecting that she was something less than
living. Her pain kept her from seeing anything that wasn't
danger. Abuse made her sexless. Paranoid. The girls at school
boiled down all of Anne's dreams into a singular desire to be
left alone. Now that she'd finished school, a deafening silence
took over.

She was finally, thankfully, alone. And she had Shandra, though she hardly counted as a close friend. Shandra was kind, but was never around much. She had her own family for most of Anne's life: her own children, her own dog, and a husband who loved her so much that he'd recently bought her a second Chanel purse. She felt more like a pleasant wind than a real presence Anne could hold on to, no different from their parents, who were always away on business. Her whole life revolved around her marriage, which she wouldn't shut up about.

"I had to quit my job," Shandra was saying. "The hours were too long. I can't stand being away from the kids."

"That's a lot to give up," Anne said.

"You'll understand when you marry. Not now, of course, but sometime in the future, I'm sure."

"I wanna be a single mom."

Shandra's pleasant face dropped. "Don't be ridiculous, Anne," she said. "I'm sure there's a million boys you like, and a million more who like you. You're always talking about that one guy from St Mary's. What's his name again? The one with the band?"

"Finn. But I don't know if I love him. I just hate him less than everyone else because he's hot and doesn't act like a total idiot. I don't feel like any less of a shell when he's talking to me, though. Isn't love supposed to make you feel better?"

"Shell?" Shandra raised an overly tweezed eyebrow. "What do you mean?"

Anne looked down at her feet, studying her purple socks with the embroidered toadstools on the cuffs. She'd never told anyone the true extent of her suffering at St. Mary's. The idea of revealing the truth this late depressed her worse than anything her worst tormentors had ever said about her looks. She desperately wanted to live out her parents' vision of how her life was supposed to be. They still thought that she was friends with Meredith and Brittany, both of whom had decided one day in middle school that they hated her before infecting the rest of the grade with their contempt.

"Anne?" Shandra was saying. "What's the matter? Why do you always look so sad?"

Anne almost felt ready to say the truth. But the phone started ringing before she could speak. It was Shandra's husband calling to ask what time she would be back home. He said he wanted to order dinner out and was there anything Shandra wanted? Yes, Shandra said. Anything with pasta would be fine with her. She had him on speaker because their mom had the hairdryer going in the other room. The walls were thin. She hung up at the same time the washer stopped. It played a short song each time it finished. Anne hummed along with it. It was so relaxing finally being left alone. The girls had stopped filling her Ask.fm page with questions on whether or not she'd had an abortion (she hadn't) and if she planned on killing herself (she didn't believe in suicide, though she used to daydream of what it would be like to fall asleep forever).

Only after Shandra left to go back to her real family did Anne finally collapse. Now that there was no threat of violence, all her emotions—the anger, the mourning and intense self-loathing—took up the space in her brain where her desperation for survival once resided. The loneliness was the most overwhelming part. She couldn't suppress herself anymore. There was no need to. She cried until her mom called her down for dinner. "Don't be sad," her dad kept telling Anne at the table. "You have so much to look forward to!"

Anne's depression only grew worse as her life improved. She spent the summer alone in her room, reading romance novels about beautiful women falling in love with handsome but troubled men. Everything after St. Mary's felt like death, though Anne didn't mourn her old life. She felt sadness for only the girl she could've been had her life worked out different, had she attended a different school and maybe learned how to make herself invisible in a way that didn't invite scorn. What St. Mary's had done to her went beyond murder. They killed the woman she was meant to be before she could even emerge.

Anne's new life was fake. She couldn't make herself into a stronger, better person, couldn't move forward when the St. Mary's girls had stripped down so much of her will. She got a genioplasty but felt unchanged. It was already too late, her reflection was telling her. She was ruined. Every passing look and whisper felt like a personal insult against her. When she enrolled at the local state college (her parents' idea; she wasn't an intellectual like Shandra), a sophomore boy asked her out, and she said yes only to stand him up, her mind overcome with irrational thoughts of him stringing her along as a joke like Alan Thomas had in the eighth grade. She didn't get what men wanted. She imagined them searching for the last scraps of her essence that weren't already destroyed. Whether they wanted to fuck her or fuck with her, she didn't care—it was all the same to her.

Anne was waiting at the campus bus stop halfway through her first semester when she decided she didn't want to go to school anymore. Some lady from the dean of studies wanted to speak to her about her poor grades. Anne had barely attended any classes and would probably get kicked out if she opted to stay any longer than she already had.

There was a pregnant woman sitting on the bench. Her groceries took up all the extra room on either side of her, but Anne didn't mind. Lately, she'd been thinking more about pregnancy, pregnant women, the whole birthing process and what it meant to be alive. The science interested her the most. Before she grew tired of the lectures, her biology class had touched upon the reproductive systems of different animals, mostly mammals but also amphibians. The professor showed pictures of fetuses at different stages of development. It disturbed Anne how similar they all looked, the human fetus overlapping with the rabbit one and the rabbit one with the frog one. She thought of them all stuffed inside the pregnant woman, making herself ill until she thought of how wonderful it would be to have a child of her own. What a magical experience it must be transforming slimy, gilled creatures into babies that sometimes became important, loved people.

What Anne really needed was a daughter. The daughter had to be beautiful and smart. She needed to be the opposite of Anne, a positive reflection of the parts of her that had withered away. She imagined a new life blooming out from inside her uterus, which for so long she'd associated with just her menstrual cycle, with blood and discomfort and the nightcapped bear on the front of the Sleepytime tea box. When the bus came, she'd already decided who the father would be.

Sex with Finn was awful. She bled after. All she wanted was her daughter; the wait was excruciating. Phantom needles stabbed her vagina for days. What kept her going was the knowledge that Finn was too solipsistic to want the baby for himself. There came a great power in realizing this each time she looked down at the swell of her stomach and the life taking form underneath. All mine, she thought. The St. Mary's girls couldn't steal this happiness from her like they had all the cash from her pencil case.

When the doctor told Anne she was having a son, she didn't mind because it was still *her* son. She could take care of him without anyone's help. Her parents gave her a trust fund, a house, and promised even more if she considered online school ("Please," her mom had begged, "for the baby, just consider it"). If the state ever tried taking away her baby, she'd kill them all with the rage she'd been saving over the course of her whole life. In her renovated basement was a gun rack and a pearl-handled Beretta. She had dreams where a pack of wild wolves broke into the foyer and she had to shoot them all before they could make it upstairs to the nursery. The wolves screamed each time she missed.

* * *

The birth was easy. She waded in a pool until her son, Harper, slipped out of her. They both cried. The midwife said she'd never seen such a beautiful child before, and though she probably told all her clients this, her tone felt like she meant her words. How could she not be genuine to a baby whose wide, pale eyes seemed to contain a whole universe of emotion. Everything about him felt pure. His bowel movements didn't smell foul. Her parents fell in love with him even though they still hated the idea of Anne being a single mother. (*Uneducated,* they kept calling her, as if she hadn't gone to school for most of her life already. Her dad brushed her off when she pointed out the hypocrisy, bouncing Harper in his lap and tickling his belly.)

What Anne's parents and preachy politicians on TV didn't want to understand about single motherhood was that most of the hardest parts could easily be resolved with the right amount of money. Years went by quick and easy. She never worried about a single bill, and could always hire babysitters if she wanted to, which she never did. Finn's band became famous. Her whole world became Harper and, by extension, Finn.

For her life to be complete, Anne had to forget Finn. Harper wouldn't let her. Neither would the rest of the world. She couldn't put on the TV without hearing about his band and how famous they'd become. When Harper wasn't asking about paternity directly, he was obsessing about Devil's Juice, how cool they were and how deeply their music touched an unreachable part of his soul. He didn't know the truth—hard to believe considering how much he resembled his father, but his ignorance really was genuine. She had to pretend to still be religious when she told him to take down the giant poster of Finn on his wall. It was appalling, she told him, shaking her head as if she, too, didn't believe the words that were coming out of her mouth. She, the single mother, the one who'd dropped out of college and gotten pregnant.

From the poster, Finn stared at her with wild eyes, guitar in hand. He was shirtless and humping a stage somewhere, the background fuzzed out so that all that showed was his body, his toned, wet muscles and body hair.

"He has cancer now," Harper said. "He says his fans are his best medicine!"

"I don't care," Anne said.

"You're being mean."

"That's not gonna make me change my mind."

"So mean," Harper said again, spitting out his words as he tore the poster up into many pieces. "You won't even tell me who my dad is."

He was only bringing up the subject to pain her. He was twelve now, an inauspicious age, the same age she'd been when all of St. Mary's started turning on her. "You're always saying he's not important, but I still wanna know. What if I need an organ transplant and he's the only one who can give it to me?"

"He's dead," Anne lied.

Harper nodded, content with the answer for a brief moment. He wasn't a tragic, lonely figure like his grandparents imagined him to be. There was no need for a dad to come home to them. Harper wasn't in need. He was just a curious child, safe, unbothered, and still filled with wonder for the world. When he asked her how his dad died, she told him he needed to change into a shirt that didn't have ketchup stains on it.

Anne took him to the pier for the distraction of ice cream and the fresh, briny air of the sea. They talked about his new school by the Ferris wheel. She'd enrolled him at an experimental place where kids sat on medicine balls instead of desks and got long, overly involved behavioral evaluations without letter grades. He was so beautiful, just like his dad. People in his grade even said he looked just like the lead guitarist from Devil's Juice, joking about Finn being his dad until the truth of his paternity felt more like a pun than reality. She felt like she was losing him already even though he was still a child and seated right beside her. All her dreams had revolved around him as a small child, and now that he was older, she was worried that he'd turn into someone cruel if not herself. She had no idea how an ideal kid was supposed act, much less an adult. She racked her brain, picking apart the roles she'd known for most of her life: predator, bystander, victim.

Anne was trying to find a way to breach the subject of his father. She had to give Harper a version of the truth that wouldn't reveal it entirely in case he went out looking for Finn. The whole time, she had to listen to Harper talk on and on and on about Finn this and Finn that. Apparently, Devil's Juice was coming to perform near them.

"I wanna go," he said. "My friends are, but I know you'll say no because it's dangerous or whatever."

"I'll think about it."

"Please, Mom."

Anne nodded mutely. She couldn't tell him no. She spoiled him, but he was never nasty like the St. Mary's kids, which only made her spoil him more. He'd recently made friends with the autistic boy in his class.

Her mind didn't process the man lingering over by the tower viewers. He was on his haunches, rustling through an oversized gym bag. She didn't see the gun in his hands until he already had it pointed at her. The crowd drowned him out as it broke apart, a chorus of screams. The *pop-pop* of the gun felt like

it was coming from all over. Anne grabbed Harper. She ran. She
didn't stop when his body started dragging along the boardwalk.
Looking back would be a mistake. She had to run, couldn't stop.
Blood all over her hands and face and all up in her mouth, the
wet-penny taste of death percolating on her tongue.

She woke up at the hospital, saw the bare white walls and
knew that Harper had finally been taken away from her. She
could feel it all: the bullets lodged in his head, the slow unfurl-
ing of brain death, the screams.

* * *

Finn was smoking in bed when he got the call from his publicist. Just some woman, said the bored voice on the other end
of the line. Anne Something. She'd kept insisting in emails that
she knew Finn from childhood. The publicist would've deleted
the messages until he read that she had a kid who'd died in that
shooting—not the one at the special needs school, but the
amusement park one.

Finn thanked him and said he'd think about it. His own
personal miseries had made him less feeling toward others,
not more. His mom would say the same. She thought he never
called enough, not even when he was sick and always staying over at her place between surgeries. There was another
tour coming up. She'd be angry at him again, comparing him
to his dad even though he was nothing like him. There was
never enough time. Music used to keep him going. Now it only
drained him. His bandmates tired him with their constant
squabbles over money.

His mind got caught up with the dogs. He'd dreamed about them again. The little one chased after the big one, growing larger in size until it was a monster. Finn could only watch. His legs were planted to the floor, slowly sinking through it until he was enveloped into blackness.

The cancer had crept up on him around the same time as the nightmare, and though it had gone away, his memory of the dogs continued to grow and mutate. The dream never changed much: two dogs, one big, the other small; the latter growing larger; Finn's body enveloped in deep, impenetrable darkness. Sometimes he emerged in his dad's old swimming pool in Rotterdam. Often, like the last time, he stayed swimming around in the dark until he woke up.

Finn called Anne's old phone number, the one she'd given him at the reunion. She picked up, sighed. "It's me," he said.

"I want to try again," she said. "I can pay."

"I don't need money," Finn said. "I have a lot of that now."

"I can give you more."

"No."

"Why not?"

No one but Finn knew the other reason, which was that he'd lost the ability to have children. It was a side effect of all the treatments he'd been through. He didn't care that he'd never be able to knock another woman up. What embarrassed him was his lack of virility. It made him feel like less of a man, like a castration almost.

Loneliness plagued Finn. He didn't understand that he was in mourning until he told her to come over. She hung up first.

He kept the phone pressed up against his ear, too tired to find the energy to remove it.

Finn arranged to meet Anne at a hotel room that was much nicer than the old one. She came with pictures of the boy. He was a cute kid, a blond reflection of Finn when he was young. His name was Harper and she was still in love with him. Here was them at the beach. And here was his first birthday, first Christmas and first Easter, the first time he took a crap and the first steps he took. It had rained at his kindergarten graduation, she said. The ceremony was indoors. Harper and his class sang "So Long, Farewell." Harper remembered all the words. Harper didn't lip sync like the others, didn't cry or wander around the room in a daze. Harper, Harper, Harper—that's all she could talk about. She claimed he'd been a fan.

Finn kept thinking about the dogs. They were their own emotion, a special combination of dread and heartbreak. He wondered if his and Anne's life would've turned out the way it had if one of them had intervened. If the big dog had ripped out Finn's throat, would Finn have had a less miserable death than the slow ones he'd witnessed at the oncology ward? Whatever happened to the vape shop guy? Was he happy? Did he still think of the dogs too?

On the night of Harper's conception, Anne had left him there in the hotel room, and Finn had cried. He thought he was all used up then, but really his emotions were just looking too far into the future. They couldn't see the fame waiting for him just around the corner. He'd cried and cried until he dragged himself to a gig he could no longer recall, refusing to touch the check, walking past his bank and feeling vindicated but still pathetic. A bald music producer tapped his feet as Devil's Juice played, an ice-filled highball glass in hand. "You put so much into your music," he'd said to Finn right after. "I could see the tears in your eyes."

Finn gasped. Anne was hugging him. She was soft and smelled like pure sweetness, like perfume mixed with some type of sugary food. He remembered the uncashed check in his wallet and said he had something for her—not the thing she wanted, he clarified, just something she needed.

"Please," she whispered, grabbing his shirt collar. "Just this one time. I won't bother you after this."

Anne was pathetic but also in shape. He should've been attracted to her. Her legs were long, the thighs fleshy and soft but not shapeless, the skin still taut after all these years. She pressed up against him. The feel of her made him sick.

He was in charge now, he kept thinking. His body took forever to get off, sapping him. He retreated to one side of the bed while she cried herself to sleep on the other. He couldn't decide if he wanted to kill her or cry with her. Perhaps it was best to just leave.

* * *

When Anne woke up, Finn had already gone. He'd left something on the nightstand. It looked like trash until she unfurled it and saw the puppies in a basket. He hadn't cashed the check. Or maybe he had. She'd never done a great job of keep track of her finances. She threw it in the garbage and walked out into the hallway.

In the elevator was a woman cradling a newborn. The newborn looked fresh, his skin still purpled and veiny with new life.

Anne smiled at it, waving. Hope filled her to the point of near insanity.

"Is that your first?" she asked the woman.

"Yeah," the woman said, laughing.

"I'm about to have my second pretty soon."

"They say it gets easier the second time around."

Anne nodded. She'd heard the woman's words many times before in parenting magazines. The second time was best because mothers knew what to expect. Less surprises. They didn't have to worry nearly as much.

The doors closed. On the ride down, Anne wondered if the meeting had been a mistake. But she was fine, she kept telling herself. She promised herself she'd move somewhere tropical if she failed again. She could buy a pet, too, not a dog but something much smaller. Maybe sea monkeys. Whatever she chose, it couldn't be big enough to leave behind a noticeable corpse nor endearing enough to be missed to the point of devastation.

Apples and Dresses

· · · · · · ·

EVERY DAY AT WORK, another homemade dress. Peter Pan–collared gingham, button-down paisley, or sleeveless satin with star-and-moon patches sewn on the skirt. Always the same Add-A-Pearl necklace. Sometimes earrings: studs of purifying crystal from her sister-in-law, Beverly, who owned this woo-woo, new age boutique online. "Let me send you something, Celeste," Beverly was always saying on their long calls, "something to cheer you up."

Celeste showed up at Green Forrest Elementary ready to perform for her second graders. She made up songs for them, dancing and getting them to dance with her—all while in a homemade dress. Her songs were about time mostly, day-of-the-week and season-of-the-year, cycled through in a minute or less to the tune of some cheesy song she'd heard on the radio.

Today's lesson: autumn. Her dress had pictures of cartoon apples with little cartoon worms poking out. Celeste and her kids were learning about different apples, how they grew and what they tasted like. Granny Smith was bitter, Red Delicious waxy-skinned, and pink lady sweet like candy. In the teachers' lounge, hidden in the fridge—top shelf, behind the Igloo cooler and next to the jar of Vegenaise—thirty-some gala apples tightly packed away and dripping still-warm confectionary goo (she'd forgotten to buy caramel at Stop and Shop). She planned on passing them out in the middle of the day, after lunch and recess.

"I want to be an apple farmer when I grow up," one girl, Venice, said.

She raised her hand but still spoke out of turn. She was loud and strange and very pretty, which was why Celeste never punished her. Celeste had a daughter whom she imagined would've been Venice's best friend.

"That's awesome!" Celeste said.

Celeste talked into the mini microphone clipped to her collar. Venice had hearing difficulties, and the microphone connected wirelessly to the speaker on her desk. Her parents had bought the set for her. They wouldn't take their daughter to an otolaryngologist for some reason. Celeste was pretty sure they were a part of a cultish church. Venice had said her mom wouldn't let her go on the lower-school camping trip because she didn't approve of girls wearing pants like boys. Spiritual corruption, she'd explained airily.

"I just wanna grow up so bad," Venice was saying now.

"You will, eventually," Celeste said. "Enjoy being a kid."

Venice stuck out her tongue, repulsed until she dissolved in her own silvery giggles. She had a toothy smile, dimples, faultless skin, and glasses. Large eyes, lashes long like a baby calf's. Her hair reached the small of her back. She was drowning in curls. They spilled all over her head so that she was always pulling them out of her face and spitting out the jet-black strands.

Once Celeste saw Venice stealing a boy's graham crackers from his lunchbox but didn't say anything. When he came to her in tears, it was easier to lie and say a squirrel snuck into the room—less fighting that way, plus now the kids didn't leave the door open after recess.

"I just wanna make money and buy a house with a horse stable and lots of land," Venice was saying. "My friend—her family is all famers—she lives on this really big farm with horses and rabbits and all sorts of stuff—and it's all hers! Her parents buy her anything. I wanna be like that when I'm an adult, except I'll buy everything myself because I don't wanna share. I have to share everything with my little brothers, and they break stuff all the time."

"Well, your friend sounds very lucky," Celeste said. She waited for Venice to calm down and stop kicking her feet. "Now let's get back on task."

"What do you want to be when you grow up?" Venice said. She raised her hand when the boy she stole from shushed her. *Shut up*, she mouthed to him.

"I'm obviously already grown, Venice," Celeste said, though sometimes bartenders still carded her.

"Yeah, but I mean, when you were a kid. Did you want to be a teacher then?"

"Not at first. Now let's move on."

This time Venice raised both hands. "Then what did you wanna be?"

"An actress."

That got the class excited. Other kids raised their hands, which seemed to act separate from them, stretching so far in the air their eyes squeezed shut like they were in pain. "Oh, oh, oh," they said, "me, me, me. Call on me."

"Alright, let's calm down," Celeste said.

Celeste called on Venice. Kids rolled their eyes. "Again?" a girl said. They were old enough to sense injustice, mostly favoritism but also increasingly the lies Celeste had been telling about Santa Claus not only existing but loving all kids around the world equally.

"You should perform," Venice said. "Right now."

"No way," Celeste said. She laughed. "It's not like I could put on a whole play with just me."

"You could just do a part of it. Like just one person from a play."

"Like a monologue?" Celeste went to the board and wrote out the word, sounding it out for everyone: "Mon-o-log. That's when one actor talks for a really long time."

"Monologue," Venice said.

"Monologue," the other kids repeated.

Celeste was onstage again. Not Broadway, maybe, but one at a child's theater that put on dramatizations of *Ramona and Beezus*, *Matilda*, *Watership Down*. She'd applied to a million of those places; no callbacks, though she did get a personal rejection from a place near San Francisco.

"Awesome!" Celeste said. "Do you know who's famous for writing monologues? An Englishman named Shakespeare. He wrote a bunch of plays that people perform on stages. Lots of monologues. In his most famous one, a man says, 'To be or not to be'"—Celeste gripped a bruised fuji apple, pretending it was part of a dead man—"and he holds up a skull like this."

Venice and a bunch of other girls squealed. "That's so creepy," one of them—not Venice—said.

"Perform a monologue," Venice said. She crossed her arms.

"We don't have time, unfortunately," Celeste said.

"How'll anyone learn if you don't show it?"

Celeste's old, wannabe actress self fought with her, demanding to be seen. "Okay," she said, "I have an idea."

The class squealed in delight. Venice pumped her fist.

"Okay," Celeste said. "Here we go."

But Celeste had nothing to perform. Her mind wouldn't let her recall all those lines she'd memorized. She thought back to her performing arts high school, then college, community theater, interviews, auditions, sitcom sets. All she could remember clearly was a commercial she'd done for a brand of laundry detergent. It never aired—the company got sued because the product made customers break out in hives—and she'd only had two lines anyway (her, age twenty-two, dressed up like a Playboy bunny to demonstrate softness: "Detergent and fabric softener all in one bottle? I'm all hopped up!").

Another potential performance: her fantasy. It involved her being on the *Jalisa Johnson Show*, which she hate-watched and coveted at the same time. In the fantasy, she was a famous actress—not the celebrity kind but a serious Method actor who just happened to attract fame through talent alone and maybe also a best-selling memoir. "You've overcome so much," Jalisa would say. Celeste would break down in tears while the audience clapped. "It was so hard getting here, Jalisa," she said, "so, so hard." Then her daughter would come onstage and hug her. They'd cry together. Everyone would: Jalisa and the studio audience, the camera people and the people watching from home, the tabloid writers and readers. No one could ever learn of her fantasy. Too dangerous—people would pick her apart for it. The dream was the root of all the other failed ones.

Celeste rattled off one of Ophelia's monologues—"*O, what a noble mind is here o'erthrown!*"—with her eyes shut. Her mind lost its grasp on the half-remembered lines, which came undone quicker than she could recite them.

She went quiet. The class went quieter, staring. She thought back to living in Los Angeles and having to walk from Silver Lake all the way to Koreatown for an audition because she couldn't afford gas. That had been almost ten years ago. She'd come here to this town when she didn't get the role, taking a Greyhound. So loud. She could still remember the fight the driver had gotten into with a passenger. Lots of shouting. Laughter, too, most of it coming from the beach-bound high schoolers on summer holiday. Her daughter, Monroe, just a baby, on her lap, crying. "Jesus, shut that baby up already!" someone said. The worst thought she'd ever had came to her as she pressed Monroe closer to her chest: What if she didn't have a kid? Could she have stuck it out longer in LA?

Celeste had never talked about her old life to anyone. However, she did briefly mention it to her landlady, who'd asked point-blank if she'd been a stripper (answer: no, not unless pretending to be one for five seconds of a Lifetime Original Movie counted). Her landlady didn't mind single mothers, she just didn't rent to loose women and thought LA was demonic save for the really good tapas she'd had there while passing through the area.

Even though she was in a bad place still, Celeste liked teaching. She smiled as she struggled. Clusters of baby faces looked up at her with a mixture of curiosity and judgment and awe in their eyes.

"Well, kids," Celeste said, "it's a bit hard to perform without props. Back to the lesson, then. Apples. What were we talking about? Oh, that's right: how the heck does pollen make fruit?"

Celeste's mind went all over the place, ping-ponging through time and space while staying closed up in her head. She couldn't remember if she'd cut off the stove that morning. And why had she even bothered becoming an actress?

"Hold on, kids," Celeste said. "I'll be right back. I forgot something in the lounge."

Celeste wasn't supposed to leave. It was against the school rules, but she slipped out anyway.

Her mouth tasted coppery like she was going to vomit. She rushed into the bathroom, hovering her head over the toilet until the bleachy smell of the water forced everything out of her. Her mouth unhinged. Out poured her breakfast. Coffee, marshmallow fluff, crackers, spearmint gum—all of it gray and ruined.

When the vomiting stopped, the tears started up. Celeste hadn't cried this hard since she was a child, not even when her husband died, nor when Monroe was diagnosed with cancer. All those years of silent regret, forced smiles, and coffee mugs that said things like, "Today's another day!" felt silly.

People were always saying a mother had to sacrifice for her child, but what happened once there was nothing left? Celeste had given away all her old possessions when she moved to the boonies. She only started really falling apart when she had to sell her husband's things to afford diapers.

All her dreams were gone. First acting, then motherhood. Monroe was still in the hospital. The oncologist said they couldn't risk releasing her because she'd gotten weaker. There was still a little hope left, but not much. Celeste had nightmares where one of the specialists called and said she could bring Monroe home forever, because if the hospital let her go, chances were that Monroe would be destined to die.

Celeste forgot about school while she retched. She remembered only after she'd finished washing up and looked into the mirror. Venice's microphone. It was still on. The kids had heard everything. Her body went light with fear. She felt dizzy. All motivation left her. She just wanted to go home. Bring Monroe home already, but not to die. Hope was tiring. It didn't feel good, just desperate.

On her way to the exit, Celeste passed by the principal.

"Good morning," the principal said, smiling. "Where're you headed off to?"

"Home," Celeste said.

"Pardon?"

"I can't stay anymore. It's difficult to explain. I don't want parents complaining about me, so it's best I just cut ties now."

The principal tried stopping Celeste. Celeste sprinted out to her car. In the driver's seat, she tried taking the mic off, remembering its presence for the second time. It was a tiny, bug-like thing, very annoying. No matter how hard she pulled, it wouldn't come off.

* * *

Celeste rushed down Main Street, running a red light and two stop signs. She struggled one last time with the microphone. It clung to her. There was no point. No point in tearing one of her nicer dresses over a mic; no point in teaching other people's kids when her own had less than a 10 percent chance of living.

The light turned green. One of the cars behind Celeste laid on its horn. Celeste did the same back, screaming. When the car went around, flipping her off, she flashed two middle fingers back. She parked by a fire hydrant and ran the rest of the way to the hospital.

Monroe was asleep when Celeste made it to her room. She was six, seven this June if she made it that long. Next year, she was technically supposed to start the second grade. Celeste could never be her teacher, not even in all her fantasies wherein Monroe wasn't sick. She taught in a different district, one she couldn't afford to live in. So many rules. Celeste understood them less and less. She didn't get how the insurance company pretended to be as natural-seeming as illness whenever they called.

Celeste touched Monroe's cheek and wondered how much Monroe missed school now that she'd been out for a while. Monroe's first grade teacher gave all her kids stationery with their names on it. Hard to believe that had been less than a year ago, a distance that felt too far and too close. All in a year: Monroe on school picture day, showing off baby teeth and a herringbone sweater from Beverly; Monroe's sickness, her sudden weakness and fevers; diagnoses and misdiagnoses; the looming presence of death swaying downward like a feather, very steady but direct.

"Monroe baby," Celeste whispered.

Monroe kept her eyes shut, but she shook her head. Her closed lids closed tighter, turning her puffy face into that of an angry baby.

"Princess," Celeste said.

"Mommy, go away," Monroe said. She swatted a swollen hand in the air.

"I have something for you."

"Is it Daddy?"

Ouch, Monroe's dad would've said. He'd been dead since she was an infant. Traffic accident. He was out late one night on his way back from seeing old friends. There weren't enough lights. His motorcycle went under a truck. The driver felt a boom then a short cracking noise that lit up the primal, panicked animal part of his brain.

"Baby doll," Celeste said, "why would you think that? I was gonna get you something from the gift shop. Do you want the chocolate drops I was telling you about? They're super yummy."

"I'm not gonna be around here much longer, am I?" Monroe asked. She talked in a bored tone that sounded unlike her.

"You sound feverish. Here, let Mommy go get you some lemonade."

"I'm gonna see Dad." She turned toward the window. "When I get out of here, he's gonna be there."

"Who's out here telling you these things?"

"The Christian lady. She came here because I was scared or whatever, and she told me about heaven and stuff."

"That's not right," Celeste said. "Proselytizing to kids shouldn't be allowed."

Celeste crossed her arms. She was an atheist who let her second graders skip over the "under God" part of the Pledge. The hospital was run by Catholics. She tried getting angry in a strictly political way as her anguish grew. Was Monroe's destiny really that obvious to people? Celeste felt herself getting sick again.

"Look," Celeste said. "You're staying right here, okay?"

"But I hate it here."

Celeste kissed Monroe's cheeks. Her daughter let her until she got tired and told her to stop it already, come on, you're hurting me. She kept whining when Celeste tried holding her.

"Mommy, no!" Monroe squealed.

"I swear, I just want the best for you. I want you to get older. I want you to outlive me. Don't you understand?"

Of course not. Monroe kept squealing. Celeste pulled up a chair to her daughter and massaged her bald scalp. Her mind drifted off, but it wouldn't let her fall asleep. She thought about when she was young. Not Monroe's age but a young adult with no children. She and her girlfriends stayed at a friend-of-a-friend's houseboat the summer before they had to split up for college. The parties were constant, Thursday through Saturday, each one bigger and louder and more sweltering than the last. On Friday, Celeste got so drunk and hot she fell overboard. The scariest part was that she hadn't felt afraid. Her panic stayed contained in a small part of her brain, screaming out until the water's coolness overwhelmed her entirely. She didn't thrash, never screamed. She just kinda floated up, letting herself go higher until she broke through the surface.

* * *

Celeste must've been sitting in an awkward position, because she felt about a million years older when she got up to stretch. Her bones cracked in odd, new ways when she shifted her weight. It was evening. Only a few hours had passed.

She saw Monroe with fresh, older eyes. At first, Monroe looked like a completely different girl. But then her familiar features took shape, first the snub nose, next the slight lips and bushy eyebrows. She was already awake. Celeste watched her daughter fix long hair that she'd never had before. Before the chemo, they'd agreed to pageboy cuts. Monroe didn't like to look girly. No dresses, no skirts, no pink, and definitely no long hair. But she loved collecting cutesy things. She was using her pink Barbie comb. She smiled into her Minnie Mouse compact, flashing healthy rows of permanent teeth.

Monroe was older. And her hair. It was so flowy, so healthy and glossy.

"Oh my God," Monroe said. She looked up at her mom, her teenage girl's voice startling her. "Can you stop staring at me? It's super weird and rude."

Celeste tried kissing her daughter one more time. Monroe pushed her away.

"What's wrong with you?" Monroe yelled.

"You're changing," Celeste said.

Monroe shrugged. She still seemed tired, though her eyes made her look more bored than exhausted. She asked Celeste when they were going home. She tore all the tubes out of herself, yawning as she ripped them away. Nothing seemed to hurt her anymore.

There were so many emotions pouring into Celeste that she could only feel the rush of their energy. All she could think was that Monroe's hospital gown wouldn't do anymore. It was too small on her.

"Can't you see you've changed?" Celeste asked.

"Yeah, Mom," Monroe said. "That's life. That's what you're always telling me." She mocked her mom's voice: "'Life is unpredictable. We gotta roll with the punches, accept change while we're alive.' Blah, blah, blah." Another yawn. "Can we get food? The eggs they serve here taste really bad."

"You can't go out like that," Celeste said.

"What?" Monroe looked down, seeing herself as if for the first time. "Oh."

"It's no problem."

"You're gonna get me something super embarrassing to wear, aren't you?"

Celeste winked and said she'd be right back. At the gift shop, she bought Monroe the only clothes in her size. They were pajamas with a pattern of popsicles shedding yellow teardrops. Monroe winced when she saw them.

"Those are for babies," Monroe said.

She dressed in them anyways, pouting, her face growing rounder, then gaunter, then rounder again as her feet stretched down to the floor. The pajamas were baggy on her, but by the

time she finished putting them on, the pants just barely met her
ankles.

"Let's go to the beach," Celeste said. "We can eat boardwalk
fries like we did with Dad. Remember?"

"Don't you have work?"

Celeste laughed. "It doesn't matter," she said. "We can go
wherever now."

"I don't get why you're acting like this. It's really freaky."

Celeste wanted to ask Monroe point-blank what was
going on with her. But she couldn't risk jinxing anything.
Her kids—her second graders plus Monroe—had imbued
her with their childhood superstitions. Ever since Monroe's
sickness, Celeste had developed a slight aversion to childish omens she hadn't thought about in years: cracks in the
sidewalk, black cats. Jinxes. After the first call from the doctors, when there was still the possibility of the tumors being
benign, Celeste bought Monroe a "Hang in there, kitten!"
card for good luck. She made sure to get the one with the
fat tabby instead of the black one even though the latter was
cuter. Avoid the cracks! Celeste kept thinking, hearing the
laughter of children as she came out of CVS. Luckily, the
sidewalks were freshly paved.

"I'm just so grateful," Celeste said.

Monroe stood up, stretching. She was up to Celeste's shoulders. They went to the elevators. No one stopped them. "Just a
friend," Celeste explained to one of the passing nurses.

Everyone probably thought the teenage-looking girl behind
Celeste was family. Monroe looked more like her dad's side of

the family than Celeste's. She had the same features as Beverly's daughter, Amelia. Celeste felt hopeful, then concerned because Amelia could be real annoying when she wanted to. Amelia's most recent misadventures: totaling her mom's car and becoming the type of girl who thought men like her dad, a serial cheater, had it the worst in society.

As she and Monroe left the hospital, Celeste's relief collapsed into disappointment. No one noticed their good fortune. They didn't even get to ring the cancer-free bell.

The sun knocked the hospital's chill out of Celeste's body and made Monroe grow. Monroe was now her height. In the car, she got a little taller. She was big in a willowy way. She sat in the back next to her car seat.

"What's on your mind?" Celeste asked.

"Hm?" Monroe was looking out the window. She drew hearts on the fogged-up glass.

They passed their apartment complex. Celeste wondered where they'd move now that Monroe's sickness didn't have them pinned down.

"What if we lived somewhere else?" Celeste asked.

"Like where?"

"I dunno."

The ramp to the freeway was fast approaching. If traffic wasn't too terrible, they'd be at the beach in two hours.

"We could go somewhere east," Celeste said. "Like New York City. You love *The Lion King*. Did you know you can see it on Broadway? The actors dress up like safari animals. Hey! You love the zoo too. New York has five of them."

"Mom, we're poor. Broadway tickets, cost, like, a gazillion dollars."

"We've always found ways to make things work."

There weren't many cars out. The endless strip of road kept going, blocking the ocean for many miles. Celeste went faster. The sun was starting to set.

"Mom," Monroe said. "Slow down. Are you trying to get us killed?"

"Hush," Celeste said.

Signs rolled by for fast food and ratty hotels. There was one for an ice cream place that claimed to have broken the world record for the biggest banana split.

"Let's get some ice cream," Celeste said.

Monroe shuddered. "So weird."

"Do you even know who you were a few hours ago?"

"Um, yeah. *Me.*"

"*Myself,*" Celeste corrected.

The ice cream place was small but had a gigantic roof that looked like a swirl of vanilla soft serve. Celeste and Monroe went inside even though Monroe insisted on eating in the car.

"People are gonna see me in this and think I'm weird," Monroe said.

She folded her arms over her swelling chest. The pajamas still fit, but became skintight when they got in line. Celeste caught a man staring at Monroe with a gross look on his face. She shot him a mean look that said, *Don't even try.* The man looked back, incredulous.

"She's a child, sir," Celeste said.

She shook her head. When she turned around again, Monroe towered over her. Other people were looking at Monroe. Her face had gotten more heart shaped and beautiful. Celeste and Monroe wound up eating their ice cream cones in the car. Celeste got chocolate, and Monroe some experimental flavor that involved tapioca balls.

"You have strange tastes, kid," Celeste said.

When Monroe didn't respond, Celeste patted her shoulder. They were both in the front seats. From the right distance and angle, they probably looked like two good friends. Celeste thought of the houseboat again. How nice the water had felt. When she'd climbed back aboard, kids, mostly boys, were diving into the water, making death into a game. "It feels so good," she kept saying, dancing to some sappy R&B song about getting eaten out until she passed out warm and safe in her best friend's bedroom.

"I'm not a kid anymore," Monroe said. Her tone was more matter-of-fact than cruel. She seemed almost sad saying it. "There's no escaping it."

"Escaping what?" Celeste asked.

"Death."

"Sweetie, no."

As Celeste reached out to massage Monroe's scalp again, her hair started falling out. The strands disappeared before they could fall to the floor. They left no trace. It was as if they'd never existed at all. This time around, Celeste didn't scream. She'd gotten used to this type of loss. It was just hair, she reminded herself. Nothing living. Really, humans were just a collection of inanimate parts: hair, flesh, bone, blood, brain matter. The parts that made them real people were just an illusion.

Monroe was still so young, so beautiful, and now she was decaying for a second time. "It's coming back," she whispered.

"Then stop it," Celeste said. "Do what you did earlier today. Come on. Don't do this to me now."

Monroe's face grew gaunter. Her skin turned sallow, first yellow, then a slightly greenish color, then gray.

"Why did you have to go and make yourself like this?" Celeste asked. She was crying again. "I do so much, and you can't even give me this one thing?"

Monroe shook her head. "I'm going away now," she said. "Stop being angry."

"I'm not angry."

"You are."

"We're getting you back to the hospital."

Monroe said nothing back. Celeste kept asking if she was okay as she tore down the road. She glanced at Monroe's arms. They puffed up like inflated sleeves, the skin purpling. There was so little time. The speedometer crept up to seventy. Celeste gagged. There was an awful smell in the car. She rolled down the window.

"It's cold," Monroe said.

Her body was unspooling. Her jaw clicked off and smacked against the dashboard. Just a dream, Celeste kept telling herself. All of today was just a bad dream to her except for the good parts, which she tried to yank free from the rotting nightmare filling up her nose. The faster she drove, the worse the smell got. Monroe was melting

They missed the exit to the hospital. It was already too late. Monroe was gone. There was nothing left. Her smell wafted out the window. All gone. Celeste pulled over to the shoulder of the road and stared at the road ahead. Her mind went numb.

* * *

Celeste didn't know where to go aside from Green Forrest Elementary. It wasn't that far, and going back to the apartment was too lonely an option.

"Welcome back!" read the blocky letters of the school pylon sign. "We missed you."

The parking lot was empty. She chose a faraway spot underneath the shade of an acacia tree. It took her forever to get out. She just wanted to lie still and never budge ever again. Every move felt like a different kind of heartbreak. And there was physical pain too. Her joints ached so bad.

What was she here for again? She wandered down the empty halls of the elementary school. The lights were dim. The aftercare room was silent. Even the janitor had gone home.

When Celeste reached her room, she heard people talking. Not children, but adults. She could tell what they were by the baritone of the men's voices. She crept closer, and the voices became whispers. For a while, she stood there, waiting them out. She could see blurs through the pebbled glass, but not much else. She glanced at her phone for the time. Six-o-five on a normal day, no parent teacher conferences or school plays or fundraisers.

People were clapping. She slipped into the room and jumped when the sound hit her head-on. They overwhelmed her: middle-aged people dressed up like they were at a show.

The fat, curly-haired woman in Venice's seat whistled. There were tears in her eyes. She looked just like Venice too. But Celeste knew this lady couldn't be Venice's mom because she'd met her at the farmer's market and knew the woman was bald due to a health condition. This woman was wild-haired. And she was wearing slacks, not a peasant dress.

"You were so wonderful out there," the lady said.

"What?" Celeste said. "What did I do?"

"Your performance was amazing. I couldn't stop crying when Monroe died."

"I don't understand," Celeste whispered. She felt her stomach contract. Her voice sounded echoey like in a dream.

"You don't recognize us, do you?"

Celeste looked down and saw the tiny speck of a microphone still hanging on to her dress. "Oh my God," she said. Venice's speaker amplified every word. "Venice! You were listening?"

Venice, plump but still radiant, clutched a kerchief. "Of course," she said. "We're your students."

"Is Monroe here too?"

No, Monroe wasn't. Celeste scanned the room as the applause grew louder. So much time had gone by, and at the same time, hardly any time at all. And her seconds graders had been waiting. Listening. She wanted to reach out and hug all of them, just reach out and squeeze them tight to make sure they never went away.

"Did you really enjoy it?" Celeste asked.

"Oh, it was spectacular," Venice said. "Every moment, every tear. Just, oh my God, I can't even find the words. You were so good out there. So genuine."

The timid Guatemalan girl, a woman now, came to the front of the class. "These are for you," she said in flat, unaccented English. She held out a child's bouquet: milkweed tied up with a hair ribbon. The roots dripped with fresh earth.

The rest of the room was still clapping. Some took pictures. Celeste bowed, her youthful, actress self coming back.

"Give a speech!" someone shouted.

"Speech, speech, speech," the rest of them chanted.

"I remember you guys when you were just little kids," Celeste said.

Her mind couldn't think of anything better to say. People cheered anyway, lifting her up while the pain of loss pulled her down. She started trembling, feeling herself begin to break.

More students came in. One of them was carrying the sugar-apples. The cheering got even louder. Celeste couldn't stand the sound. She started to leave when she caught her reflection in the bay window. She couldn't stop looking. She'd gotten so old. Had she always been this old?

A rancid smell wafted toward her, not as pungent as death but still unbearable. Celeste made herself look happy as Venice went around the tables, passing out dessert. The apples looked rotten. And the sugar coating had turned a strange gray color. People ate them up anyway. Celeste watched them lick their fingers and lips.

Venice gave Celeste the biggest apple. Celeste tried to turn it down, but Venice insisted.

"Just take a bite," Venice said, and of course the rest of the class joined in, all of them telling Celeste the same thing: "Come on, just one bite, take one bite, you made them!"

Celeste forced her best stage smile. She closed her eyes and bit down hard on the overly ripe flesh. The flavor was sweet to the point of foulness.

Melissa, Melissa, Melissa

....

THAT WAS HOW Dad greeted the apartment when he came home from work, singing my name to the tune of "Maria." Melissa, Melissa, Melissa: me, his favorite child, his only child. He'd wanted me to have siblings, but Mom said no way, the money wasn't there, which was fine, he said, because I was worth three good kids.

Though she never mentioned it, I think his illness was another factor in Mom's decision. I'm not supposed to tell anyone this, but when I was a baby, he tried to take his own life. We didn't lose him then. He disappeared gradually, continuing to live as his mind left him, us.

Right before he went away, when I was sixteen, a sophomore, president of the Key Club and an honors student, there was an evening Dad didn't call my name. He slipped back into the apartment quietly. It was Sunday. He'd started going into the office on weekends to keep up with the heavy workload, though I don't think this helped progress his career much.

The 1970s had just gotten started and I was growing older, my curiosity of the world blooming out of my limited life as a latchkey kid. I was in my room listening to a radio drama on the old Sylvania. I forget the name of the show, but the plot had to do with a princess on a quest to save her parents' kingdom. What I remember well is the last scene and how the announcer had described it: rolling hills, the smell of sunshine. A delicate princess sitting atop an Arabian horse, her hair golden. There was going to be a battle soon.

I didn't hear Dad riffling through the cupboards, but if I had, I'd have told him to stay away from the fudge I'd hidden in an empty packet of frozen sausages. They were edibles I'd gotten from a friend. She was dating a much older boy who was no good but had managed to make himself an indispensable part of the drug scene that was going on in San Francisco at the time. I hadn't even tried a piece yet.

The radio show ended on a cliffhanger. I went to the kitchen feeling sort of hungry, already aware that there was nothing good to eat. I spotted the sausage package sitting on the table and approached it slowly, feeling the same gut-in-throat apprehension I'd had at recess as a little girl when I pushed a dead squirrel down a storm drain with a stick. The package was empty. All the fudge was gone. I looked toward the living room.

Dad was watching TV—a baseball game. The apartment was a mess, pure disorder, last week's clean laundry strewn on the couch, the floor. Thank God Mom wasn't there. She'd gone back to Germany to see an old, convalescent friend. Before she left, she told me to put the clothes away, but I hadn't. If she came through the door right now, she'd make me clean all night.

"That candy tasted like absolute shit," Dad said frowning at me as I hugged the empty package to my chest. "You should take them back for a refund if you can. I don't know why you'd wanna hide something like that. Not even the rats would want it."

"Dad! You ate it all?" I said.

"What? You can always buy more. It's not caviar."

I didn't know what else to say to him. I remembered that one story of a guy in NYC who took so much LSD that he dove off his apartment's roof and onto a blue milk truck that he mistook for a swimming pool. The thought of my dad's pancaked corpse made me ill. I couldn't stop thinking that he might go insane. I realized how little I knew of the world, of drugs, and also of Dad's state of mind. I kept waiting for him to soil himself and start speaking gibberish.

My throat stopped up so that all that came out were ragged breaths. I closed my eyes and promised myself I'd remain sober for the rest of my childhood, which wasn't long but felt like forever. I'd be good. No more drinking with friends, no sneaking out late, no unfiltered cigarettes or miniskirts with thigh-highs.

I sat down next to Dad to keep an eye on him. The game dragged on, inning after inning after endless inning. I was never too big on sports—I considered myself more of an artist than an athlete. In the top-right drawer of my desk was the novel I'd been working on. It wasn't very good. The plot was almost identical to the radio show only more melodramatic, lots of declarations of love and hatred for no good reason. I let Dad read through the sections that didn't have sex in them, smiling when he nodded and said, "Interesting" and "Very good, Melissa" and "You really have an advanced vocabulary for your age."

As Dad zoned out, I studied him closer, searching for signs that he sensed what had been done to him. For the first time, I could see him as a complete person who lived separately from me. The pieces of him grew foreign to me: his gray eyes, his aquiline nose, his chestnut hair. He looked tired. Or dead. I couldn't tell.

"Dad?" I asked.

"Huh?" He startled and kept blinking, looking around. I didn't know what to say, so I asked him about the novel I was working on.

"What did you think of my book?" I asked. My voice felt squeaky and foreign. "You never said if you liked the characters or not?"

"Oh."

"Oh?"

"Sorry, I just have something on my mind."

He started scratching his face a bunch. His eyes drifted from the TV screen. An ad for instant coffee came on, and he started talking to me about his childhood in fragments that felt almost poetic.

"My dad bought me coffee," he said. "I used to help him out at his job and we'd work real late."

"What was your dad like?" I asked.

"I never really liked the taste of coffee," he went on like I wasn't even there, like he was talking to someone else—maybe a ghost. "Too bitter, no amount of sugar or milk could help the taste. I preferred salty things. Chips."

"What else do you like?"

Dad had to stop to think. I thought he forgot the question, but then he said, "I love drawing. And painting. I get to use my hands." He showed me his hands, wiggling his fingers. The sleeves of his dress shirt were still rolled up from work.

There were faint lines and puckered scars all over his arms, but I preferred not to reflect much on them. For so long, I believed that they'd always been a part of his anatomy just like his eyes or his smile. I had no memory of him without them.

"What else do you love?" I asked.

He shrugged. "Nothing, really."

"Nothing?"

I couldn't help but take his words to heart even though I knew he cared about me. I was extra sensitive to rejection of any kind. I'd never had a boyfriend even though most of my other friends at school did, even Marlena, who was forever talking about saving herself for marriage. The world kept pushing me away. Though I wanted to be a writer, my new English teacher was indifferent to me. Nothing I did seemed to impress her. She was fresh out of teacher's college, too, which Deana, my other friend, said was supposed to make her more lenient, but I'd gotten a B-minus on my last essay.

"Dad," I said, "do you love me?"

"Yeah? Aren't I supposed to?"

"But, do you love me?"

He cocked his head, smiling. "I don't know," he said.

I waited for him to say something else. The light faded from the windows. He started snoring. He made me think about what Ramona's work friend had told me about each individual person's mind being its own separate universe, a lonely space that could feel emotions for others but never understand them. Sitting there in the ruined wingback easy chair, I began to see myself as a ball—not a planet, just a small, spherical thing—that was orbiting around an indifferent world.

Mom would be home early tomorrow. I didn't want to disappoint her and risk her love too. I picked up the clothes from the floor and smoothed out the wrinkles as best I could, folding everything away into my parents' dresser and my own.

Dad was at peace. There wasn't any drama like in the anti-drug PSAs. He didn't fall out a window or chase me around the room with a knife or see dead people hanging from the ceiling. He was the picture of calm. Still, I hovered over him, waiting. When his eyes opened suddenly, I almost cried out.

"How long do you write for?" he asked. He was so normal sounding, and yet nothing about him felt normal anymore.

"It depends," I said. "Sometimes an hour. Sometimes the whole day on a weekend. Whenever I feel like it, I guess."

"Interesting," he said, already falling back asleep.

When I went to bed, I didn't feel relief. If the edibles didn't cause any drama, I knew something else would. Something always did at home.

* * *

Morning came without incident. My mother arrived home very early and so quietly I didn't wake. It was Monday, which I loathed, though I enjoyed its freshness that unraveled from the soft scent of laundry soap and the fresh bread Mom bought from the bakery near her old job. My blouse was freshly starched, the hem of my skirt just mended but also wrinkled from its time on the floor.

But the memory of the previous night wore on me like an infected tooth that was too deep to pull. All my senses were heightened as my mind filled with all the headlines of people on drugs doing dumb and dangerous things. I still remember what we had to eat that day and how it tasted: Mom's hurried attempt at huevos rancheros—sulphury, rich. She'd used leftover red beans from last week's dinner instead of black ones, which grossed me out, though I ate it anyways. I didn't want to complain. She'd barely slept at all, having just gotten back a few hours ago, her temperament so short and tense that it would surely break any minute now.

Dad still had his clothes on from the night before. He wouldn't eat. All he did was draw. He used supplies from his work, a prestigious architecture firm that paid him very little because he was a new hire. Last week, he'd told Mom there'd been whisperings in the office of the higher-ups promoting him to a more senior position. Though he didn't believe in rumors, he still considered them to be a sign of something positive to come.

"David?" Mom said.

"Sorry," he said. He didn't look up from his drawing. "Just working on something personal."

Mom craned to get a better look. She frowned. "What's gotten into you?"

"A dream," he said. "Last night. Melissa was with me when it struck me. I was watching a game, and the world just kind of dissolved. I thought I was dying from fatigue, but then I remembered how I used to love drawing as a child. It used to make me so happy. I'd forgotten."

Mom shook her head. "Let's not talk about this in front of Melissa," she warned.

"It comes through in my art. I have to express it."

"What time did you say you were supposed to be at work?"

The answer was about two hours ago. He'd been going to the office at dawn to work overtime on this new project, a public library they were building way out in the boonies. I'd seen sketches. It was a brutalist structure that was all concrete save for the courtyard, which the head developer had modeled after how he imagined the Hanging Gardens of Babylon to have been except modern and way smaller.

"I was thinking about taking leave," Dad said casually.

Mom laughed and asked if he was joking. Her face got serious when he started talking about turning the spare bedroom into a studio. That room was where she went when her migraines were bothering her because there weren't any windows. It was more like a big closet with a daybed.

"And how are you gonna pay bills without a real job?" she said.

"Savings."

"Savings?" Mom pinched her temples. "Dave, that money's for emergencies. We can't just live off savings forever so you can go off and do whatever. It runs out."

"Relax, Thea. Don't be such a Nazi."

"Don't you call me that, and no, I won't relax. We've been over this when you said you wanted a new car. We're not rich."

Dad turned to me and did the cuckoo sign, circling his finger around his ear until Mom told him he was the crazy one—not her. That was when I finally relaxed. Nothing about him had changed. The drawing obsession was new, but not the abruptness of his wants. He'd almost gotten that car, an Oldsmobile with an all-leather interior, but Mom threatened to sell everything in the house and use the money to leave him.

"We can downsize," Dad said.

"Downsize?" Mom asked. "Downsize to what? A cardboard box? The street?"

Our place was already tiny. There were two bedrooms and the spare room that was really just a closet. The living room was also the dining room and the kitchen. Outside was worse. We lived dangerously close to the Tenderloin, far from the school Mom had enrolled me in with a false address. "Zone of Terror," people called this area. Last week, someone discovered a dead woman in the trunk of an abandoned jalopy, her life so thoroughly snuffed out I can't find any record of it even after the internet. In ten years, a drifter named Richard Ramirez would start his killing spree just a short walk away from my bus stop.

"You're sick in the mind if you think there's somewhere lower than here," Mom told Dad.

Dad smiled. Mom left, slamming the door to the spare room behind her. I heard the click of the lock, her and the small daybed sighing in unison as she collapsed on top of it.

For a long time, until I was running late for school, I watched Dad's hands maneuver his varyingly sized pens and pencils across the paper. His movements were delicate, his fingers long and slender. The scratching sound of the pens was familiar. Reassuring. *Shh, shh, shh*, went the paper, long white, gridded sheets. I was used to him drawing buildings he wanted to erect if he ever made partner at his firm, but when I looked down at his pad, I saw an elephant. It was very realistic, the elephant's pebbled skin standing in contrast to the background of palm fronds, which were abstract, the edges fuzzed like in a dream. Dad didn't use a reference. I think his mind sort of just came up with everything on its own.

The elephant's eyes were sad to the point of being human-like. They were just like Dad's on his worst days, repulsing me in the same way the sound of my parents fucking did. I didn't like it when they revealed too much about themselves. I didn't like it when any adult I knew did. I stopped worshipping my third-grade teacher, Ms. Agata, when I caught her crying. It didn't matter to me that she'd lost her husband in Vietnam because she was an adult.

"I like the trunk," I mumbled. "It looks like it's coming off of the paper."

Dad stopped working. For a moment, I thought he was angry at me. I expected him to look me in the eye and tell me he knew I'd had drugs in the house and that I'd poisoned his mind with them. It wasn't like him to call me out—he didn't yell at me like Mom had when I broke the lazy Susan fiddling with it too much—but he was mercurial.

"Thanks, Melissa," he said. "Really appreciate it. Really. You're keeping me going."

I didn't feel relief, only the continued pressure of guilt smashing down on me as I let Dad muss my hair. I told him that he was welcome, though I wasn't really sure what he was thanking me for. I knew he found my compliment nice, but I sensed that there was something deeper to his gratitude that I wasn't getting.

* * *

At school, I kept thinking about Dad's father, a mysterious man who didn't feel like a grandfather to me but a specter. I couldn't figure out who he really was or why Dad had mentioned him. I knew that he and his wife were Lithuanian Jews, that they'd immigrated here sometime before the war, that they were poor, and that their children had spent time at orphanages. And they were still alive. They just wouldn't talk to us because they didn't like Mom's background—her Black half in particular, though I'm sure the German one didn't help. All this information came from my mother, always in a hushed, quick voice to explain away Dad's idiosyncrasies: he ate food past its expiration date because he'd grown up hungry; he slept with the side-table lamp on because the mean kids at the orphanage were known to attack the weak ones in the dark.

Mom's past, however, felt complete to me. She'd spent her early childhood in Germany in a town near Cologne. She was half-Black: her mom was a German maid, her dad unknown except by race. During the war, she had to stay hidden in their house because her skin color made her an enemy of the regime. She and her mom wound up fleeing to the States, where they lived for a time with a family in Bakersfield who sponsored them. Then they were in Los Angeles, then New Mexico, Arizona, Oregon. One of the rich people her mom used to clean for was a well-known politician in Santa Fe. I can't say his name, but he had an obsession with ladies' feet and used to pay my mom to come to his house when her mom wasn't there and walk barefoot on his back. She was fifteen.

Then Mom's mom died and Mom went back to California, where she met Dad. She dreamed of going to college, but she had me instead. Dad went to architecture school. Mom took care of him, washing his clothes, cooking his meals, keeping him sane. And she took care of me.

Unlike Dad, Mom's still alive today, though her mind's left her. I can map out her life better than she can now, except I still don't know why she'd chosen Dad to love. I didn't think to ask her until it was too late. I'd always just assumed all adults got married out of a mixture of loneliness, convenience, and boredom—the same reasons why they broke up.

* * *

But I know exactly what Mom was thinking when she decided to finally end things with Dad: my well-being. Instability concerned her. She'd grown up with it all around her, lived through it, and now she'd had enough. She could only tolerate him for one last week.

When I came back home from school, Dad was in the kitchen drawing again. I don't think he ever left. Maybe he went to use the bathroom, but not to go to work or anywhere farther than the front door to the apartment. Same shirt, same pants, same detached smile that I saw in a new, perplexing light.

"Melissa, Melissa, Melissa."

The words made my stomach bubble. Mom was leaning against the kitchen sink. The sink's gingham skirt matched the pattern of her housedress. She'd swaddled her hair into the silk-print scarf he'd bought her ages ago. I stared at the floor until the pea-green tiles had imprinted themselves into my mind.

"Please talk some sense into your father," Mom said. "He'll listen to you."

"Thea," Dad said, "please."

"No. I'm sick of the arguments. They never go away, they just get more ridiculous."

"Look, I was just saying that maybe you could work for a change."

"Doing what?!" Mom yelled. "You think I'm gonna scrub other people's floors again just for you?"

They went back and forth like this. I just stood there, waiting for my turn to speak. Mom said Dad was destroying her, and Dad said that if she was that easily disturbed then maybe she was the one destroying herself.

I tried my best to detach myself from my body, thinking of school, of my dear friend Ramona with her drug-dealer boyfriend and all the gossip we'd heard about other kids who had it way worse than us. We still couldn't believe it when this religious girl we kind of knew started doing blue films—this according to a friend-of-a-friend whose brother worked at an adult theater. She was so pretty, too, we said. She could've been a real model had she tried.

"Fucking nigger Nazi!" Dad yelled.

I laughed so hard that I choked on my spit. It wasn't funny, it was just that there wasn't any other way to respond. Or maybe *he* was funny. The best jokes were always the ones that had no answers, and Dad's outbursts toward Mom often turned spiteful to the point of absurdity.

The laughter left me when Mom started crying. I thought of the white-trash kids at school calling me a spic until they found out who my mom was—who I really was underneath the bone-straight hair and off-white complexion—and started saying that other word minus the Nazi part. I felt bad for Mom, then worse for myself when she started screaming. She got so mad her English became more heavily accented.

"Your father quit his job today," she said, "but you laugh! He called over the phone. I watched him, and now he's insulting me and you laugh because you think this is all a joke like TV."

"That's not true," I said. I turned to him. "It isn't true, right?"

"It is!" Mom said.

Dad's pencil rolled off the table and fell to the floor. I picked it up. When I handed it back to him, Mom tore it from my hand and broke it in half. Dad applauded her like she'd uprooted an oak tree with her bare hands, his sarcasm so loud and over the top the people next door pounded on the wall for us to be quiet.

"How are we gonna afford anything now?" I asked. My saliva started choking me. I had to focus just to swallow. "I thought you wanted a nice car and a nice house. You even showed me the car you wanted in a magazine. You said you'd take me to the dealer and that I could pick out the color."

"Yes," Dad said, "but that was different. I hadn't had the dream yet. The inspiration hadn't struck me, but now that it has, I know what I'm after, and it's something bigger than even the biggest mansion in the world."

"What about me?" I asked. "You still want me, right?"

"Of course, Melissa."

I wanted to tell him no, to please just stop already, but Mom spoke over me. I was so focused on trying not to cry that I almost didn't hear her.

"I want a divorce," Mom said.

Dad said nothing. He just breathed heavily with his eyes closed. I got flustered for him, willing him to speak with my mind. Do something, I thought. Say you're sorry at least!

I don't think he ever apologized to Mom for anything. Not when he called her filthy names just to get a rise out of her; not when he went behind her back to make big, confusing purchases like the antique set of fishery books; not when he poked fun of her anger, dressed her down, or lied to her. He had other ways of expressing his sorrow, his love: gifts mostly— that and also manic declarations of affection that felt genuine but also deeply unsettling like a shout-out in a suicide note. It was just that they hurt worse and worse.

I wanted him to tell the truth and say that he cared for us in his own selfish way. I knew deep down that he had to feel sorry for being such a fuckup. My want became so huge that it crushed me. I considered telling him about last night. The drugs. Mom would kill me. What was the point of upsetting my parents even more? Mom despised the bums on the street for the heroine needles they left behind.

"Dad?" I heard myself say.

"Tell me when you get the papers ready," he said to Mom.

"Dad!"

I'd become invisible to my parents. Only our neighbors noticed me, their banging getting louder.

"I'm being serious about my plans, Thea," Dad said. "I'm not working at that place anymore. Talent doesn't matter to them, just the type of school you went to and who you know. It's hell on earth and I'm tired of it. I want paradise."

"Well, you make my life hell," Mom snapped.

"So leave then. There's the door. Go on."

"Okay. I will."

Mom didn't leave, though. She stayed in my room, in my bed while Dad locked himself in his new studio. I'd thought Dad had spent the whole day drawing at the table, but I was wrong, he'd spread out. I peeked inside the spare bedroom before he closed the door. Sprawled out on the bed was a long swath of cotton fabric on which he wanted to paint the birth of Jesus Christ in the modern day. I think that had been what set off Mom. She'd probably called him all sorts of words before I came in the door. I tried to sleep on the sofa, but I was too tall; I had to put either my neck or my calves against one of the hard arms. Dad's lights were all on. Their yellow glow puddled underneath the door and seeped out onto the living room carpet like a piss stain. I couldn't relax. I caressed my face as lovingly as I could but felt nothing but my own hand.

The apartment went quiet, which was rare ever since new people moved upstairs with their brood of stompy, squealy kids. I could hear the sound again, the *shh, shh, shh* on the paper coming from my parents' room. It did more to console me than my parents could. It told me that everything was as usual, everything bad Dad did was just a phase that separated him from the type of father we all needed him to be.

But paper was just paper, its sound a false consolation. It didn't prepare me for when I came home from school the next day to find that Mom had packed away most of Dad's possessions. She'd bought him used suitcases and a trunk from the thrift store.

Dad was in the kitchen, oblivious, drawing again. I don't remember what because I didn't care anymore. Mom and him were making me question the point of art. He looked pathetic and she devoid of joy. Was this the world I was supposed to be writing about? The tension building between my parents denied me access to my imagination, erasing my fantasies and replacing them with more of the ugliness that had surrounded me my whole life. At study hall, I'd set aside the drafts of my novel and started redoing my math homework, comforted by its logic and predictability.

"He's leaving soon," Mom said.

Dad looked up. "Melissa, Melissa, Melissa," he said.

"Be safe," I told him.

I didn't want to cry just like I hadn't wanted to laugh at his meanness. Of course, I bawled like a little kid. I let him hug me even though his touch stung.

"Don't go," I said.

"I'm not going anywhere," he lied.

Dad left in stages, taking only a few things with him. He had a lot of stuff. For a few months, he made many small trips to the apartment when he wanted something. One time, he took a salad bowl he said he needed to make soup. Another time, just a pair of socks. He'd try to reason with Mom, promising her he'd find part-time work to support us as well as his wants, but she wouldn't have it.

"Do you believe in God?" he asked her.

"No," she said, throwing a dishrag in his face. "I don't believe in anything anymore. Now get out!"

When Mom started working—a doctor's office, she got a receptionist job there thanks to a friend of a friend's recommendation—he tried talking to me. I felt hope, but also anger, fear, dread.

Dad explained to me the intricacies of gouache painting, Georgia O'Keeffe's vagina flowers, and the vastness of the San Francisco Museum of Modern Art. Everything else about his or our personal lives was incidental, a footnote to the grand epic he thought he was starring in.

He said that his acrylic painting of Venus was coming along quite nicely and that he might be homeless soon, that he wanted to learn to sculpt and also that he was terrified of dying alone. He was adamant that he wasn't after fame because he knew it would come to him on its own eventually.

"I don't care!" I said one day. "Just get your shit and go already. I'm tired, Dad."

* * *

Dad stopped coming by. I think he was supposed to be paying child support, but he never did. I became fatherless.

To sublimate my pain, I wrote. Short stories mostly, all of them about rejected girls who find out that they're magic or warrior princesses or magic warrior princesses. My childish heart fell deeper in love with fantasy, which was anything but juvenile. At a party in Mission, Ramona's boyfriend introduced me to the Lord of the Rings books. He showed me his copy of *Return of the King*, which he said he took with him everywhere. "There's dragons and shit," he said. "It's pretty far out." He relayed the whole plot while Ramona poked fun at him for being a nerd. A perfect combination: the easygoing language of friends and a fantastical universe where elves existed. I read all three books in a month. I giggled at the parts he'd described the most in-depth, like Sauron's all-seeing red eye, which he'd compared to that of a stoner.

* * *

Dad sent me messages, long letters that read like artist's statements and always with Polaroids of his latest creations: paintings, sketches, jewelry made out of discarded bits of smoothed-down glass. I tried to write back at first, but he never answered my questions. He didn't congratulate me when I told him about the progress I was making on my novel, which was still terrible but also cathartic. His handwriting grew more erratic until it was almost as indecipherable as what he was saying.

He liked talking a lot about religion, about God and evil. He said a force outside of himself was guiding him. I realized that my father was another mentally unwell man with a fixation on the spiritual. But I also knew there was more to him than his delusions. I could sense his regret bleeding through his words.

I thought of Dad less and less. As the memory of him faded, dissolving from my conscious mind, it spread to the rest of my body. I suddenly couldn't stand the rustling of papers. My heart rate jumped when Mom crumpled up one of his letters.

Eventually Mom and I moved. We didn't tell him our new address. No more letters. I told people at school my dad died of cancer. Ramona paid a delivery boy to bring flowers to my home since she knew me well enough to know where I really lived. It came with a note, two sentences: "You're the worst liar ever, Brazdauskis. Condolences." She'd even spelled my surname correctly.

Mom met a new man, a Black priest. He was kind and unshakable, so stable I never learned of any of his childhood issues. He ran a Bible study that was just for bums. They'd come to eat, some of them staying to hear about Jesus but most of them not. Mom cooked, I served. I got to see her around other people. The other workers found her accent intriguing. One volunteer, Black, thought she was faking it because she looked so much like one of his sisters from down south.

One time, Dad showed up. I recognized him through his overgrown beard. He was dirty and sunburnt. I said nothing, didn't make eye contact, just filled one of the square pools in his tray with creamed corn and wished him a good day.

Melissa, Melissa, Melissa.

He took the food outside with him. He wasn't supposed to, but I didn't stop him.

I think Mom saw too. She was coming out of the kitchen and did a double take at the door before coming up to me.

"Watch out for the needles," she whispered to me in Kölsch. "I heard bad people are purposefully pricking people to get them sick."

* * *

I'm still not sure if I love Dad, but I also know that I can't not love him even though I have a lot of hate for him. My body shook when I found out that he lived out the rest of his life in a ratty hotel—not the Cecil but one just like it that's since closed down. I wanted to kill the people who took his life away from him, away from me. The police report said there'd been a break-in and a struggle. The intruders-*cum*-killers were never found. There was a brief search and some articles about the case. Other than that, nobody cared. It took over a year for the people who mattered, powerful people, to notice Dad's absence, and even then, they were only really after what he'd left behind. As I grew up, his name got bigger, mostly in intellectual circles, but still.

Mom and I ignored the calls we got about all the junk-slash-art he'd left behind in storage lockers. We didn't want any of it, didn't care if strangers bid over his life's work. Even if we'd known just how valuable all that trash would become, Mom would've just sold everything. If I could, I'd destroy it, just burn every piece like a bunch of bloodsucking ticks that won't let go.

I told Mom this as we were taking the elevator up to the new exhibit to see his art: Dad's life's work hurt me so bad I could barely breathe, and not because I thought it was any good. The memory of him dug deeper than any piece of art I'd ever laid eyes on.

The exhibit was housed in a sprawling baby-blue Victorian that used to be the residence of a late almond heiress. Now it was a museum named in her honor. The ride was slow. I thought the elevator might break. It kept stopping randomly, but Mom didn't seem to care, so I pretended not to either. Breathing became a conscious action for me. Mom looked at peace. I hadn't even wanted to come, but she did. Her curiosity got to her. She needed to know.

"Doesn't knowing he's dead make you feel bad?" I asked.

"Why wouldn't it?" Mom said, riffling through her purse. The crinkling sound of old receipts and gum wrappers agitated me.

"Because you hated him!"

"Yes," Mom said as if it was obvious, "but that doesn't mean I never loved him."

She fished out her handkerchief. She wiped the excess sunscreen off of my face. "Stop," I said, but she kept going, getting on her tippy-toes to reach me. She didn't look satisfied when she finished.

By now, I was an adult. I studied comparative literature at San Francisco State even though Mom wanted me to do something in the sciences. I still wanted to be a writer, though my professor said my stories were weak, their structure confused, and the prose purple.

The doors opened. I wanted to go back down, but Mom insisted I come with her.

The exhibit was called *Unforgotten* and it featured work from Dad and people like him: dead, mentally ill loners who'd tried creating beauty while living ugly lives. The museum owned multiple storage bins' worth of his pieces, of which we'd seen a fraction of a fraction before he left. Only a few were on display. "Masterworks," the informational pamphlet called them.

"You can close your eyes if you want," Mom said, giving me her hand. "It'll be like when your father took us ice skating at Union Square. You were so little then. Remember? I bought you a pink snowsuit."

"Yes, Mom."

I closed my eyes and let Mom guide me. She called me silly, as if the idea had been mine and not hers. I didn't care. The feel of her skin relaxed me. I could see it in my mind: a warm, even, brown complexion, on her face zero blemishes, zero pimples, her wrinkles so fine I could only see most of them up close.

"Oh my God!" Mom said.

She spoke the words as if Dad himself had jumped out in front of us. My eyes fluttered open. I almost ran away.

The canvas took up most of the wall. I don't know how he'd managed to fit it all in a tiny hotel room. I kept staring at the girl made out of rigid, jagged pieces. She was sitting at a typewriter. Above her head, a halo made out of flowerlike weeds he'd glued on, all of them wilted but beautiful in a sickening kind of way.

"God," Mom said. "He was such an asshole."

The description didn't reveal much. I reread it anyway. Medium: acrylic. Date: around the time I spotted him at Bible study. Title: Melissa, Melissa, Melissa. There was a short bio, too, but it was vague, and the parts I recognized were lies. It said he'd been an orphan and that his family—his wife and one child—left him.

"It's powerful in a way," I said.

"How?" Mom asked.

"Because it hurts?" I shrugged. "It kind of makes me want to write."

"About what?" Mom asked.

"Myself."

Anita Garcia-Barnes

. . . .

THE PRETTIEST GIRL at St. Catherine's was Anita Garcia-Barnes, the one Pat called difficult. There were others too probably, but I didn't feel like looking through the whole yearbook. It got predictable after a while: pages of acne and milkmaid skin, braces and crooked baby-toothed smiles.

"Where's Anita from?" I asked.

Pat was grading papers next to me in bed. I didn't know high school theater classes had homework, but his did. He'd been teaching stagecraft at Catherine's for two years. "Anita?" he asked. "I think she lives in Hialeah. I don't remember. But her and the Black girl I was telling you about never show up on time. It's ridiculous. Sometimes they come when class is halfway through."

"Are they nice?"

"No."

"I was like that too. Willful." I leaned in to Anita's picture, studying the familiar dimples, green eyes, and full lips. "I could pass for her mom. I'm thirty-five and she's like, what? Sixteen? We look related."

"Mhm."

"One of the teen moms at my old school had her son get into all the Ivies. He was on the news and everything."

"Wow."

"It's weird, because my parents were always freaking out about me going down a similar road. Not the Ivy kid's, his mother's. Then the tumors spread everywhere. But sometimes I wonder, like, what if? I mean, I would've wound up sick no matter how many bad decisions I made. Why didn't I have a kid while I still could? They could keep me company if my cancer ever comes back. Maybe I'll adopt. I don't know."

Pat nodded. He wasn't listening, but he wasn't grading anymore either. He was doing that thing where he stared into space and swished his mouth. I guessed he was thinking about his divorce. We'd been seeing each other on and off for a few months, and though we were close, he was still in love with his ex-wife, the Australian. Sometimes she sent him pictures of their two-year-old doing cute stuff like wearing a bowl of oatmeal as a hat. They flashed on his phone in the middle of the night when he was asleep, I was awake, and she was taking pictures of breakfast halfway around the world.

I felt him on my thigh. His hand was cold, probably from the ice pack he'd been using to nurse his sprained thumb. I shivered. The cold was part of the reason, but not all of it. I grabbed on to his hairy leg and took in his warmth. He kissed me.

"Pretend I'm Anita," I whispered.

"What?" he asked.

"You're you and I'm Anita. Come on, it'll be fun. I'm bored."

"Meredith, that's fucked." He pulled away. Hypocrite. I'd seen the porn he watched. Stepmother stuff, a real Freudian nightmare. We couldn't stop laughing when the old lady two doors down bent down into one of the washers in the apartment's basement.

"What?" I said, laughing.

His frown lines deepened. I kept wondering what was wrong, didn't he get the joke? Because I didn't know that I was joking until now. Or maybe I wasn't. I stopped laughing.

"You shouldn't say that kind of thing," he said. "People kill themselves over abuse. It's a parent's worst nightmare."

"I'm not trying to hurt anyone." My voice came out squeaky. I should've said sorry. Either that or tell him about all the messed-up experiences I'd had with older people growing up. There were so many of them too: my first boyfriend, and before that my old driving instructor, my sister's friend, a neighborhood boy who'd invited me up into his treehouse where his mother couldn't hear me. "I just want to be someone else," I said. "I'm tired of this."

"Of what? Our relationship?"

I shook my head. "This," I said, slapping my shoulders, chest, legs.

"Oh," he said.

Pat knew what I meant. After the last cancer scare, I'd called him up and asked him how I could make sure my organs went to medical schools for dissection. My parents were hardcore Christians who didn't believe in organ donation. Pat's were lawyers. He said he'd have them look into it, but by the time he got the answer, Dr. Livingston called me to say false alarm—my cancer was still in remission.

"Why be something so messed up when you can pretend to be literally anything?" Pat said. He put all the papers on the messy nightstand.

"So I can't be me at sixteen? I was a stunner then. Big boobs, super skinny. It's rare for a girl to have that and a pretty face too. I almost got kicked out of Miss Christian Beauty for being that way. The people in charge thought having me do the bathing suit portion was salacious since the whole point of the pageant was modesty. I had a one-piece like all the other girls, so I couldn't figure out what the problem was."

Pat smiled. His eyes looked sad. He shook his head slowly. *No*, he mouthed.

"Fine," I said. "I'm Pam Anderson."

He made a face. "Someone else, please. I can't stop associating her with my old roommate, the real odd one back at FSU. He had this huge poster of her. I mean, you should've seen the size of it. It was like Big Brother watching you 24/7."

"Jerry Hall."

"These references keep getting more retro. Are you trying to make me feel ancient?"

I pulled the covers over my head, blocking out his voice until he pulled them back off of me. (Him: "Come on, you can't be serious, Mer.") "I don't know how to make you happy," I said. "Just let me sleep here, and then I'll go home and you never have to see me, and even if you want to, I just won't respond."

"I guess I like you the way you are," he said.

I rolled my eyes.

"Seriously."

"You would've liked me better when I was in my prime."

He sighed. "I like you now."

"Would you have messaged me if my profile pictures weren't touched up? Like if I posted one of me without any hair and all bloated? Or of me right now?"

"I didn't even know the pictures were altered. Your essence is still there. That's what counts, right?" When I didn't answer, he started touching me again, leaning his mouth toward the crook of my neck and speaking into it. "Right?"

"But wouldn't I be better looking if I weren't so sick? If the medication hadn't blown me up and I didn't have to get cut up, I'd be . . ." I didn't know how to finish the sentence. I'd be what? Happier? More loved? Even when I was beautiful, I'd gotten hurt. I think I just wanted to be miserable in a way that made me feel beautiful. "I should probably stop," I said. "I'm being a stereotype. Can't be the washed-up woman regretting things." Then, in a low voice, so quiet that even I couldn't hear fully: "You've never called me physically attractive."

"You're perfect the way you are," he said.

"You're such a good actor."

"Not sure if that's a compliment, but I'll take it."

I let myself give in to him, hugging him, kissing him, believing his lies. "You should audition for parts again," I told him. "Don't teach forever. Get in contact with your old agent again. Whatever happened to that teen action film you were meeting about?"

"It's been almost twenty years," he said.

"So?"

He laughed through his nose. "So I don't think football-jocks-slash-secret-agents are supposed to be balding."

"What're you talking about? I see a head full of curls." I rubbed the thinned-out part of his scalp. In my head, I was Anita flattering him for a good grade. I gave him a fantasy within mine, running my fingers through his salt-and-pepper hair. "So pretty."

"Okay, now you're just pulling my leg."

"Are you sure you don't still go to FSU? Are you a freshman?"

"Come on."

"Sophomore?"

"Meredith, seriously."

"Oh, so you're a senior, then. Ready for the real world? I bet you already have the perfect job lined up. Has anyone told you that you should act? I'm sure you get that a lot. You could totally play Prince Charming at Disneyland."

Pat kept laughing until he put his Serious Actor expression on. His eyes lit up. "Did I ever tell you that I was in a hair-care commercial?" he asked "I mean, wait, no—I got the role recently, yesterday actually. It's for a conditioner that's just for men. We're shooting tomorrow on the beach."

"Oh my God! I know a real TV star. This is unbelievable."

Pat got real excited at that. He told me that he was a junior studying musical theater and that he'd been single since his girlfriend back home in German Village, Ohio, ended things. He talked a lot about making homecoming court in high school. I couldn't stop focusing on his eyes. They were so pretty. That and also the shape of his face, which was angular in a feminine way. He was probably kind back when people let him be who-ever he wanted because of his looks. He didn't seem like the type to bully others just because he could.

"I feel so humbled," he said. "I can't believe I'm talking to the woman who was too hot for Miss Christian Beauty and— wait, where you going, babe? We just met. Can I get your number at least?"

"I'll be right back," I said, and went into the walk-in closet.

I was so excited that my body vibrated. My fingers shook and my vision pulsated as I searched for my old clubbing dress, the powder-blue one I'd bought during my last cancer-less semester at Pensacola. I'd meant to give it away, but couldn't part with it completely, only partially, so I'd asked Pat to guard it until I lost twenty pounds.

It didn't fit. The bodice cinched my middle too tight, but I didn't care anymore. Pain felt invigorating when I was having fun. It was just like when me and my girlfriends danced in sti-lettos until our feet blistered, all of us high and drunk out of our minds.

"I'm back," I said, slinking up against the closet's entrance.

Pat's mouth dropped. His eyes sparkled. "Wow," he kept whispering, which worried me until he said, "I didn't know women could look so good in real life."

I climbed onto the bed. The dress kept squeezing me. I looked in the mirror and saw Anita staring back, big-boobed and baby-skinned. The truth was I couldn't remember myself from childhood. I didn't like looking at old pictures, so the only memories I had rested in other people. Pat's amusement felt the same as the looks I'd gotten from men when I was young, which made me wonder if they'd secretly found me kind of ignorant too. The dress started hurting me worse. Glittery nylon straps dug into my flesh. I couldn't breathe all the way in.

"We should probably stop," I said.

I started undressing, redressing. I'd come to his house in the same outfit I'd worn the last time I saw him, an oversized tunic with jeans, nothing special. He didn't object. Pretending had been enough for him. He often told me how the rush of being onstage or on camera was better than sex.

"Where're you off to now?" he asked.

"Bathroom."

I closed the door behind me. Water spots dotted the medicine cabinet's mirror. There's Anita, I thought. I cupped the air where my breasts had been pre-double mastectomy. My insurance at the new place where I worked would cover part of the cost for reconstructive surgery. The problem was that I didn't want to go under the knife again. Too many bad memories. I had nightmares about people touching me.

The fantasy of Anita played out in my mind, dwindling. I imagined myself, Anita, being passed down a line of people: teachers and neighbors, boyfriends and friends, stepfamilies and flesh-and-blood families and driving instructors who stuck their hands in her shirt. People lined up like they were at Disneyland, pulling down their pants, shorts, skirts. The fantasy grew larger until it popped. I arched my back, making sex-faces, and then I was frowning again. The woman in the mirror judged me.

I closed my eyes and thought back to when I first believed I was going to die. I was twenty-two and still religious. In my mind, people's bodies were tin cups and the souls Jell-O stuffed inside, and when the cup broke apart, the Jell-O stayed whole. At first, the soul clung to the past, keeping the shape of the broken cup. But then the sun melted it and it got to go to heaven.

"Are you coming out soon?" Pat asked.

Jell-O souls were something I came up with when I was seven and bored, nothing too deep. But the thought of them terrified me in the hospital. I didn't want to turn to goop. I didn't want my body to be broken.

"Mer?" Pat knocked on the door. "Come on, I need to take a leak real quick."

I ran my finger over the scars on my chest, imagining what I could be now that my tin cup was breaking. I hadn't died yet. I could be anyone. My soul expanded as it melted across an endless world, growing thinner. I couldn't stop crying. Poor Anita.

Softie

....

BEFORE I WAS born, I tried to kill myself.

My dad told me how, according to the social worker who'd taken me, I'd wrapped myself up in my birth mom's umbilical cord as a baby so that I almost choked to death. He said that I wanted to scare the doctors into keeping me in her womb forever because I knew she was dangerous but didn't yet know how much purer his love would be than hers. I wasn't allowed to ever see her because she'd tried to kill me when I was too young to speak or remember.

"And now you're mine," he said, patting my hand with his sweaty one. "What's the matter? Come on, Clio. Don't do that here. Quit being such a softie and have a good time."

I'd just turned seventeen. We were at the Pasta Palace for my and Rosa's birthdays, which my dad had consolidated into a single celebration even though Rosa, his latest live-in muse, had turned sixteen when she was still living with her grandma. We would've done it later in the week, but then I told Rosa I was thinking of killing myself again and she told my dad while fighting with him over money.

I crouched over my plate, trying to make myself as small as possible as the large family in matching Hawaiian shirts walked past us. They'd already seen me, my dad, and Rosa a thousand times, throwing us judgmental looks from one of the low-slung booths by the bar. They probably recognized him from TV interviews. Or maybe they didn't and were wondering how someone so pale could be connected to me. The mom had a look of knowing on her face. Her eyes narrowed. She'd probably read the tabloids about my dad, Carter Banks, the film producer who threw scuzzy parties.

Their youngest kid stopped in front of Rosa, cocking his head. His mom grabbed his small hand. He swung back as she dragged him away. His eyes were fixed on Rosa, who was pretty in an extremely common way that even little kids could notice. Rosa yawned, oblivious as she cradled a sweating glass of watery Coke Zero underneath her chin. My dad, who was once handsome, liked to say that beauty was a topic that bored the beautiful. He'd said this so many times I felt nothing when he said it again.

"Isn't that right, Clee?" he said, rubbing my back.

"I don't know," I said.

"You would know best."

I shrugged. I yearned to be seen like Rosa, but also detested being noticed. I liked to think I was pretty, too, but it was difficult to know for sure. I'd overheard a boy that I didn't know call me hot at a water park. But then a school friend said that I looked like a boy when I wore my hair pulled back.

"Don't let people get to you," Rosa said, as if reading my dark thoughts. She'd been staying with my dad long enough for us to become attuned to each other. "Stupid people infect you with their problems. We're hot bitches from the coasts who don't care about anything, remember?"

I laughed.

"It's true, though."

"I feel fat. I ate too much."

"It's supposed to be a celebration," my dad butted in. "Come on. You love this place."

My dad thought the gauche chain restaurants from my early childhood might cure my suicidality. His time in the film industry had made his logic less grounded. He believed in healing crystals, free love, and the power of positive thinking. According to him, his varied political beliefs—no to feminism but also the fanatical silliness of the GOP; yes to free health care within reason and eugenics—made him a classicist who transcended political labels. Though he worked in film, he detested unbridled emotion of any kind, which he found self-ish. He said he thought therapy was a racket. He couldn't trust me to be alone with someone prodding into his business. I had too many of his secrets.

"I love you," he said.

"I love you too," I said back, which made him smile like a little kid being told he was the handsomest and smartest in his grade.

The waiter brought out a chocolate soft-serve cake topped with sparklers. Rosa and me blew them out together and, for a second, I imagined we were sisters. Here we are, I thought, narrating the inner monologue of my made-up TV life. Here we are, two schoolgirls from Silver Lake or maybe Burbank sharing a moment that deserved to be dubbed over with music, ideally something from Rosa's Spotify account because she had better taste in music than anyone I'd ever known.

"I don't want any," I said when Rosa started cutting the cake into sloppy, falling-apart pieces.

I watched as melty soft serve waterfalled down the slices, pooling onto the platter. My stomach hurt with hunger. *Softie, softie,* my mind kept chanting. I'd only ordered a plate of plain salad, no dressing, because I was convinced my thighs weren't supposed to be touching. I looked down at my lap and saw two overinflated, burned sausages staring back at me. It was hard for me to believe they were part of my anatomy.

Rosa plopped a giant piece of cake onto her dirty plate.

"Woah," my dad said. "That's a lot of cake, Rosie."

"I'll eat what I want," Rosa said.

My dad nodded, but I know what he was thinking, which was that Rosa wouldn't last with us much longer. She'd grown tired of his pretend syrupiness and he her candidness. I tried to make a distraught face that said "I'll jump out a window if she leaves" but he wasn't looking at me. His attention was on Rosa.

Despite Rosa's appetite, she was rod thin like a model. Waif-like, my dad called her. He said she was the perfect star for a film he was funding. It was the one about the girl who keeps leaving voicemails on her late mom's cell. I forget the name. I think it was *Missing Your Call* or maybe *Missed Call.* The girl freaks out when she gets a text back, believing it's her mom's ghost contacting her from the grave. But then it turns out the telephone people reassigned the number to this hot quarterback who just happens to go to the girl's high school.

I went to put my head on Rosa's shoulder, watching her text her grandma pictures of the cake. I couldn't understand what she was writing. It was all in Spanish. Still, I knew enough about her to guess that she was making up another tale about my dad being a pious Christian woman who was letting her stay the summer. I tried reading the words aloud to make her laugh, though the joke had grown old since she first started teaching me Spanish.

"That was actually better," Rosa said. "If you roll your Rs, you might be able to talk to Javi and Mike."

"No way," I said, burrowing my head deeper into her skin. She smelled like the strawberry-scented bodywash I'd lent her.

Javi and Mike were the groundskeepers at my dad's estate. I liked Javi; he reminded me of someone's grandfather. Mike was cool too. But he could also be terrible when he wanted to be, which had been all the time lately. I found him increasingly annoying because of how much he liked trashing my dad, always saying I was addicted to his money. Rosa, however, thought he was the anti-Christ because he was the first self-described socialist she'd ever met in real life. He liked to talk to her and Javi about the coup going on in Bolivia even though Rosa was Cuban and Javi left Bolivia years ago when he was still a teenager.

"I hate Mike," Rosa said. "He doesn't know what he's talking about. I hope there's a revolution soon just so he'll go hungry. Then he'll be quiet. He won't be able to go to school either. Communists hate education, you know."

I nodded even though I found her views crass. Last week, she'd said that she'd rather die than go to most colleges that weren't Pepperdine because they were all filled with socialists. To preserve our friendship, I pretended not to care at all about politics. I believed that her essence went deeper than the bland complaints certain kids had at my school about wokeness. Of all my dad's muses who'd stayed with us, all the pretty actresses and singers and influencers, Rosa was the only one who'd talked to me first. The two who'd come before her used to team up against me. They used to throw my books and clothes in the trash up until my dad kicked them out for stealing his Rolex.

I became so lost in thought I almost didn't hear Rosa saying that Mike was here. Or rather, I didn't feel the need to respond in a genuine way. We were always making the same joke about people we didn't like popping up in the places we least suspected them. I'd be like, "Oh my God, Rosa, is that your grandma wearing a thong again?" at Carbon Beach even though her grandmother lived in Miami and was so religious she found most other Christians sinful. And then on Hollywood Boulevard, she'd point to a random Black woman who was usually tweaking out or panhandling, and she'd be like, "Your mom's come to get you, Clee." The game was only supposed to be fake mean.

"But really," Rosa said, gesturing over toward the host table, "he's here."

Mike was arguing with one of the hostesses, gesturing wildly, his face flushed. She smirked at him. A group of old women came in behind him, laughing and complaining loudly about the traffic on the Hollywood freeway. The hostess walked over and greeted them, flipping her ombre hair all up in Mike's face as if it had the power to erase him from existence. He caught me looking at him and started walking, marching, up the small set of stairs in Bean boots so unsullied they looked new. My mind thinned out into a haze of random observations. I thought: he must keep a separate pair outside of work, maybe he prefers wearing boots all the time, maybe his wardrobe is all lumberjack outfits because rugged looks were in fashion.

My skin started itching. I had the urge to chew on my braids again even if I looked juvenile doing it. The hostess was talking to one of the waiters now. She pointed at Mike and made the cuckoo sign. They were looking right at us. A small audience formed around them, customers and workers united in their love of drama that didn't affect them. Mike took out his phone. He was filming.

"So how does it feel?" Mike asked.

"Is everything okay, Mike?" my dad asked, his face impassive.

"You're disgusting, man. Some of those girls you bring over are underaged. You know that, don't you? That's what you prefer."

"You're, like, actually insane," Rosa said, her voice even. "For real."

Mike ignored her. He got closer to my dad, so close that his abdomen pressed up against the wobbly table. The drinks rattled. I stuffed my face with leftover spicy andouille and concentrated on chewing so the anxiety didn't take over me completely. I looked up at Mike, pleading, trying to transfer my panic onto him so he might freeze up too. But he wasn't looking.

My dad pushed his plate back. He cleared his throat. "I don't know what you're talking about, unfortunately," he said.

"I have evidence," he said.

I started choking. An invisible force pressed up against my chest, stopping me from breathing. Chewed-up food spilled out of my mouth. I tried to say Mike's name, but all that came out was choking. Rosa's eyes went wide with fear. She tried beating my back. The blows hurt, but I felt like I deserved them. I felt happier when the hitting and choking stopped. The feeling was the same relief I got during my period when my cramps let up and gave me a renewed appreciation for not being in pain.

Mike left on his own. The owner gave us coupons to apologize, and then we left. On the drive back home, as Rosa and me sat in silence, my dad started muttering to himself. I could sense his rage bubbling up inside him. He pulled into an office park and I felt my body melting into a hot liquid that quickly became polluted with the emotions of everyone around me. I felt his rage, Rosa's disgust and fear, Mike's outrage. I wondered if my dad found out that Rosa had been telling her friends back in Florida about dating him. I looked at her. She feigned obliviousness, studying the creamsicle-colored manicure that I'd given her just yesterday.

The door slammed. Dad got out and started screaming. He kicked the car's fender hard enough for the body to bob and sway on its tires. Rosa tried to say something when he came back into the driver's seat, but I squeezed her hand, willing her to be quiet just this once.

* * *

I fell asleep in Rosa's room on the trundle bed's slide-out mattress. My room was too close to my dad's to sleep comfortably in. When I woke up, she was gone. The air still smelled sweet of unwashed bodies, Chloé Eau de Parfum and the shampoo we shared. I was pretty sure she smoked last night after I'd gone to bed. When I opened up her bathroom, the stench of weed struck me.

I went into my dad's room and found her glasses sitting on his nightstand. The bed was still unmade. Marie, the new maid, came in and started mopping the parquet floor with lemony wood soap. When I ask where my dad had gone, she said that he was eating breakfast on the patio.

"Is Mike here?" I asked.

"I'm not sure, love," she said. "Why?"

I shook my head. "It's nothing."

"Are you sure?" She cocked her head. She was so new. There was a good chance she didn't even know about the rumors yet. She looked too old and proper to read tabloids.

I shook my head again, trying to hold back tears. Not because I was trying to tell the truth this time but rather because it was easier to repeat a simple gesture than make up a whole lie. Before she could say anything else, I ran down the stairs and out the French doors toward the balcony. My bare feet burned against the sunbaked brick floor, which I didn't mind because they reminded me of summer. Not this summer, but the summers when I was young and lively and used to spend all day throwing my dolls off the railing and into the infinity pool, which I imagined was a pit of ice-blue acid. The tingling sensation made me temporarily forget myself.

Both Rosa and my dad were silent. I surveyed what was left on the table: half a gallon of OJ, no pulp; whole wheat bread with embedded seeds I used to try and fail to extract from the sandwiches the cooks made me; the leftover pasta Rosa had doggy-bagged from last night, the cream of which she'd revived with too much oat milk, creating a soggy mess she'd barely touched.

I closed my eyes and pretended that by falling asleep I'd pressed the universe's hidden reset button. I leaned up against Rosa's chair. When I went to put my head on her shoulder again, she pulled away.

"Sheesh," I said.

My dad was glaring at the marigolds Mike had planted by the pool. They were in full bloom now. They were so pretty. I had the urge to pluck them from the ground and make them mine forever. I knew that ripping them from their beds would only make them wither up and die, but I still wanted them at my bedside. Even if my dad didn't trust me with his crystalline vases, I could always press the flowers between the pages of a book. Or maybe I could wring out their sweetness and make perfume.

"What a waste," my dad said, shaking his head and pointing to the lone, weak marigold whose stem Mike had reinforced with a small stake and string. "And they only last for one season. I don't know what Mike was thinking when he did that."

"I think they're nice," I said.

"I'll have Javi remove them."

"Can I keep them, then?"

"No."

I nodded, trying not to cry again. He was always giving flowers to his muses, exotic colored roses he rewarded them with even if they weren't that talented. Gift giving was a whole language to him. I wasn't entirely sure of the meaning behind the Madame Alexander dolls he kept giving me when I'd told him a million times that toys didn't interest me anymore.

"I hate flowers," Rosa muttered, acting as if she hadn't posted endless Snapchats of the Venus et Fleur flower box my dad had gotten for her. "They're gaudy."

My dad's glower turned to her, its intensity spilling onto me. He always blamed me when his muses left—or, rather, when he felt like he had no choice but to kick them out. He didn't care even if they hated me, their passive hostility coursing through the air like a radio frequency that only I could pick up on. In his eyes, I was always corrupting them with my negativity.

I went on my phone, Instagram again, pretending to be unaware of his eyes, which were striking, one brown and the other green. I'd only created an account to look at other peoples', mostly friends but also celebrities. My life online was uninteresting. I didn't have any current photos of myself until yesterday, just old pictures and some snapshots of my late cat, Mitchell.

Overnight, gained thousands of followers, which meant I'd been purposefully sought out. The most popular post was the picture I'd posted yesterday morning when Rosa and me were still on good terms. My dad had let me have a small role in one of his lesser-known films, a dramedy about an aging opera singer. I played a Girl Scout who sells the singer cookies.

There were so many likes, and even more comments. My mind started racing. I tapped on the photo and squinted as I tried to read what people had written without the aid of my contacts. A famous podcaster thought I had dead eyes. Some lady from Kansas called me a doll baby. Lots of people believed I'd been adopted from Somalia for some reason.

All my other photos were well liked too. For the first time in a while, I felt wanted rather than just consumed or discarded. My heart grew light. A bunch of commenters remembered the trailer for the straight-to-TV movie I was supposed to star in ("I thought it was a fever dream until I saw the trailer online lol," "Does someone have the link," "She was so great in that, I used to want to have the same sunflower hat as her," "Omg! I forgot about that!"). I played this girl who transfers to a new school and starts a rock band. The network pulled the movie last minute for some reason—something about contracts. When my acting career died, my dad said that I'd study nursing when I got old enough. I felt crushed like all the muses he sent home.

My dad got up and left, storming away for the millionth time. He slammed the door closed, and I jumped even though he was always doing that: making noise without talking, just like a little baby.

Rosa showed me her phone. She was on my Instagram page too. "They all found out," she said.

"I don't get it."

Rosa rolled her eyes. "Haven't you seen Mike's video?" She didn't wait for me to shake my head. She tapped on her iPhone's cracked screen, sighing and puffing her cheeks as she waited for it to finish loading.

I watched even though I didn't want to. I hated seeing myself from the perspective of somebody else. I caught a glimpse of me wearing the oversized velour coveralls I'd thought would hide my body in a chic way. Instead, I looked dumpy and wholly irrelevant to the main point of the video, which was that my dad, one of the most influential men in the state of California, had a predilection for young girls. Mike's words felt new even though I'd heard them before. Since I was young enough to learn what acting was, I had become skilled enough to separate myself from the memories that threatened to ruin the bland type of girl I'd been playing for most of my life. *You're messing with them*, he yelled through the phone's tiny speakers. *That's what you do. I've been watching you. I have evidence.* The video started buffering. Rosa gave up and put her phone away.

"He's just jealous," Rosa said. She winced as the sun's intensity grew brighter. "I hope he dies. Yeah, I hope he burns in a fiery car wreck and they can't identify his body."

"That's so specific."

"Not really. It's pretty common. It happened to my parents."

"I'm sorry."

"It's fine. I was too young to remember. My grandma says they were heading in the wrong direction."

"What was wrong with them?"

"Nothing, really. My mom just drove in the opposite direction by accident and then a truck hit her car head on. They think she was high, I don't know."

"Oh."

"That's what happens when people make mistakes like that. Doesn't matter if they're good or not. But it's always nice when people get what they deserve."

"I miss Mike," I whispered.

Rosa leaned back in her chair, raising a perfectly tweezed eyebrow. I desperately wanted to tell her that I'd gone to second base with Mike last week in his work truck. Was it possible for one to lose their virginity for the umpteenth time if the taker felt different? I didn't even like Mike that much—he was too conceited, too judgmental—but I felt like the choice had been mine.

I'd been the one who'd come to him. I told him he was pretty like a girl in the face, put my hand on his crotch and gave him permission to go down on me. He asked me why I liked him, and I had to make up an answer about love at first sight. In reality, I'd just read a bodice ripper about a woman who could make men bend to her will just by batting her eyes at them. I wanted to see what it was like to initiate sex. I didn't think I could fall in love with Mike until later when he pretended not to see me whenever I waved. His apathy made the memory of his attention feel oppressive.

I decided I'd make a joke out of Mike like-liking me, smirking and giggling madly to myself until Rosa asked what I was thinking. I'd learned from her how to make a new, funny, almost unrecognizable story out of a depressing one, carving out the strange details that were almost lighthearted on their own.

"Nothing," I said. "Just something Mike did before he left."

"What?"

"He showed me this weird porn site in his car. It was so weird, oh my God. Like, I can't even say."

"Okay, now you have to. Is he into furry shit?"

"No. It's this subgenre of women trying to put on clothes that are too small for them."

"Is there sex?"

"No. It's just videos of women with huge tits and hips and everything forcing themselves into Brandy Melville–type clothes. And then they're all like, 'Oh my God, why won't it fit?'"

"That's all? Like, there's no fucking?"

"Nope."

"How do they get everything off if it's all that small?"

"The clothes rip. I don't know. It's weird."

Rosa threw back her head and laughed, which allowed me to do the same, doubling over from the pain of it all. As we laughed, I imagined myself folding up Mike into a tiny ball and rolling him toward the very back of my subconscious. There was so much to forget even though I'd only known him briefly: his warmth and his softness, his attention and sudden withdrawal, the pleasure and pain of being temporarily wanted in a way that didn't feel violent. The tiny balls of awful memories rattled around, sticking stubbornly to each other as they tried to make themselves large again.

Rosa's laughter grew wilder, more unhinged. I wasn't sure what mine sounded like. Maybe it wasn't as strong as hers. One of the maids came running out as if she thought we were drowning, then scowled and left when she saw that we were fine.

Rosa turned the joke on me. "You fucked him," she said. "Didn't you?"

"No," I said. I stopped laughing.

She rolled her eyes.

"Okay," I said. "But it only happened once."

"He probably sensed something from you. That's how he found out about your dad. Girls like you send out signals when you do that."

"What do you mean?"

"You give yourself away way too easily. Like, seriously? Mike? Of all the dudes in the world."

"I'm sorry," I said, and left before she could say anything else. "I need to go to the bathroom."

The world grew dark around me as I went back inside the house. My eyes took their time adjusting to the dimness of the old, winding corridors.

I went to hide in my bedroom. A dark shadow came in behind me and passed over me. My mind grew fuzzy. I ran toward the window. My fingers fumbled with the window's lock—I wanted to jump, I didn't care if I was on the fourth floor—but the shadow pulled my fingers away.

Girls like you send out signals. The words echoed in my mind. I didn't understand, but I also did. It was as if my brain had been split into two halves: first, the girl I presented myself as at school, a normal but quiet kid who read cheesy romance novels and manga; and second, the girl who lived in shame.

* * *

"What did he do?" Rosa asked too loudly.

The music's volume lessened as the DJ played a softer, gentler song about love instead of partying. I shook my head. The back of my neck ached. She already knew the answer because he'd gotten violent with her too. Now he was fine. He was hosting an important function on the house's main level, inside and outside, around the pool. Huge crowds, lots of famous and almost-famous celebrities.

"Did he at least use protection?" Rosa whispered.

I shrugged. I remembered breakfast and having to go to the bathroom, and going to my room instead for some reason. I didn't remember closing the door, but I did remember him knocking. He made me delete my Instagram account, which had never been a secret like the tabloids were saying. It was just some inconsequential thing that I hadn't thought of telling him about. He wouldn't listen.

"Do you want to cry?" she asked.

"No point," I said.

"What happened? Why did you go to him? You should've stayed outside. You know how angry he gets."

"I don't know."

"You should've just taken a dump in the yard."

I tried laughing. Only this time, it sounded all wrong, like I was choking. I wanted to leave so badly.

"Are you sick?" Rosa asked.

"No, I said. "I thought—you—it's just, I thought you were joking about the bathroom thing."

"Why would I be?"

"Because it's so pathetic."

The party was for someone important, I forget whom, though I'm pretty sure they did something with politics. Rosa and me hung around the bar. The bartender had said we were too young to drink, but we stuck around anyway, waiting for someone to forget their martini so we could split it.

My dad was trying to do everything at once, schmooze and attract a new muse. He sat in the conversation pit with a group of men and some women. The women were all girls according to the depositions that came about later. I thought I saw a freshman girl from my school, but I was probably mistaken. I went to Agnes Tomlinson Day, this super wealthy Ivy-feeder. Why would an A&T girl attend one of my dad's parties when she could just use her connections to get a part in a movie?

"Look at him," Rosa hissed. "He's such a con."

I desperately wanted to feel her contempt, but couldn't. I'd been infected by him for so long I could only feel sorry for him the same way he did for himself and maybe me to some extent. He looked like a little boy even though he towered above the squat businessmen sitting with him. His hands were folded politely in his lap. He nodded. His eyes look worried. His back was hunched. I felt so humiliated for him that I wanted to kill him just to stop feeling. Everything about my dad was heavy, so burdensome. He was hard and soft at the same time. After he'd hurt me, he declared he wanted me and only me for the rest of his life because I didn't run away from difficult matters.

"I'm leaving tomorrow," Rosa said. "There's a bus that leaves at six in the morning, which will be hell, but who cares? I don't care about his dumb movie anymore. Let him put on a dress and play the part himself."

"You can't just leave. You signed a contract!"

"Chill, Clio. It's paper. And he has way bigger things to care about than me now. I had to watch TV in his room all night yesterday. He smashed it up when Mike came on for this interview. Fuck Mike. He's so annoying."

"You have to stay."

"You're acting like him."

I started crying. I had the urge to run outside and drown myself in the deck's oversized Jacuzzi, which glowed and bubbled like the wish-giving magical caldron I'd pretended that it was as a girl. I used to wish I was normal whenever I got to relax there, slipping pennies into the water until one coin broke the machinery. So useless. I still didn't know what normal looked like.

"I'm sorry," Rosa said.

"No you're not," I snapped. Then, in a lower voice: "Please stay."

"No."

"I just don't know what I'll do without you."

"I'm sure you'll be happier. He seems to like you a lot. Maybe he'll give you the part."

"I don't want it," I said. I didn't know if I was telling the truth or not anymore.

The last time my dad had gone without a muse had been hell. Too much attention, I couldn't bear it all alone. I tried killing myself with pills, which made him sad, then enraged, then sad again. He didn't understand that taking my own life was the only way left I had to make it feel like it was still mine. At home, he'd made the chefs guard the kitchen from me when he thought I was overeating; wrapped up my arms in packing tape when he wrongly assumed that I was cutting; fondled my breasts when I told him I wanted reduction surgery.

When he showed me the pictures of girls someone had sent him, asking me who I thought was the prettiest, I quickly picked the one of Rosa.

"Did you wanna come with me?" Rosa asked. "I'm taking the bus. Come if you want. You'll have to wake up early because I'm walking, probably."

"I don't have any money."

"So? Steal from him."

"But what if he won't take me back?"

"That's the point."

"Where will I go?"

"I'm gonna strip. That's where all the money is. Screw acting. I still have the fake ID your dad gave me."

"That's insane. The sex industry's bad. Haven't you seen that documentary about it? It messes with your confidence."

"Clio, look around. All the girls here are already messed up. You and me too. We can't get any worse. This is rock bottom, and I'm leaving it behind. See that girl over there? The one in the purple? She legit looks like she's twelve."

"What if there's worse people?"

"There's nothing worse than what he does to you."

"Yeah," I whispered, feeling my throat grow raw. "What do I do?"

"Call girls like her make mad money cosplaying as ugly guys' dates. They get paid and they get to eat at the Capital Grille."

"I could have my eyes gouged out. That's worse, isn't it?"

"At least you wouldn't have to look at him anymore then."

"No way." I shook my head. "I think I'm gonna try to finish high school early. Then I'll just get a scholarship for college. I heard nursing school is a good investment."

"Not if he refuses to sign your FAFSA."

"What?"

Rosa bugged her eyes. "It's this thing your parents have to do to let you go. The government won't give you money unless they sign it. It was like that for my sister. My grandma wouldn't help because my sister wanted to go study something really dumb at this school that accepts literally anyone and costs way too much money anyways."

"What does your sister do now?"

"Stripping."

"I read somewhere that the most common nightmare is being in your underwear in front of a huge audience."

Rosa lost interest in me. I was being too dumb for her again. She started going on her phone. I wondered if she was going to ignore me for the rest of the night.

"But anyway," she said, still looking at the screen. "I'm peace-ing out at dawn. You can come. Or not."

Rosa got up and stretched, her arm narrowly missing Javi's wife, Ana, who was rushing back to the kitchen. I watched Rosa go up the stairs to her room. I didn't want to follow her at first because what if I did something else wrong?

My dad didn't notice Rosa leave. Or maybe he didn't care about her anymore. He was already with another girl, an actual grown woman for once. They were over by the bar. He stood too close to her as they talked.

The woman was Black. I could tell from her tightly coiled hair even though she was blue-eyed and very pale. She was too young for him, though she was still older than most of the girls he surrounded himself with. I'd never seen her around here before, though I was pretty sure she was from those toothpaste ads with the cheerleaders singing amount minty freshness. Or maybe she was just a call girl. Whenever we were in LA, my dad liked to say that it was impossible to tell apart the film stars from the porn stars and the porn stars from the hookers. They all dressed the same, took orders the same. The way he saw it, the whole world was a brothel.

I became so devastated that I couldn't even cry. I knew there was almost no chance he was attracted to her, but the thought of her made me want to kill myself again. I didn't want to believe there were people like her in the world who could be so free. She wasn't desperate like Dad's muses. But she wasn't drab like the A&T moms with their brunches and business casual.

When the misery passed over, I went to introduce myself to the woman. She had horse teeth, but they looked endearing on her. She'd be too doll-like if her smile was as perfect as the rest of her. I wanted to say hi, but all I could do was wave and simper, shrinking back into that annoying little Black kid who drank soda out of champagne flutes at Daddy's parties.

"Sandra," my dad said to her. Or maybe he said Sandy or Sarah or something. It was hard to understand him over the thrumming sound of music. "This is Clio. My girlfriend."

I'm sure that's what he said. Not girl but girlfriend. He said the word while the DJ was changing songs. The woman frowned and pulled away from him before I could think of something to say. *Let me come with you,* my mind screamed. *I want to be normal again. I'm not messed up. I can be good.*

"I should probably get going," she said, her voice deep and velvety. "My kids. They're waiting for me at home."

She walked between us, leaned down and whispered into my ear, "Go home too before you get yourself into any more trouble."

"I can't," I whispered back.

I waited for her to say something. She left. I was this close to giving up.

Dad downed another shot. Alcohol made him worse. His face was red like a stop sign. His eyes lingered on me more.

"I'll be right back," I told him.

I ran upstairs before he could stop me and pounded on Rosa's door. Rosa didn't answer, but I knew she was there. Bass-filled rap music blared from the other side of the door. I texted her and waited for what felt like forever.

A minute passed, then another. I kept looking at my phone, waiting for something to happen. I seesawed between hoping she'd answer and wondering how much more I'd have to endure from my dad for him to sign my FAFSA. I was seventeen and hadn't yet realized that having more options didn't mean that my life was my own. Freedom was just a feeling—fleeting—and I was freer than ever before.

Age-Defying Bubble Bath with Tri-Shield Technology

. . . .

A SMUDGY SIGHT, distant but still in view—that was her mom's casket, pine and silk and flowers bathing in stained-glass colored light. Alda had become separate from all of her thirty-four years including this one moment in which she is high at her mother's funeral. She was looking down and they were pooled on the church floor: bright, iridescent circles of psychedelic light that sounded like voices from the past as they rose and popped like bubbles. Did they really belong to her? They were so sad.

It had only taken one pill for Alda's life to slip off of her like a loose-fitting coat. She couldn't believe her mom had really passed. Last week, they'd talked of visiting Utah to see the famous grove of quaking aspens. Science said the trees didn't have much longer to live because of global warming. Something about the root system decaying, Alda couldn't remember.

"Alda?" Alda was pretty sure her sister, Maureen, was speaking. "Alda. I can't believe you. You said you were sober. Were you lying this whole time?"

"I'm fine," Alda said.

She thought of adding that she really had been clean for most of all those years since college. This one time was just a slip up. For real. She wasn't "lying to herself" like the addictionologist said.

"What did you take this time?" Maureen asked.

"Just something for stress, nothing to freak out about." Alda swatted her hand as if to say, *No big deal!* and almost fell over. It was the shoes that made her this way. Stilettos. They were so hard to wear. She was teetering on the edge, on thin plastic stakes.

But that didn't stop her little sister—five years younger but taller, married, more together, a homeowner and dog-mom of two—from going off on her. They were near the line for the guestbook. Lots of people, over one hundred signatures. Their mom had been very popular. She'd taught for twenty years in the public school system here and won awards for her dedication. Her students got excited when they saw her around town, both the little kids and the adults. They liked to ask about the daughters she always spoke of so warmly. One of the former students, a lady in a tasteful black jumpsuit and matching heels, kept staring at Alda. Alda could feel the woman's eyes. She was never oblivious to judgment.

"You're beyond ridiculous," Maureen said. She was whispering but managed to make her voice harsh like when she yelled. "First you make me plan everything all by myself, then you ghost me, and now you show up like this. Seriously, what's wrong with you? I don't get it. Like, I'm genuinely trying to understand."

For a long time, Maureen stood with her arms crossed. She was always the same when she got mad: arms crossed, lips pursed, eyes clouded with a childlike vulnerability she could never hide completely.

Alda used to help Maureen with her math homework. That had been ages ago, a backward time when their mom conflated Alda's age and academic talent for maternalism. She worked late—there was her main teaching job and a string of second jobs. Maureen learned to stop showing fear after Alda almost burned down their mom's place trying to boil pasta. Better to be angry than scared—the latter was the worst type of incompetence. She never admitted to feeling this way, didn't talk about emotions, but Alda could sense the distress behind Maureen's anger.

The cause of Alda's substance abuse issues was either too much responsibility or not enough—the therapists she saw were pretty split. The addiction hadn't gotten bad until she went out of state for college. She would've flunked out if not for her natural gift for figuring out problems so long as they were mathematical. She'd gotten all As in all subjects save for Chinese, history, and glassblowing.

"Maybe you should go," Maureen said. "Just leave."

Alda nodded. She couldn't tell if her sister was being serious or not. She didn't try to. Nothing felt real anymore. She wouldn't have been surprised if her mom were waiting outside. Somehow, she managed to find the door.

"I can't believe her," Maureen was saying, probably to her husband, an accountant. If it wasn't him she was complaining to, it was their half sister, Joyce (different mom, same dad; Alda's mom raised her like one of her own when he walked out on all of his women for who-knows-where). Joyce, the middle child, the one who bickered the most, refused to speak to Alda. They'd gotten into a fight last week over something really silly—broken dishes, it wasn't worth recounting because they were bargain-bin trash—and would've made up if not for their mom's death, which had transformed the argument into something apocalyptic, a premonition, and now Joyce blamed Alda for everything.

The sun was setting. Alda had work tomorrow. Her mind got noisy thinking about all that she still had to do. On the walk home, as the pill's effects dissipated, she stopped by the supermarket for brandy and other things.

Even when she wasn't consciously thinking about death, a hidden part of her mind was. The knowledge of her mom's end hummed in the background of her life nonstop like an overworked machine. It tainted even the memories that had nothing to do with her mom—making paper snowflakes in nursery school, cooking deviled eggs with Maureen for a fundraiser— so that they felt kind of sad too. She almost cried trying to remember the brand of teriyaki sauce she'd had at a party. The aching was nostalgic. It felt good in a painful way. She hadn't felt this distraught since she was a little girl still trying to understand the world.

When she saw the long line for the one open checkout lane, her mood soured to the point of physical illness. No worries.

She slipped a bottle of brandy into her bag. A lady passed by pushing a stroller filled with bags of rice. She was giving Alda that look, the same one from the funeral. Alda pretended to be shopping for real. She searched the store for nothing until she happened upon her reflection in the glass of one of the freezer doors.

Alda was getting older. She'd known this for a while, except now she could see her mom's face emerging from her own. There she was, tucked right there in the deep folds of Alda's nasolabial folds: death herself.

The wrinkles alone weren't the scariest part. Alda wasn't beauty obsessed like Joyce, didn't fear the diminishing quality of her just-above-average looks or the uncertainty of what came after their decay. Joyce's worries were more carnal. Her latest plastic surgery had been a facelift. Joyce, like most people, didn't like that time progressed. And she hated the idea of being single forever.

Alda told herself that she was different from everybody else. There was no way she could feel this lonely and alien and still be a part of the world. And even if she could, loneliness was still loneliness even if millions felt the same way. It was isolating regardless of how close she got to other people. She thought briefly about getting a Brazilian butt lift like Joyce had. Something to make her feel more memorable. Eternal. She couldn't stand the idea of fading away from people's memories.

Psychedelic swirls of Day-Glo pink and green screamed out at Alda from across the cosmetics section, half convincing her that she was still high. The candy-colored bottles had their own special display by the face masks. The marketing wasn't very clear, though. She had to read the description all the way through to understand it was bubble bath.

"New serum," said the labels in curlicue letters. "Age-defying, tri-shield technology." It all sounded very scientific. Alda took—stole—three bottles and fast-walked all the way home. No one stopped her. She felt invincible. Quickly, the emotion turned into more loneliness. By the time she got home, all the levity had evaporated from her body. No one had called her to see if she'd made it home okay.

Alda took a shower before filling the tub for the bath. The stopper. She'd only used it once before when she tried to do laundry by hand after a racoon snuck into the basement where the coin-operated laundry machines were. The memory brought back her fear of rabies, adding weight to her fear of death so that its presence felt even more overwhelming. The tub filled up slowly.

How many years had it been since she'd last had a bubble bath? Alda couldn't recall. What she did remember was one specific instance, neither the first nor last, very mundane: Her mom had bought Strawberry Shortcake shower gel for her girls to share. Alda and her sisters had laughed like screeching animals at bath time, letting the warm, fruity-scented flotsam pour over them. "Look at me!" Maureen squealed. She'd made herself a beard out of bubbles. "I'm old!"

The directions on the bottle said to add a small dollop. Alda didn't know why she could only have so little. Something about the serum being strong and effective. Every part of the bottle was a marketing pitch down to the warning label. She ran the water and squeezed out a stream of pearlescent bubble bath. The room started to smell like lavender and vanilla. Her body unfurled when she lowered herself in the tub. The water turned flesh-colored as she sank all the way down into its warmth.

Time went faster when Alda got comfortable. There were no windows in the bathroom, just the overhead light, no candles. Only more darkness could get in. It slipped soundlessly under the door when night came. She drained the tub with pruned hands and watched the water swirl into a mini tornado on its way down the drain.

Alda's reflection didn't scare her. She didn't have the energy to scream out in horror or happiness like the women in the cosmetic ads. Though she looked different, younger, she felt unchanged. Nothing would last, she thought, not even this new—old?—face, which time would surely claim again. What would her sisters think of her now? She drew a blank as she massaged her newly taut skin in essential oils and moisturizers.

What had happened to her was a miracle. She'd literally de-aged—that was how far skincare had come since her childhood. She was living in the future! She yawned and used the mini electric razor on her nose hairs. Back in the kitchen, she drank brandy out of an espresso cup, shot after shot until she was downing the dregs straight from the bottle. The primal, baby part of her brain started screaming for her mom.

Time for bed. Alda put on her nightclothes and looked at her new form in the full-length mirror. She hadn't been like this since she was sixteen, seventeen: skinny to the point of being somewhat shapeless. The bubble bath's special formula had melted off the extra pounds. Her Relay for Life shirt clung loosely to her hanger-like shoulders. She had to tighten the drawstring of her sweats.

There were always health hazards with these sorts of products. If she got cancer, she thought, she wouldn't have to care if the illness killed her before she even knew of its existence. That was how it had been for her mom. The aneurism had taken her out just like that. She was making her bed, and then she was on the ground. A week later, the funeral. All the attendees would be home by now. Maureen would be complaining about her to her husband over chilled White Claws.

Alda smiled, her fear of dying becoming less oppressive and more flexible—more like a worldview than an emotion. She decided that she was alive because she could do things people said she wasn't allowed to. Dead people—all they could do was be dead. Her theft reassured her of her own existence.

When she was younger, she used to shoplift, always with friends so that she felt protected. Only once had they gotten in trouble, and it wasn't with the law but her BFF Madison Apodaca's mom, who threatened to call Alda's but never did. Alda and Madison and Madison's cousin had taken a bunch of freckle pens from Sephora.

"But we already told you," Alda said, "they're just colored pencils. From school."

"That's some real BS," Madison's mom shot back.

Alda was at the woman's slippered feet, begging her to please, please, please not tell her mom. It wasn't that she was afraid of punishment like Madison. Alda's mom's silence scared her worse than threats or punishment. She didn't like having to sit in silence at the kitchen table while her mom asked everyone but her how their day went, what they wanted from the spice drawer, whether they needed bus fare for the next day, etc.

She'd been so silly then. So young and desperate for uncritical acceptance. And the worst part was that she'd stayed like that up until last week. Now she had no one. This was the longest she and Joyce had ever gone without speaking to each other. Alda had no idea how to make things right. It was usually her mom who brought her daughters together again. "Now go and hug your sister," she would say. Or, later, "Oh come on, you guys. I need both of you to come over and help with this. You're not little girls anymore."

These memories were so comfy they made Alda ache. She closed her eyes tight.

* * *

Morning. Sunlight cutting through the gaps of the venetian blinds. Birdsong, car engine grunts, her downstairs neighbor playing *Guitar Hero* at six in the morning.

Alda drove to work even though the weather was nice. She didn't want to feel good. She couldn't. The windows stayed rolled up. She blasted the air until she was freezing, and then she turned it up some more.

Nothing had changed even though she had. Her mom was still dead. Her sisters still hated her. Maureen texted her saying to call her, but refused to say why, only that Alda needed an intervention, that she was out of control, first the drinking and now this. *This*, she kept writing. You need to stop *this*. She was convinced that Alda would lose her job doing *this*.

Alda taught physics at a Catholic school downtown. It was a nice place, way fancier than the schools where her mom used to work. The campus had a recording studio, and the kids were allowed to wear their own clothes now. The whole world had flipped around since her childhood so that now her old public school had uniforms while the kids at the bougie prep schools got to wear ripped jeans.

One of the talkative girls in her morning class had on a baby-tee that showed off her belly ring. "Girl Empowered," read the front.

"Let's all stay abreast of the dress code," Alda said, speaking to the whole class but really just to her.

That made the whole class giggle. Alda wasn't even trying to be funny. The belly-ringed girl bugged her eyes and put on a sweater with the school's insignia.

"Question," one of the boys said to Alda. He was the one who always wore a silver chain around his neck. He could be very annoying. He liked pushing people for laughs. "What did you do to your face?" he asked.

The class was polite enough not to laugh this time. Later, when some of them were eating lunch together or drinking at some kid's house party, they'd laugh belatedly at his joke. Or maybe they'd talk about him behind his back. It was hard to tell what they were all thinking. The exchange student from France shared knowing smiles with the soccer boys, but another boy's mouth dropped like he'd just witnessed a murder.

"Let's not worry about my face right now," Alda said.

"I think the change looks nice," the belly-ringed girl said. Her name was Katie. She bugged her eyes again. "It's a free country. People should be allowed to do what they want to themselves."

Alda cleared her throat and asked for last week's homework. The annoying boy with the chain flashed a quick smile as he handed in his work. It was more sheepish than mocking, like he was trying to impress her. She pretended not to notice. *Sorry*, he mouthed.

Today's lesson was linear motion. The kids separated into their lab groups. They pushed rectangular blocks of wood with wheels affixed to the long ends, timing them with stopwatches. Alda went between groups. "Make sure to use the chart to record all your results," she told a group of five.

The day went fine. People complimented her new face, the women asking which products she used, the men trying to say she looked good in an acceptable way that wouldn't get them in trouble, the students telling her how pretty she looked, how different and new (not that she wasn't nice-looking before, of course).

It was the girls who were the most interested in Alda's transformation. They kept asking to touch her hair, her skin. One of them asked if this was what Alda had always wanted, and Alda nodded without getting what "this" really was.

By the end of the day, Alda felt well enough to stop at a bakery by her home. She peered into one of the fridges, marveling at the rainbow rows of macarons inside. She wasn't sure if she wanted the lemon ones or the vanilla. Or maybe she'd get a pastry. The cinnamon rolls here were huge.

"Hey."

One of the workers was looking at her from behind the counter. He had ginger hair and a matching beard, one earring, two flower tattoos—a wreath around a wrist, a rose on his forearm. Alda's mom had been a ginger. Maureen, too, but not Joyce, who was dark-haired like Alda.

The worker made her feel judged even though he was acting nice. He looked her age, maybe younger but definitely not early twenties. But he was gross. He winked and asked her which high school she went to and whether or not she liked to party on the weekends.

"Where're you going?" he shouted after her.

"I think I want something else," Alda said.

"We have aquarium cookies. Wanna try one? They're real popular on Instagram."

"Not today."

"See you next time?"

Alda shrugged. She left without saying good-bye. On the drive home, at a stoplight by the shoe store that closed down: a rainbow. *Make a wish!* Her mom would've said. She used to confuse rainbows with shooting stars no matter how many times Alda and her sisters corrected her.

In her apartment complex's parking lot, Alda heard that same noise again. It wasn't *Guitar Hero* or birds, but children. Little children. There was a whole group of them playing in the tiny oasis of grass within the roundabout. One was trying to climb a tree. The others watched, cheering, a little girl throwing fallen leaves like confetti. A woman approached them. She called out their names as she told them to stop fooling around. Her voice felt like Alda's mom's even though it was too high pitched. Funny how randomly her mom could turn up, and always in fragments, never as a whole person like in movies about ghosts. The woman's jeans reminded Alda of how her mom only wore dresses.

Alda's loneliness made her discomfort worse. Her face ached. She couldn't stop thinking about having to live out the rest of her life alone. She washed her hands in the apartment until they felt dry. In the mirror, she saw an angry rash of acne on her left cheek. It was so painful. So gross too. She heated up a wet washcloth in the microwave and put it over her face like her mom used to do. Sweat beaded all over her.

When the achiness didn't go away, when she felt that she was going to cry again, she took another bubble bath. She added one capful, then another, a third, a fourth. While the water ran, she added almost the entire bottle and watched the suds get frothier.

* * *

Wake up, get dressed, take the car to work. No time to look in the mirror—that would only distress her, she didn't have time to make herself look right. Park, go to school. First period, second period, third. A break before lunch. Another email reminding her to turn in grades, which were now three days overdue. "Is there an issue?" the secretary asked. She'd cc'd the director this time.

Alda went through the day without feeling. People looked at her different. She kept her eyes trained on her feet except when she was teaching and had to look her kids in the eyes— every one of them, even the annoying boy, even Katie, whose face was filled with sympathy and a little bit of disgust.

The control panel for the projector was too high for Alda to reach. One of her honors kids came up and pressed the power button without her having to say a word. She thanked him. He didn't say anything back, just cleared his throat awkwardly and went back to his seat. She talked until she saw how little the class was listening. One of her best, most sycophantic students was on her phone, smiling, oblivious, the screen lighting up her face. Alda didn't have the nerve to call her out.

There was a video Alda was supposed to show her honors class. It was the middle part of a WETA documentary on these engineers who were trying to lower the temperature of helium to zero Kelvin. She wound up showing the whole thing. She couldn't lecture anymore. Too much talking. Her throat was too tight. She went on her phone, looking up all she could find on the bubble bath's side effects.

"*Used too much and now too short to drive?*" somebody had written on drugrecall.net. "*What to do? Please help. Desperate.*"

Too bad for them. All the comments were the same: should've followed the label's instructions—one capful per week, no more, no less. Just accept the change, people kept saying. Time will re-ravage your face eventually—it always does.

Alda stared at her phone until the screen went dead. She could see her reflection, the chubby cheeks and baby-clear skin. Her fingers were those of a small child's. She looked like an elementary schooler. She was lucky she'd been a tall kid. Her feet had just barely touched the gas pedals of her Ford Fiesta this morning.

When the bell rang this time, it was time to go home. Kids cheered for the end of the school day, packing their bags before she could dismiss them. Her second transformation had made them rowdier. They acted like her smallness made her not only invisible but also unintelligible.

"Wait," one girl said, "what did she say about the midterm test banks? I wasn't listening."

"No clue," her friend said.

They spoke airily as if Alda hadn't explained everything to them a million times. She'd even written out the information right there on the whiteboard.

"Make sure to put up your chairs," Alda said.

"*Make sure to put up your chairs*," someone said back in a mocking baby voice.

Alda took the long way to her car this time, still scrolling through drugrecall. Apparently, the bubble bath she'd bought wasn't allowed in Canada or the EU. Too strong. There was an on-going class action lawsuit, but the company refused to pull the product, and the FDA's hands were tied. There probably wouldn't be an issue at all if there was a solution, an anti-antiaging serum, but why would anyone with a brain want that?

This group of kids ran into her without apologizing. They were laughing. She couldn't tell if they were laughing at her pain or in spite of it. She'd become both invisible and a spectacle at the same time.

"Hey!" Alda said. "Be careful. You could seriously injure someone."

The tallest of them rolled her eyes. These kids weren't students that Alda knew. They were younger. Meaner. She was pretty sure they were from the middle school. Sometimes she saw kids their age playing basketball in the courtyard. They were small from a distance, but now they towered over her.

"Maybe you should be careful," a boy shot back.

"That's it," Alda said. "What are your names? I'm reporting this."

"Mr. None-of-Your-Business, that's what."

They laughed, this time at her for sure. She called after them as they left, throwing empty threats. "Don't think I won't tell your teachers! I know what you look like!"

"Why's she even here?" they were whispering. "I've never seen her before. Is she, like, new? And why does she dress like that? Her clothes are all baggy and weird."

The sound of their laughter stayed with Alda long after they'd left, lingering, growing. Their memory connected to those of her sisters, the funeral, the pill, her drinking—so many layers of sadness; they crushed her. When she was in grade school, this one group of girls kept threatening to jump her, and though Alda never told her mom, her mom knew. She'd stay in bed until her mom came home and massaged her scalp. *Just let me drive you to school,* her mom said. *No,* Alda said. *You get up way to early and I'm lazy.* She wanted to tell her the truth so bad. But even more, she wanted to protect her mom from the truth.

In college, Alda had read once about amputees being able to feel their lost appendages. No matter how hard they tried, they couldn't internalize their loss completely. She felt like they might understand her. She was still half convinced her mom would pick up the phone when she tried calling her in the car. All she wanted was to hear her voicemail greeting but also maybe her mom if God allowed it (he didn't).

"*Sorry I can't come to the phone right now,*" her mom's voice said, "*try calling again later. Okay, thanks!*"

Alda played the recording on the way home, in the parking lot, the stairwell, living room, kitchen, bath. The whole time, she was thinking the same thing: One day, I won't remember what she sounded like. Then she'd forget her mom's face, her purple eyeshadow and unique smell. The perfume her mom wore came by special order from a boutique whose name Alda had never thought of asking.

Sweat pooled under Alda's armpits. In the mirror, she studied the chubby-faced little girl in the ill-fitting clothes. She was an orphan, she realized. She poured two shots of brandy, throwing away the first.

Orphan, orphan, orphan—the word got stuck so deep in her head that it became part of her. She was an orphan, and she'd relapsed. She texted her sisters. To Maureen: "I'm sorry." To Joyce: "I was stupid." She called her mom again, but this time the voice was different. A robot lady said that she was sorry, but the number was no longer in service.

This time, Alda used up all of the bubble bath. She stepped into the tub before it was ready, doused her face, filled the emptied bottle with water to force out the dregs. She let the water unravel her completely, becoming a part of it, her temperature dropping. She got smaller, smaller—so small that she couldn't see over the bathtub's rim.

To be small and safe again—that was all she wanted. It wasn't that she was trying to die. What she was after was the opposite, a new chance at life. She let her desire shrink her down until there was nothing left but dirty bathwater. The faucet was still running. The tub overflowed.

Acknowledgments

. . . .

Writing is a solitary, lonely endeavor, but the process of becoming a writer involves many. I wouldn't be where I am today without the people who taught me how to express myself. Thanks to all the instructors and classmates who believed in my potential. From grade school to grad school, they've been a beautiful, shining light.

Special thanks to the creative writing MFA at the University of Maryland: to my professors Howard Norman, Emily Mitchell, Gabrielle Lucille Fuentes, Maud Casey, and Rion Amilcar Scott; to my incredibly talented workshop peers; and to the founders of the program, Michael Collier and the late Stanley Plumly.

I'd also like to thank West Virginity University Press. Not only have they championed my work, but they continue to exist under a hostile state government intent on eliminating public education. Thanks to my editor, Sarah Munroe, for her guidance and thought-provoking feedback; to Natalie Homer for answering all of my many emails; to Than Saffel for providing the cover art; and to the entire staff for keeping the press alive.

Other special people I'd like to acknowledge: my parents for helping me achieve my dreams even when they didn't understand them; all the literary magazines who've published my work, much of which appears in this collection; the Iowa Writers' Workshop Summer Session; my funny, witty students at UMD and Lycée polyvalent Raoul Vadepied who continue to inspire me; my Vassar friends who kept me from giving up after a very traumatic sophomore year; and my Stone Ridge girlies.

Megan Howell is a writer. She earned her MFA in fiction from the University of Maryland in College Park, winning both the Jack Salamanca Thesis Award and the Kwiatek Fellowship. Howell's work has appeared in *McSweeney's*, *The Nashville Review*, and *The Establishment* among other publications. She is based in Washington, DC.